D0685281

Amanda Craig is the author of four other novels, including *A Vicious Circle* and *In a Dark Wood*, which are linked to but independent from *Love in Idleness*. Her website can be found at www.amandacriag.com

Love in Idleness

AMANDA CRAIG

To Giles Gordon

An *Abacus* Book

First published in Great Britain in 2003 by Little, Brown
This edition published in 2004 by Abacus

A CIP catalogue record for this book
is available from the British Library.

ISBN 0 349 11585 0

Typeset in Sabon by M Rules
Printed and bound in Great Britain by
Clays Ltd, St Ives plc

Little, Brown
An imprint of
Time Warner Book Group UK
Brettenham House
Lancaster Place
London WC2E 7EN

www.twbg.co.uk

Yet mark'd I where the bolt of Cupid fell.
It fell upon a little western flow'r,
Before milk-white, now purple with love's wound,
And maidens call it love-in-idleness.

Oberon, *A Midsummer Night's Dream*, II.i

Chapter One

The long wooden shutters of the Casa Luna, bolted against heat and crime, were flung open, and the light of a new day flooded in. Pia turned her back to it and began to sweep. There was always dust: dust from the ancient, crumbling plaster, dust from the great, dark oak beams of the ceiling, dust from long-forgotten visitors and dust from the bone-white roads of the country. As Pia's plump figure bent and stretched, a fine cloud of glittering motes rose, swarming, as if alive. She knew they'd be back, as they always were, but she captured what she could with her broom.

Now the cobwebs twirled like fine yarn round a long-handled duster, their spiders scurrying to temporary hiding places in the rafters. Now the scorpions scuttled from the rough stone walls, to lie invisible on burnished stones outside. The death-watch beetles stayed their clocks, and the mice that lived behind the stairs vanished in a furry blur. The bathroom taps were rid of slime and lime, and the kitchen

1

had its sink scoured, its cooker chastened and its fridge defrosted.

'Ai, ai, ai, ai,' bawled Serafina, Pia's sister-in-law, listening to the local radio station, 'why do you always make me cry?'

Pia joined in the chorus.

'You naughty love, you little boy,
You treat my heart just like a toy!'

They sang with relish, vigorously whacking rugs out of the window with stout cane beaters. A lizard, basking on the warm window ledge like a tiny dragon, shot off and vanished into the star jasmine. As the sun rose higher, a miniature orchestra of cicadas in every tree began to shrill the midsummer music it would play until nightfall. Swallows darted round the house and its cypress trees with high shrieks. It was going to be another very hot day. The two women worked at a steady, untiring pace. They wore flowered pinafores, and an expression of concentration and satisfaction, for they were at peace, unlike those for whom they were preparing the house. How strained these foreigners always looked when they arrived! Of course, travel was never pleasant. Pia herself had never been further than Arezzo, and had felt most uncomfortable there, surrounded by alien faces and buildings, so much so that she had never returned. The poor foreigners had no doubt suffered far worse, hurtled through the air from one country to the next. But it was their complexions that really made her pity them.

'They live in the dark, like mushrooms,' Serafina speculated.

Pia doubted this.

'They don't know how to be happy, poor things.'

She had an approximate idea of what the rest of the world was like from the large colour TV set that was permanently switched on in her kitchen; it seemed to be a place best avoided. The wisdom of this was confirmed by the extreme reluctance of those who stayed at the Casa to leave.

She counted up the sheets that she had bought from the market in Camucia. It was a nuisance that the burglars had taken the antique linen Signor Bill provided, but Pia had supplied the deficit with new, fitted poly-cotton sheets from the market – so much easier to wash and iron. Burglars were an annual pest, always striking at the holiday homes of foreigners – an easy target because they tended to be isolated and unguarded. They knew that Signor Bill worked in Hollywood, and all of Cortona was immensely proud of this, living in the hopeful expectation that one day he would make a film in which they would all feature. The Cortonesi had a lively appreciation of the photogenic qualities of both their town and their own features, which remained largely undiscovered by the outside world. On discovering that Signor Bill only had a twelve-year-old television and clapped-out hi-fi, the criminals had taken the sheets – luckily, the antique furniture was both too heavy and too sparse to be worth bothering with. Pia sorted through her replacements. One double pair for the king-sized bed. The husband and wife would take that room; it had the best views out across the hills and an en suite bathroom. Three pairs of buttercup-yellow single sheets for the children – two boys and a girl, according to the note left her by the estate agent. Foreigners still had big families, unlike Italians these days . . . Pia, who adored children, sighed. After some thought, she brought out a tiny china tea-service on a silvery tin tray. It was nothing special – just a white teapot, a jug, and four cups and saucers, each no taller than a child's thumb and decorated with a miniature purple flower that might or might not have been a violet. The girl would like it, Pia thought. Perhaps she would have tea parties, as she herself had done, once upon a time.

She returned to bed-making. There were the two smaller double beds, each with its headboard carved from chestnut wood. One of these would be for the children's grandmother, no doubt. The other was for the couple's friends. It had been left vague as to precisely how many of these would be staying, so Pia left the beds unmade in the last three rooms. There were enough sheets to go round, but only just. The white waffle towels she carried to the bathrooms were old and balding in places, but generous in size. Nothing in the Casa was new except for the sheets, and the swimming pool that had been carved out of the garden in order to attract a higher rental. Before that, foreigners had been reluctant to come and spend the summer months there; it had been the gentle insistence of the estate agent that had persuaded the owner to see it as an investment.

'Who's coming this time?' Serafina asked.

'Americans.'

They exchanged grins. Quite apart from the large tip they could expect at the end, Americans were always extravagantly grateful for a tiramisù left in the fridge, or the fresh vegetables from the kitchen garden they were paying to keep up. They only ever used the shower, and treated Pia as if she, rather than the Signore, were their host. Upon departure, they left quantities of strange food in the fridge – boxes of yellow grease that no sensible person would dream of ingesting, and cans of fizzy drink – but the remains of many pleasant soaps and shampoos as well. The Germans, too, were punctilious, and so clean that it was rare to find anything left for them to do. The English, on the other hand . . . Pia grimaced. Some English people were charming, even if they never understood that money was always better than a bottle of whisky, or that they were wasting precious water filling the baths. Others made her shudder. She hadn't forgotten the English party of the previous year which had left beer bottles surrounding the swimming pool, overflowing dustbins and the plumbing blocked with contraceptives. Italian Dream didn't care about which nationalities booked the Casa Luna as long as they had the money to pay for it, but it was always the English who caused trouble. Usually, they just weren't rich enough for Tuscany.

Pia and Serafina delighted in contemplating other people's wealth, which they felt reflected honour on their own labours. This would be a busy time, with so many houses let to foreigners. A distant car was sounding its horn. Pia looked down the hillside, past the pool where her nephew Rico was toiling, stripped to the waist, to clean the filters and replace the chlorine, past the long avenue of cypress trees bordering the road below. There it was, a long pale car, the kind that was always driven by a uniformed chauffeur from a top hotel in Florence or Rome. It would be with them in half an hour, once Rico had helped it round the sharp bend in the road. She surveyed the drawing room before closing the shutters again. Her labours were done, for the time being. All traces of the people who had stayed here just a few hours before – eating, sleeping, laughing, crying, loving, hating and forgiving – were eradicated, just as they always were. That was the way the owner wished it; and the guests, too. It gave them the illusion that the house and its gardens and woods was really theirs, and that nobody before themselves had ever discovered its charms, or its mysteries.

Theo and Polly Noble waited for their luggage to appear through the slatted curtain of the carousel at Pisa airport with mounting apprehension. Tania and Robbie had been restrained so far by a combination of story-tapes, colouring books, unbridled ingestion of sweets and, inevitably, forcible mid-air separation. They were now boiling up to a fight. Polly, aching with tension and exhaustion, waited for the right moment to pounce.

'Are quite you sure you don't need a wee, darlings?' she asked, again.

'Can you turn the volume down, dear?' said Theo. 'You're embarrassing them.'

The children, far from looking embarrassed, took no notice.

6

'Sorry,' said Polly. 'They just don't seem to hear me unless I talk in a piercing sort of voice. Children! Do you need the loo?'

'They're smart enough to decide for themselves, aren't they?'

Polly clamped her lips shut. They weren't, of course, but she didn't want Theo to go into one of his cold rages. If her children ignored her, they would have to stop on the burning verges of the *autostrada*, ankle-deep in rubbish, for one or both of them to empty their bladders. If they could just make it to the villa before the Demon Queen, all would be fine. She so longed to find peace. In her heart, she knew this was highly unlikely. Sweat saturated the fine blue-and-white stripes of her blouse. Oh, why did it have to be Italy? Of course she adored Italy, but not in midsummer; you never came in midsummer, not if you were sane. However, people with young children never were sane. They were driven crazy by not getting enough sleep. Half the time Polly didn't know if she were awake or dreaming, she was so weary, and now she had to cope with being Abroad again. Why couldn't they go to Scotland or, better still, go to their lovely house on Rhode Island, with those perfect sandy beaches? Why endure the soaring temperatures, the mosquitoes, the foreign language? But Theo had insisted.

'I have to take this vacation in Europe because of the deal we're working on. Chances are, I'll be flying to Milan or Frankfurt in the middle of it, and that's so much easier if I don't have to cross the Atlantic. Besides, they'll enjoy the paintings.'

Theo had a charming belief, untainted by experience, that their children would thoroughly enjoy trudging round the Uffizi with a horde of other sweaty tourists, looking at Renaissance art. Polly was too tired to argue. She wondered what a Tuscan farmhouse would be like, dreading the prospect of valuable antiques and china which would have to be protected from sudden childish arm movements. Perhaps it was a good thing that the children were getting some exercise now, chasing each other round and round the carousels. It was important to look on the bright side.

'If you'd stuck to hand-luggage for the kids, we'd be out of here by now,' Theo said. 'I don't get why there has to be such a lot of stuff. These temperatures, all they need is T-shirts and shorts.'

'I'm sorry, darling, I did try. But you know how Tania insists on bringing her entire summer wardrobe.'

'There is a washing machine there, you know.'

'I know.'

Polly was all too aware that much of her time on holiday would be spent doing the laundry and the cooking and the child-care and all the other chores that back in London would be shared with her cleaning lady. A holiday with Theo and the children represented two weeks of domestic and maternal drudgery. She did hope the kitchen would have a nice view. Continental kitchens, like continental breakfasts, usually left much to be desired.

'Why did they bring their tennis racquets?' Theo demanded.

'You promised to play with them, remember?'

Robbie tugged on her arm.

'Mummy, Mummy, Mummy, it's my turn to sit on the trolley.'

'It isn't, you great big fibber, it's mine.'

'Get off! I was here first.'

'Guys, guys,' said Theo. They took not the slightest bit of notice.

'Fuck, fuck, fuck, fuck,' chanted Robbie.

Theo turned on his wife and hissed, 'Where did he learn That Word?'

Polly flushed. She couldn't bring herself to admit that it was one that occasionally escaped her lips during the school run.

'I think he decoded those advertisements for French Connection,' she said, in a flash of inspiration. 'You know the ones? FCUK?'

Theo's expression of fury changed focus.

'In that case, I shall certainly write to their Board to complain,' he said.

Robbie began to scream.

'She's pushing me off the trolley! Mum-meee!'

'Time out now, time out,' said Theo, making the T sign.

'Shut up, butt-head,' said Robbie.

Polly, who now appreciated why the phrase 'going off your trolley' was synonymous with madness, said, 'Lamb, you can't sit on the trolley. We need it for our suitcases.'

'Then I want a trolley to myself!' said Tania.

'You'll have to fetch it.'

'All right then, I will!'

Polly watched her daughter's figure retreat in an exaggerated flounce of fury. It was still flat and childish, but during the past year her nine-year-old daughter was behaving increasingly like a teenager. From one month to the next she had mutated from a sweet little girl who wore pinafore dresses and talked to her dolls, to a terrifyingly sophisticated creature who demanded that her ears be pierced and her social life enhanced by a mobile phone. When Polly had refused, she screamed, 'I hate you, you fat loser!' and sulked for weeks.

Outside school hours, Tania now wore metallic varnish on her soft, childish nails, and smeared sparkly gel on her flawless cheeks. Her long, coltish legs terminated in lumpen platform sandals, and her body was barely covered by a skimpy lime-green top and a white mini-skirt, dotted with rhinestones, carefully pulled down to reveal the waistband of her Calvin Klein knickers. She looked, Polly thought, like a miniature hooker. Worst of all, she was always so angry and sulky. What had happened to her beautiful, cheerful, innocent child?

At least Tania still had a child's imagination. Theo, in fact, worried that she lived too much in a fantasy world – 'off with the fairies', as the English called it. Polly blamed herself for this, having struggled to continue with her career during the earliest years of her daughter's life. Tania had had a succession of uninspired nannies, who had never known how to contain or control her – not that Polly did either, only she did love her with an awkward, wary passion. Tania was forever inventing long, elaborate games, which she condescended to play with Robbie when they were not quarrelling. Sometimes, the strength of her beliefs was unnerving. She was quite convinced, for instance, that she could fly, and had sprained her ankle jumping off a high wall to prove it.

'Too much imagination can be bad for kids, just like too much of anything,' her father said. 'She should be concentrating more on her math.'

Regrettably, Tania hated maths almost as much as she hated vegetables.

Polly observed her son, who, now that his sister had ceded his right to the trolley, was looking angelic. There was nothing unusual about this, for Robbie always looked angelic. Strangers would stop them wherever they went and exclaim at his beauty, unaware of his propensity to bite if the whim took him.

Robbie beamed up at her now from his position on top of the trolley.

'Love you, Mum.'

'I love you too, scallywag,' she said.

Nothing had prepared Polly for the passion that had taken possession of her when she had a son. She felt bad about it, because modern women were supposed to value daughters more than sons, but it was inescapable. She loved Tania, but with Robbie it was adoration. He could literally make her heart beat faster just by smiling at her. She wanted to keep every lock of his hair, she shed tears over the small discarded clothes when he was at school, mooning in his bedroom and burying her face in his pillow. However, he too was changing. He still allowed her long cuddles, but recently he had stopped coming into bed with her first thing in the morning as a matter of course. The exquisite pleasure of holding him for as long as she liked was gradually slipping away. He said 'ugh!' and 'yuk!' when he saw people kissing on videos and this embarrassment was spreading, so that half the time when she held out her arms for him, he giggled and hung back.

Thank heavens Meenu was coming. It was such luck to have persuaded her, and Ellen too, of course. Ellen was the best person in the world to go shopping with. She could also speak Italian. Oh, it would be good to be together again, just like the old days when they shared a flat. Perhaps they could manage a girls' trip to Florence one day. Besides, Bron was bound to get on with Tania – they were the same age. Slowly, as the smells and sounds of a foreign country filtered into her consciousness, Polly began to feel more cheerful. This was Italy, after all, and Italy was always divine. She hadn't been sure about the way Ellen would fit in, but Polly had a shrewd suspicion that the real attraction was the presence of Theo's half-brother, Daniel. They seemed to have something going. Polly drifted off in a haze of hopeful thoughts. Both Ellen and Meenu were single. What if she could make a match between Meenu and Ivo? Ivo did have something of a reputation, but he was interesting, and good value as company. On the other hand, so was Guy, though she did rather hope she could keep Guy to herself. That was the point about having a house party. It meant that you weren't lonely or alone.

There was the usual despondent rubber plant doubling up as an ashtray by the car rental booths, and the usual haggling with someone who spoke heavily accented English over whether or not he had booked an air-conditioned people carrier from London. Whatever company you travelled with, they always seemed to lose your booking and took up to an hour to find it again. Theo hated the inefficiency of travelling Economy. Polly joked sometimes that if there were Club Class seats on a lifeboat, her husband would insist on having them, but there was no such thing as Club Class anything on family vacations. Of course, he should have booked Club for himself and Economy for the rest; he could have justified it to his internal accountant, no problem. His legs were too long for the cramped seats in Economy, and there was that research about the danger of blood clots while flying. Theo had taken care to buy himself a pair of support stockings, because it stood to reason that he was the one most at risk from a stroke, and he now included an aspirin as part of his daily schedule, but it still made him antsy. His nerves were soothed at first by reflecting that at least all their tickets were free on Frequent Flyer Miles. He could even have brought a nanny, but, much to his relief, Polly had insisted she no longer needed one now she had given up her career. He'd never expected Mary Poppins, not exactly, but if there was one who didn't come with multiple piercings and a built-in hatred of her employers, Theo hadn't met her. The child-care problem was something else the British really hadn't licked, not having a willing army of Mexicans on their doorstep. Needless to say, as a partner at Cain, Innocent, he couldn't have employed one of those either, but still . . .

Two weeks away from the office with Polly and the children was enough to make anybody's heart sink, he thought. It wasn't as though he didn't love them all, especially the kids, but going on vacation with them was another matter. Some of the guys had wives that managed the whole summer alone, occasionally dropping by for the weekend but otherwise keeping well clear. He needed his own space, and the office was where he found it. But Polly would have gone bananas at the suggestion. The trouble was, whatever Theo cared for his spouse and children, he cared more about his work, and his other life. Nothing, but nothing, compared to the adrenalin highs of a deal going through. Polly didn't understand; she thought that he was working for the money, or to prove that he could be successful on the other side of the pond, far away from Mother. But to him, a vacation was just that: a vacancy; an empty, unoccupied period of time, and even if people were coming to stay, it didn't lessen his frustration. At work he was somebody. He had a position, a function, an occupation; at work he had stress, yes, but stress was good for you, Theo believed. You were up against the best of the best, and you gave it your best, even if it meant meeting people at seven in the morning on a Sunday. That was how a white-shoe firm worked.

Polly got what was left over from that, and because she was so placid, so calm and undemanding about all the petty domestic matters a partner couldn't be bothered with, she was the ideal wife, even if she cared more about music and art than was strictly necessary. He occasionally got the impression that the difference between Polly's experience of their life together and his own was like that between one of them sitting in the auditorium of a theatre and the other seeing the same play on TV. Of course Theo went often to the theatre, as he did the opera. It was the kind of thing you did, much as you went to the barber and the tailor, as a partner at Cain, Innocent. Life management was all about staying on an even keel, rolling with the punches and keeping one's sunny side up, and culture was therapy in that situation. He wasn't passionate about music like Danny and Polly. He sincerely hoped that he wasn't passionate about anything. Theo had long ago learnt that whenever anything seemed likely to disturb him he could simply watch what happened with perfect detachment. There were some people who might have found this uncomfortable, but he found it essential. How else could a rational person function appropriately?

So now, waiting for the Avis girl to find his booking, he concentrated on remaining calm. This didn't matter. He remembered what his favourite professor at Harvard had quoted him, 'The law is reason without passion.' That was the way to live a lawyer's life. He loved Polly while never being in love – a condition he thoroughly disliked as bad for business and destructive of property, stability and conformity. No lawyer, and especially not a partner at Cain, Innocent, could believe in romance. He thought about Polly as the Avis girl finally filled out the requisite forms. Going on holiday was downtime, something they both needed. They shared so much – the same interests, the same values, and the kids who were (by and large) absolutely great. Theo looked back at Tania, who was now perched on top of his big squashy Mulberry suitcase, with her headphones on. She beamed at him. The upside of going on holiday with them was being able to do things together, like teaching them both how to play baseball, getting Robbie going on his crawl. Theo had always wanted children, he was as involved as a working father could be, and this vacation meant that they would be able to catch up on some friends too. No, all in all, thought Theo, having returned his blood pressure to normal, just as long as Guy fitted in with the whole scenario, this is set to be a really great time.

'Uh-oh,' said Ellen von Berg to Hemani Moulik, one hand clenching the strap of her handbag. 'Look who's coming with Danny.'

'Who?' said Hemani, turning and seeing only a heaving blur of brightly dressed tourists. She really ought to wear contact lenses, as Bron kept saying, instead of these granny-glasses, but she never seemed to have the time to sort out her own eyes, only other people's. Just now, she was too excited to care. She was in Italy, the country she had always yearned to visit, and the light and heat and sounds and smells sent an unfamiliar thrill of hope through her.

'Ivo Sponge,' Ellen said, groaning. 'God, don't tell me he's coming too . . . If so, this holiday will be a disaster. How could Danny do this to me?'

'Who? Why?'

'Oh, Meenu, I know you live like a nun but you must know Ivo. Everyone does. He's famous for being the worst flirt on either side of the Atlantic. You must have heard of the Sponge Lunge?'

Hemani, not really listening, watched Daniel approach them across the pale floors of Rome airport. She began a flood of bright, nervous chatter, until Bron rolled his eyes and told her, silently, to stop. She looked at her son's grave, beautiful profile as he scuffed the floor with his Nike trainers. I must try not to be silly, she thought; and I must not humiliate Bron out of nervous social ineptitude. She, who was so confident and competent as a doctor, still found she fell to pieces when confronted by a man. She forced herself to concentrate on what Ellen was saying. She was still complaining about Daniel's friend.

'. . . biggest slime-ball and a total loser.'

'He doesn't look boring. That's what I most dread about going on holiday with people.'

'Oh, sure, he isn't boring,' said Ellen sarcastically. 'One thing you can guarantee is that Ivo will be the life and soul of any party. Also the death and damnation of it.'

Hemani looked at her friend shrewdly.

'You used to go out with him?'

'Are you kidding?' was Ellen's answer. 'You know, I introduced him to one of my friends in Manhattan who was seriously desperate, and she called me the next morning and said she was going to try for a sperm donor instead.'

Hemani, who had a sinking feeling that Polly was once again trying to set her up with a spare man, looked at Ivo with reluctant interest.

Even at a distance his eyes snapped with a particular live-
liness and perhaps a hardness too. He was plump and tall,
dressed in a crumpled cream linen suit and a Panama hat. A
figure out of a Somerset Maugham story, she thought,
amused; or perhaps someone not quite at ease in the modern
world, like herself. Beside him Daniel, in chinos and a polo
shirt, looked the quintessential American academic, his
floppy hair framing both a classical profile and a perpetually
diffident expression. Who was the woman in black gliding
along beside him, though? Hemani squinted. Oh – it was his
cello.

'I didn't think he'd bring that on holiday,' Ellen said.

'What?'

'His, um, instrument,' Ellen said.

'He must have bought a ticket for it.'

'Pardon?'

'You can't just put a cello in the hold, you know. It'd
destroy it.'

Ellen shrugged. 'Whatever.'

She didn't really understand this obsession with music,
but just seeing him stride across the airport floor was
enough. She had two weeks in which to get him to propose
to her, and if she failed in a setting like Tuscany, well, she'd
be very surprised.

'Hi, sweetheart.'

Ellen beamed at Daniel. He smiled vaguely, as he always
did, then registered Hemani and her son. He never looked
quite in focus, Hemani thought, even close up.

'Good flight, angel?' Ellen asked.

'For a sardine-box populated by psychotic toddlers specialising in projectile vomiting, it wasn't all bad,' said Ivo.

Hemani, who had travelled Tourist Class with her son, grimaced in sympathy, but Ellen, who had been astonished that Hemani had failed to take up her darling little man who could get her Club Class tickets at the bargain price of $1000 each, only shrugged.

Daniel said, addressing the space between the two women, 'Hi, how are you?'

'Great!' said Ellen enthusiastically. 'My media profile has never been higher. Did you see the article about my new shop in *Vogue*? I clipped it for you.'

Daniel looked at Ellen with the dazed gaze that most men seemed to have when they saw her, then smiled nervously. Ivo, on the other hand, lifted his hat to reveal short coppery curls, dampened by sweat.

'Ellen, my darling. So good to see that if you took your top off you could still model for the prow of a Viking ship, terrorising the Saxon peasantry as you thrust through the waves.'

Ellen said, 'Ivo,' in tones that would have made most men shrivel into dust. 'I'm glad you haven't forgotten me.'

'How could anyone possibly do that?'

Hemani caught Daniel's eye, and gave a small snort of laughter.

'Hi,' he said. 'Er – I don't think you've met, have you? Hemani, Ivo.'

Ivo seized Hemani's hand and, to her bemusement, kissed it. She wondered whether she had imagined a slight flick of his tongue on her flesh as he did so.

'People call me Meenu,' she said.

'And this is?'

'My son, Auberon,' she said, holding him in front of her with both arms crossed over his chest, as if to protect him. She looked hard at Daniel, to see whether he would be surprised. However, the expression on his face was one of perpetual mild wonderment, so she couldn't tell. She suspected he had looked like this ever since he had discovered Shakespeare.

'Hello there,' said Ivo.

'Hi,' said Daniel. 'How old are you?'

Bron smiled shyly, and made no reply.

'Nine,' said his mother.

'Ah.' Daniel rubbed his nose. 'Well, that's a great age to be.'

'Is it?' said Bron.

Daniel suddenly remembered that he had been nine when Mother had left his father. 'It can be.'

There was an awkward pause, which Ivo filled.

'So, we're all travelling to Cortona together, how delicious, how delightful, how delirious. You don't need to hang about for another hour. Dan has hired a car.'

'Oh, Danny, but I hired a car too,' said Ellen. 'That's why we're in the queue.'

'Ours is bigger and better,' said Ivo at once.

'You could come with us,' said Daniel. 'That is, unless you'd prefer—'

'Oh Mum,' said Bron. 'Can't we go? I'm so bored of waiting. I just want to get there and swim.'

Hemani looked hopefully at Ellen. It was agony being with a hot, tired, bored child, even if he was as good as Bron, and she felt very sorry for him. Ellen was clearly torn between her loathing of Ivo and her desire to be with Daniel. She had already taken his arm possessively, and was gazing up at him.

'Well . . . Wouldn't you mind, honey?'

'Not at all.'

'I take it neither of you have been there before? Nor have I – that makes us all equals.'

'Oh, Ivo,' said Ellen. 'You have no equal, surely.'

'You flatter me, my darling, you flatter me.'

Hemani felt sorry for him. She flashed him an encouraging smile, then wished she hadn't because Ivo immediately squeezed her hand convulsively in his own warm and pudgy paw.

She said to Ellen, 'Can't we just go? After all, how many cars do we need?'

So it was settled. They wheeled their triangular trolleys out into the car park together. It was like walking into an oven. Daniel gingerly opened the driver's side, and turned on the air conditioning.

'Is it OK with everyone if I sit in the front? I get motion sickness,' Ellen said; although Hemani remembered that in the plane over she had boasted of never getting it at all.

'Excellent idea.' Ivo beamed. Hemani nodded to Bron, who scrambled into the back with her. It was stuffy, but he was too fascinated by all the palm trees and bright flowers to notice. 'You two hop in, and I'll handle the cases. You do at least trust me with those?'

'No,' said Ellen; 'but I can't resist seeing you try to lift mine.'

Having extracted the cream limousine from the deep dusty ditch into which it had swerved, the sweating chauffeur from the Hotel Excelsior took his leave without the expected tip. Betty's face was frozen into an expression of perpetual displeasure thanks to the Botox injections which maintained a marmoreal calm in her visage at all times, but her irritation at having to wait was magnified by the realisation that the maid did not speak a word of English. She neither displayed nor felt the slightest degree of interest in the smiling peasant woman before her who was jabbering away in unintelligible Italian. Where was the agent? Not here, it seemed. Presumably Polly had not thought to arrange details such as these. She looked around, taking off her straw hat, scarf and sunglasses.

Throughout her childhood, and during each of her marriages, Betty had demanded the best. Naturally, as she rose in the world her ideas about what constituted this altered, but she hated anything that fell short of her expectations. The Casa Luna was far too small and rustic, although the large garden, glimpsed below, was pleasing enough. The woods beyond the olive groves looked far too overgrown, and were bound to be seething with snakes, if she knew anything about this kind of climate. She went indoors. No, not much better. The architecture was, dismayingly, that of a farmhouse with pretensions: some jumped-up farmer had enlarged it, she guessed, before it had been converted.

Betty's heels clacked impatiently across the tiled floors. She had to admit that the drawing room with its great stone fireplace and large sofas was pleasant enough in a distinctly Greenwich Village fashion, but those vases! Not a decent light fixture anywhere, either. That was Italy for you.

Betty sighed. The things she did for her sons! None of them was quite as much trouble as her youngest, Winthrop, but she was still willing to sacrifice a fortnight in order to ensure Daniel got engaged to that charming girl Ellen von Berg. Everyone knew that Ellen was mad about him, and they had been pictured together in *People* magazine leaving the Ivy restaurant in London, which these days was as good as an engagement. Didn't she deserve to have at least one of her children married to someone respectable? Polly had been such a disappointment. She had never understood why Theo, who could have married anybody, had chosen such a homebody type. Even a cheerleader would have been preferable, at least first time round. She must also have a word with her daughter-in-law about the unbecoming quantity of weight she had put on since having Robbie. Her own hips were as slim as they had been when she had first captured the heart, and wallet, of Theo's father more years ago than she cared to imagine. But the new generation was almost as ill-disciplined and indulgent towards themselves as they were towards their children. She was not looking forward to sharing her space with Robbie and Tania. She didn't imagine that time had improved their disposition or their habit of creating havoc wherever they went.

The chauffeur had deposited her seven suitcases in the hall. This was a matter of indifference. Somebody would be along to take them up to her room. The main thing, Betty thought as she ascended the twisting marble stair, was that she was free to choose the best room. The corridor was long, with a large window at the end giving on to a view of the opposite hills, of no interest save for the castellated tower of somebody's palazzo. Now that was the sort of scale she expected for a partner of Cain, Innocent. But Theo, like everyone, was hurting in the recession. She tried the doors. One, to her mild annoyance, was locked. She inspected each of the rest, flinging back the shutters and leaving them open so that the precious shadows were dispelled, and quickly discovered that the room with the largest bed also had the best view and the only really tolerable bathroom.

'Here,' she said aloud to herself.

Gingerly, she sat down on the mattress and bounced a few times. It was firm. She felt the sheets between finger and thumb and noted with distaste that they were not pure cotton. With a sigh of martyrdom, Betty closed the shutters again, severing a frond of wisteria as she did so, then kicked off her Jimmy Choos and stretched herself out for a session of meditation that was almost as revitalising as sleep, only infinitely more fashionable.

Chapter Two

Wow, this is wonderful, this is great! Look at that lizard zipping along the wall at one hundred miles per hour, almost as though it was a snake, Mum keeps on warning us about snakes and not going into the wood, there's a syringe full of anti-snake stuff in the fridge, wish I could see a snake, Tania says she's spotted one but I bet she's telling a great big fib to impress Bron and anyway if I do see a snake I'll whack it with my big stick before it can bite me, wow what a cool stone, bet it's got gold or something in those coloured specks, I wonder if there's buried treasure here, Tania and me can look for it and there's the pool, a cool blue jewel, oh water, oh man, now I can dive straight in, thought Robbie; and did.

The children had taken to the Casa Luna at once. Its vast downstairs living room, stretching almost the entire length of the house, soon resounded to their cries, and just as soon was emptied of them. They vanished into the garden, where the presence of the swimming pool immediately dispelled any shyness with one another. The adults wandered around at a more leisurely pace, commenting and admiring and generally feeling relieved that the Nobles' choice – made on the basis of three blurry photographs on the Italian Dream website – seemed, after all, to have been a good one. The house was L-shaped, with a square tower rising above the kitchen and main bathroom. (Tania, as soon as she had had a swim, immediately went to investigate this tower, envisaging herself sleeping romantically in its topmost room, and perhaps growing her hair like Rapunzel, but the door was locked. Presumably this was where the owner, one W. Shade, kept his or her private possessions.) The stair to the first storey spiralled up within this tower, but there was also an external stair, accessed by a balcony. It was overgrown with an old vine, laden with sour green grapes like clusters of flawed marbles, and Betty had already made it clear that this area was to be hers.

Downstairs, apart from a bathroom and the kitchen, there was an enormous living room, with a table at one end and an arrangement of sofas and chairs before a large, square fireplace. The walls were painted white, and it was furnished simply, the sofas with loose linen covers and a few solid-looking chests and cupboards in dark wood. There were no knick-knacks or obvious breakables, other than the crockery, which was plain. The relief felt by Polly and Hemani on discovering this was considerable. Both agreed that the very first thing they should do, after unpacking and finding the all-important fuse-box which the

26

Owner's Notes warned could cut off at unexpected moments, was to find a tablecloth in order to protect the oak table. They searched, but could find only drip-dry sheets in the airing cupboard.

'Not quite what I'd have expected, somehow,' said Hemani. 'I suppose the owner must keep the proper linen locked away somewhere.'

'At least there's no satellite TV or video. Robbie will be forced to get reading.'

'I'm not looking forward to sleeping in these sheets, are you? It's hot enough as it is.'

Polly nodded.

'I don't think we can really use one of the blankets either.'

'But won't we be eating out of doors all the time?'

'We will, but you never know what Robbie will get up to,' said Polly. 'He's death to furniture, and Tania's into arts and crafts. They'll be carving their names into that oak and expecting praise for it before you can blink. We'll have to go into town.'

Nobody objected to this. The restiveness of travel was still in them, and they wanted to explore; the Owner's Notes, unattractively bound in greasy transparent plastic but friendly in tone, mentioned several good trattorias and pizzerias in and around Cortona. The cool white rooms with their thick black beams seemed like blank pages to be overwritten, and the evening sun bathed everything in an unreal beauty. Ellen and Daniel were already walking through the lush half-wild garden on the terraces below, where the blues of love-in-the-mist wavered above the knuckles of iris roots.

There were clumps of speckled orange canna lilies, oleanders whirling with white blossom, a small formal rose garden edged with box and large terracotta pots of lemon trees. At the end of the house a pergola of iron hoops thickly overgrown with wisteria shaded a ping-pong table crusted with pigeon droppings. Two scabby bats, but no balls, lay waiting to be used.

'We could probably walk to Cortona, you know,' said Daniel, with what Ellen felt was ominous enthusiasm. 'Look, I can see a path going all the way up on the opposite hill.'

Ellen shaded her eyes. She could think of nothing more unpleasant than a walk, and had brought only the flimsiest and most fashionable of sandals, but if that was what it took, she would do it, even if it meant going barefoot.

'I wouldn't like to try it when the sun is high.'

'We'll have to get up early, then,' said Daniel with his diffident smile. She returned it.

Ellen had made sure to grab the room next to his at the end of the house – it didn't do to be actually sharing a bed, particularly not with his mother around. (Those Southern belles were always conservative.) After all, although Daniel hadn't exactly invited her, they did have a sort of thing going, and Ellen was not used to being resisted. She wound her slim arms around his neck and said, 'Happy?'

'Sure,' said Daniel. Her hands dropped lower, and she giggled.

He said uncomfortably, 'Uh, Ellen – there are other people around, you know.'

Ellen whispered, 'I don't care about them, though.'

He detached her and held her by the wrists, so she laughed.

'I'm serious.'

'Too serious! You're on vacation!'

'But with other people.'

'Only Ivo,' said Ellen, 'and he doesn't count.'

While Theo, mindful of potential fraud, measured the swimming pool to make sure it was twelve metres, Hemani and Polly, temporarily released from care, wandered around the garden below the house. It extended down the hillside in a series of wide steps or terraces, punctuated by olive and cypress trees that eventually gave way to a steep valley. Looking down, they could see the topmost branches of chestnut and oak waving enticingly, but the two women felt no inclination to explore just yet. The woods might be lovely, dark and deep, but right now they wanted sunlight and safety. The garden was contained within a structure of descending stone terraces, former olive groves, where ancient gnarled trunks lifted sprays of silvery leaves into the sky, their bases ringed by bird-of-paradise flowers. There were paved areas and grassed areas, punctuated by large terracotta pots brimming with scarlet geraniums; there were small stone outhouses, and just outside the kitchen a long, vine-shaded terrace on which to have barbecues at a large round table adorned with concentric circles of blue mosaic. There was a vast complicated cactus with serrated edges bearing bright red prickly fruit, and another spiny-looking plant from which a spear, thickly encrusted with creamy

29

flowers, rose into the sky. It looked familiar, and Polly, who loved plants, realised with surprise that it was a yucca, which normally looked so miserable back home. They passed under a wide stone arch billowing with apricot roses to see the swimming pool, a slab even bluer than the sky. Its waters seemed to extend to the very brink of the hillside, pouring in perpetual motion over the edge to be magically replenished. Below this was a small orchard, whose trees were laden with peaches, hard as tennis balls, and plums like dull opals. Beneath the kitchen was a vegetable garden, with tomatoes and runner beans scrambling up wigwams of canes. Clumps of basil, thyme, sage, lettuce and rosemary seemed to boil up within their boxed confines, backed by the silvery jet of artichokes, whose vast thistles were promising a rich crop to come. Banks of lavender hummed with furry bees, and butterflies shimmered among the lilies.

The two mothers forgot their weariness.

'Oh, I'm so glad you could come!' said Polly, happily; for what was the point in being rich if you didn't share it with your friends?

'I'm so glad too,' said Hemani, a little awed by what money could buy. Bruce's family had been wealthy, but in a dismal, costive and (she believed) Scottish way, meaning that they lived in the countryside and never turned on the central heating for fear of spoiling the antiques. She'd only ever seen pictures of places like this in magazines.

The most striking feature of all was the grass, as dense and soft as moss. They could see a parched landscape on the opposite hills but here it was green and fertile. There were no sounds apart from children laughing, leaves rustling and birds singing.

'This is paradise,' said Polly as they returned to the terrace. 'Isn't it?' she said anxiously to her husband.

'You did good,' said Theo.

'Sheer luck,' she said.

He put his arm around her, and her anxiety drained away. It was worth anything, she thought, even having the Demon Queen, if only Theo was happy and could relax. Perhaps, perhaps Betty would give them some much-needed time alone together. Perhaps she could even turn out to be a benign grandmother. Surely a woman who could curdle mayonnaise at thirty paces would instil some discipline into her grandchildren? A blissful daydream of Tania and Robbie transformed into quiet, polite children engaged in constructive activities downstairs while she and Theo actually did more than fall asleep together drifted across her thoughts. It was possible . . . In paradise, anything was possible.

'Two weeks,' she said, luxuriating. 'Two whole weeks of this, imagine!'

Ivo laughed.

'It seems such a short time when you're working, doesn't it?'

'And such a long one when you're not,' said Theo.

Naturally, they at once began to make plans to leave. Siena was only two hours away, according to the Owner's Notes, and Florence easy to get to by train. These were insignificant distances to those who had just flown a thousand miles. Their holiday seemed full of limitless adventure. Every time

31

someone looked out at the shimmer of the olives below, at the shining skies, at the exclamation marks of cypress winding up and down distant roads, he or she felt joy. Yet there was also a town to explore, a household to possess and food to be bought. An hour after arrival they were all once more bumping back down the road to go up into Cortona, the Nobles and Bron in the Renault Espace, the others in the car Daniel had hired.

Tania, whispering in her brother's ear, said, 'Let's make a gang against the grown-ups, OK?'

He grinned, and she whispered the same thing to Bron, as much for the pleasure of whispering to him as anything. He nodded. They were both shy of each other, without understanding why. Tania had met Bron at various intervals throughout her life, the last time a year or so ago. His mother was her godmother, and Mum was his, not that they believed in God or anything but Mum had explained that it was important because that way you had a grown-up friend who wasn't your parents to talk to. Meenu gave really nice presents, but Tania hadn't registered Bron before. Then, he had been boring on about trains and planes. Now she thought he was really cool, so cool that she had immediately decided to make him her boyfriend. Disappointingly, Bron did not seem to have noticed. He was gazing out of the window, so that all she could see was his shaggy hair, and the super-cool leather thong round his neck.

'Five, four, three, two, one, blast off!' cried Robbie.

'This is my little brother. He's a lunatic as you may have gathered,' said Tania.

'You're the loony,' said Robbie. 'Nah-nah-nah,' he added.

'Quit bugging me,' hissed Tania fiercely, adding in martyred tones, 'I've got a headache.'

'Poor lamb, you're tired,' said Polly, seeing Tania's face. 'You can have an ice cream when we get there.'

Tania shrugged.

'So what?'

The car, which had reached the valley, now began to climb. They passed a farmyard filled with waddling white ducks, the high stone walls of private estates, niches at crossroads with small ceramic Madonnas. Suddenly, they crested the hill. The town lay before them, its ascending horizontals interrupted by the verticals of cypress and pine, and the fragile grey bubble of a church dome. Flowering hibiscus and oleander wound up the side of the road.

'Oh!' said Tania, as she too saw it for the first time. 'This is really pretty, isn't it?'

Polly squeezed her daughter's hand, and received the faintest of squeezes back.

They parked beside a church just outside the city walls. Daniel followed them. Everyone emerged into the warm evening, into the shrill screams of swifts chasing each other through the luminous skies.

'Wow, what a fantastic view,' said Ellen. Daniel and Hemani each felt a private flash of irritation at the banality of her words, but perhaps, thought Ivo, fantastic was the right adjective after all.

The whole of the plain, which before had been partly concealed, now lay beneath them, with the pearly corner of Lake

Trasimeno just visible to the left. Light poured down on it, shafts as strong and marked as spotlights on a stage except where great violet shadows drifted slowly across the distant fields and hamlets as soft hazy clouds moved in the sky. Far away, on the very edge of sight, some other hill-town or castle raised its profile among a chain of mountains. Otherwise there was just air, a blue melting into blue, and radiance.

'No wonder they painted angels,' said Daniel, but his eyes were not on the view but on Ellen. Her blond hair shone like a nimbus around her face. Ivo made a sound very like a snort.

'There's an angel here,' Ellen said. 'One of Fra Angelico's Annunciations.'

'Does it look like you?' Tania asked.

Ellen, who had majored in Art History at college, was about to say it didn't but thought better of it and smiled archly.

'You'll have to judge it to see.'

'Actually,' said Ivo, 'it features a stunningly camp bloke with curly blond hair in a pink and gold dress that even Ellen wouldn't dare wear.'

'I thought you'd never been here before?' said Hemani.

'Spotted it on the tourist posters coming in.'

'Get down, Bron, you idiot!' Hemani snapped, suddenly seeing her son scrambling up on to the parapet.

'There's ground underneath, Mum.'

'Yes, and a million broken bottles. Come down, sweetie-pie.'

Bron shrugged.

'Hey, there, I thought you wanted ice cream,' said Daniel. Bron's mutinous expression softened. He got down, unhurried, ignoring the offer of help. Hemani put a hand on her son's shoulder, but he shook it off.

'What is it?'

'You promised,' he hissed at her. 'You promised you wouldn't talk to me as if I was a baby, Mum.'

'I'm sorry,' she said, 'but it was dangerous.'

'It wasn't, but if I'd fallen it would have been your fault.'

'Of course,' she agreed. 'I'm your mother, so everything must be my fault.'

They glared at each other, then a small smile crept over each face.

'Just don't bug me, OK?'

'OK.'

They left the little piazza and approached the main street, Via Nazionale. Across it hung a large banner announcing CORTONA WELCOMES THE STUDENTS OF ATHENS, USA!

'Isn't that your mother's home town?' Polly asked Daniel. She noticed that Betty paused, momentarily, to read this, before walking on ahead.

'Yes.'

'I wonder whether she'll meet anyone she knows?'

'I doubt it. She hasn't gone back.'

Via Nazionale began at the foot of a slanting, tree-lined road, and ran nearly level until it reached the main piazza. Alleyways, stepped or cobbled, plunged off it up and down the hillside, giving glimpses of the plains below, interspersed with flapping lines of laundry. Polly stopped and read the names: *Vicolo della Notte, Vicolo del Silenzio, Vicolo del l'Aurora*. Night, silence and dawn, she translated, wanting to turn into each one and explore. There was a smell of hot dust and cool stone, of roses becoming wet and drains becoming dry, of varnish, sawdust, sugar, coffee, aniseed, liquorice, oleanders, frying onions, cat pee, grilling meats, ripening fruits, rotting vegetables and growing basil. The children ran ahead fearlessly, for there were no cars.

Hemani said, again, 'Thank you for asking us to this lovely place.'

'Yes, thanks for asking us to this lovely place,' said Ivo. Ellen looked daggers at him.

'You're welcome,' said Theo, kindly.

'It's lovely that you could come,' said Polly. 'We never see enough of our friends – our real friends, that is. Mostly it's just Theo's colleagues. Last year we went away with two and, well, you can imagine.'

'It is great, isn't it?' said Ellen. 'No matter how many times I come to Italy, it still gives me that special feeling.'

Theo sneezed, and made a groaning sound.

'Honey,' said Betty anxiously, 'is it your allergy? Are you sure you're OK?'

'I don't know, Mother,' said Theo. 'I think I may have caught something. My glands are swollen. I'm not feeling too good, as a matter of fact.'

'We must find a drugstore right away,' said Betty. 'I can see one right ahead.'

Polly sighed. Of course she was sorry for poor Theo, but she knew that he always went down with a bad cold when they were on holiday. For 344 days a year, while he was at work, her husband was in the peak of good health, springing up at 6 a.m. and racing off to the office or the gym and not returning until 10 p.m. No sooner did he take part of his holiday allowance, than he collapsed. It was a pattern familiar even on their honeymoon.

'I brought some medication with me,' she told Betty, but Betty ignored her.

'We'll see if we can get you some antibiotics over the counter,' she said, and hurried along the street.

'Do you think I should go too?' Ellen asked. 'They don't speak Italian, do they?'

Polly shrugged.

'Betty will make herself understood,' she said, dryly. 'She always does.'

'Hypochondria, now that's the collective term for men, isn't it?' said Ellen, and the other women laughed.

'Oh, like hysteria is for women?' said Ivo.

'Only when they've been in your company,' said Ellen.

They wandered on, drifting with an increasing number of people who were emerging in two and threes now that the sun was setting. Some were obviously tourists or foreigners like themselves, and there were a handful of shops selling tie-dyed clothing and ill-made leather goods designed to appeal to them. For the most part, though, the shops along Via Nazionale served the townspeople, who now gathered to walk or talk, show off babies and dogs, drink in its small bars or simply get some fresh air in the doorways of their homes. Polly and Ellen stopped by a greengrocer's to buy fruit and salads, while Daniel, Hemani and Ivo ambled on with the children towards the main square.

'Look out for a supermarket!' Polly called. 'We need bread, milk and breakfast cereals, remember?'

'Oh, look at those heavenly albums,' said Hemani, to whom it all still felt dizzyingly unreal. 'You'd pay twice as much in London for that.'

'Shopping already?' said Ivo.

'Well, only window-shopping.'

'I can never understand why women do that,' said Ivo. 'Either you want something or you don't, surely?'

'What women want,' said Daniel. 'Isn't that the oldest riddle of all?'

'The handbags aren't nearly as pretty as yours, Ellen,' Hemani said.

'Ah, the handbag, a metaphor for the vagina,' said Ivo.

'Great!' said Ellen. 'So I can carry a laptop, a cosmetics case, a mobile and a bottle of mineral water in mine? No wonder you guys are envious.'

She put her arm into Daniel's and walked ahead.

'You asked for that,' said Hemani.

'Heigh-ho, I suppose I did,' said Ivo. He looked after her with mingled scepticism and regret. 'Not just a pretty face, is she?'

'No woman is just a pretty face,' said Hemani with asperity.

Ivo sighed.

They came to the first of two large, irregular squares, the Piazza della Repubblica. Here they found, as they had hoped, a small supermarket and two cafés, each with seats outside. The children flopped down at the closest wobbly round table and demanded ice cream. It being suggested that they should go inside the Bar Signorelli to choose their own, they rose like a flock of sparrows and whirled off.

The remaining adults heaved a sigh of relief, and ordered drinks. The waiter, when he brought their order, presented them with the bill, and stood stolidly waiting to be paid at once. He had a nice face, but one already worn by the tourist season.

'Dan, old chap,' said Ivo, 'I haven't bought any euros yet, do you mind?'

Ellen, who had arrived with bags of fruit, rolled her eyes, but Hemani felt a pang of fellow feeling. She was undoubtedly the poorest person present, and knew she was the only one to have looked at the café's prices before ordering a mineral water. Ellen and Polly never realised what a struggle it was not to be rich, not that she wanted to make them uncomfortable by reminding them of this.

'I've got some,' she said hastily. 'Let me.'

'It's OK,' said Daniel, taking out his wallet. 'Please.'

They settled down to watch the square. To one side was a flight of wide stone steps ascending to a building with a clock tower and a balcony. Numerous youths, probably the students of Athens, Georgia, were sprawled around this area, chatting or sketching. In the square itself there were older people dressed in dark clothes, standing or sitting, gossiping or fanning themselves, and children, darting and laughing between tubs of shrubs while pigeons crooned and strutted at their feet.

'It's like the stage set for *Romeo and Juliet*,' said Daniel. 'I could just picture her there, on that balcony where the Communist Party headquarters are.'

'Or an opera,' said Polly.

'Or a film,' said Ellen.

'Quite,' said Ivo. 'At any moment now the Three Tenors will break into "Just One Cornetto" before driving away in a Fiat to buy some Olivio margarine from a toothless but cheerful crone of a hundred and one who turns out to be Helena Bonham Carter in a monkey mask. Inspired, one of us will suddenly take the decision to abandon our well-paid careers to buy a ruined but picturesque hillside farm and, despite knowing nothing about olive presses, create an organic environment where children can grow up untainted by TV dinners, microwaves and other curses of modern existence. There's nothing more glorious than seeing a cliché come to life, is there?'

'Do you know,' said Ellen, to nobody in particular, 'that in New York we have a cliché called The Great British Sponge Fleet?'

'My fame goes before me,' said Ivo, easily. 'Polly, my darling, shall I find out where there's a butcher, or shall we eat out tonight?'

'Oh, do let's cook at home,' said Hemani, mindful of the budget she had set for herself and Bron. 'The house is so lovely.'

'I quite agree,' said Daniel. 'I'll go buy the meat.'

'No, no,' said Ivo, 'meat should be on me.'

'But I thought you hadn't any euros, Ivo?' said Ellen.

'I expect the butcher will take Visa.'

Ellen asked the waiter for directions to the butcher.

'There you go, Ivo, just round the corner,' she said.

Ivo rose. So did Daniel.

'I doubt they take credit cards,' he said, awkwardly. 'I'd better come too.'

The two men walked off, just as Theo and Betty arrived.

'Thanks,' said Ivo, when they were out of earshot. He was more annoyed by Ellen's needling than he cared to admit, though resolved to keep his cool at all costs. 'I only got back from New York yesterday. It's bad enough having to keep dollars and pounds in the same wallet. I'll get myself sorted in the morning, and pay you back.'

'No problem,' said Daniel easily.

He was used to Ivo sponging off him, and was slightly amused by it – although their friendship had taken a knock some years back when Ivo had not only not paid the rent on Daniel's New York flat, borrowed for three months, but left unpaid a $1000 phone bill. Ivo was so charming that in the end you had to decide whether it was worth the occasional feelings of outrage his behaviour engendered. Much of it, Daniel knew, was pure affectation, and often, just when you decided he was too stingy to go on forgiving, he would do something unexpectedly generous, like sending a crate of vintage champagne. Daniel was very fond of Ivo, whom he counted as his first real friend in London, valuing his good qualities while being in no way blind to his defects. Both of these sprang from a liveliness of mind that he himself lacked, and rather envied. He couldn't help being straight and serious; it was Daniel's nature. Ivo, on the other hand, had once told Daniel that he saw him as his conscience, 'bloody irritating but the only thing that makes me human'. Not that Ivo cared much about his finer feelings. It was as maddening as discussing literature with him.

Before his current incarnation as a film critic, Ivo had been a literary editor. He had read everything, yet he seemed to remember so little of each book, he might as well not have tried. Daniel had smiled on rereading Coleridge's *Lectures on Shakespeare*. Readers, said Coleridge, may be divided into four classes:

1. *Sponges, who absorb all they read, and return it in nearly the same state, only a little dirtied.*
2. *Sand-glasses, who retain nothing, and are content to get through a book for the sake of getting through the time.*
3. *Strain-bags, who retain merely the dregs of what they read.*
4. *Mogul diamonds, equally rare and valuable, who profit by what they read and enable others to profit by it also.*

It was Daniel's ambition to be such a diamond, and to surround himself with others of like mind, but Ivo seemed determined to live up to his name. Of course, he was quite different in print, where he was elegant, intelligent, gallant and wise. This led his friends to suspect that the persona he displayed was not the man within. Daniel could not help feeling curious as to why Ellen seemed to be so mad at him. Impossible to ask, given that he was now sleeping with her in the strange on-and-off way of Transatlantic romances. Ellen was so beautiful, funny and clever that Daniel did not really want to find out more about her past; he was guarded with his feelings, and aware, as only an English academic can be, of all the manifold clichés and booby-traps of love. At least Ivo had been happy to come to Italy with him. That was one of the things Daniel valued about British men: they didn't seem to be rivalrous about women. A fellow-American would be locking horns with him, not keeping him company. Which was just as well, because he was too tired for any problems right now.

The two men looked at the chops displayed on the butcher's gleaming white counter. Ivo's eyes popped out as he saw the price of a Florentine beefsteak, and converted it into sterling.

'How many do you think we'll need?' he asked. 'They seem awfully big.'

'I don't know,' said Daniel, who had never been good at cooking. 'One each?'

'Oh, surely not,' said Ivo. 'The kids will never eat even half, and your mother doesn't look like a big eater.'

'Do you think Meenu eats meat?'

'Well, why shouldn't she?'

Daniel said, 'Isn't she Hindu? Aren't they vegetarians?'

He tried to remember whether she had eaten meat when they had had dinner together, and couldn't.

'Actually, I've no idea, never having met her until today,' said Ivo. 'One could be too sensitive in these matters though. She seems completely Westernised. Well, let's say five, then.'

He held up his hand, and pointed with the other at the steaks. The butcher understood.

'I guess,' said Daniel helplessly, pushing his round spectacles up on his nose, as always when uncomfortable. 'Er – maybe a few sausages as well? Just in case?'

The sausages, marbled with fat and smelling powerfully of garlic and herbs as well as of pork, were duly cut off, and wrapped, first in waxed paper then in a mauve sugar-paper tied with string. The steaks, after careful trimming with an enormous knife, followed.

'Do you take Visa?' asked Ivo, gulping.

It was just as well that Daniel had bought the sausages, for when the steaks were unwrapped in the kitchen of the Casa Luna Ellen counted them, pointedly.

'One-two-three-four-five. Gee. Is anyone here a vegetarian?'

'They are pretty big steaks,' said Hemani.

'Look, the moon is following us, Mummy,' said Robbie, gazing out.

'It isn't really. It's just so much bigger than we are, it seems to.'

'You and Dad are bigger than me, but you don't follow me everywhere.'

44

'That's because we're not up in the sky.'

Bron said, 'Mum? I'm starving.'

Polly gave the children a bowl of crisps.

'Take these outside, and don't quarrel over them,' she said.

The children ran out of doors.

'Really, Polly,' said Betty, 'you might as well give my grandchildren poison as junk food.'

'They'll go into melt-down if they don't have something now,' said Polly.

'My boys never had any snacks but fruit.'

'Perhaps Theo would like some fruit now, then,' said Polly. 'He's out on the terrace, getting the barbecue going. Though I expect he'd rather have wine,' she muttered, as Betty click-clacked out on her kitten heels with an apple and a knife.

'Well fielded,' said Hemani. 'Er, is she staying for the whole holiday?'

Polly laughed, shortly. The spell of silent endurance that Betty's glittering eyes had laid on her from the moment of her engagement did not last once she had left.

'No idea. She invites herself, you see. Theo wouldn't dream of saying no.'

'Uh-huh,' said Ellen. 'How does Dan feel about that?'

'Oh, Dan, bless him,' said Polly, 'is like a soft cushion – always bears the imprint of the last person to sit on him.'

Ellen said stiffly, 'I can't say I've noticed.'

It came into Polly's mind to say something sharp about this, for after all Ellen had been going out with her brother-in-law for only a few months, as far as she could discern. But

45

she didn't want to spoil their first evening, and in any case she knew perfectly well that love is always blind.

'I HATE YOU, I HATE YOU, YOU FAT B-I-T-C-H!' shrieked Tania, the next morning.

'Now, darling, just calm down and pass Robbie the milk.'

'No, I WON'T!' howled Tania, and flounced out on to the terrace, slamming the french window. The adults still lying in bed trying to sleep winced, but evidently it didn't make a loud enough bang, for Tania returned and slammed it again, harder. The lower pane of glass cracked.

'Oh hell,' said Polly.

'She is awful, isn't she, Mummy?' said Robbie. 'She's your bad child and I'm your good child, aren't I?'

'I'm sorry, I'm not well enough to take this,' said Theo. 'I'm going back to sleep.'

The other guests wished they could do the same. They had never before been exposed to the fact that a child of Robbie's age could scream so piercingly if his mother had put insufficient Coco Pops in his breakfast bowl, or that a nine-year-old could have a tantrum just as irrational and prolonged as a toddler's. Everybody had stayed up too late, and although the adults tried to sleep in, it was impossible. Tania, Bron and Robbie were far too excited to stay asleep and, besides, the adults had forgotten to provide them with mosquito repellents in the bedrooms. Nobody had slept well, and at an impossibly early hour the youngest members of the house party had decided that it was time for a swim. Deprived of videos, computer games and above all routine, all three now wandered everywhere. Ellen and Daniel had each been mortified to find themselves being scrutinised while in the bathroom.

'Why are you using tweezers on your chin, instead of a razor?' Tania had asked Ellen; whereas Robbie had simply exclaimed, 'Ugh, yuk, a smelly one!' before diving back out again.

'Pity there isn't a child-repellent, as there is for mosquitoes,' Ivo muttered at lunchtime, and they all laughed guiltily.

The children returned this simmering resentment, particularly during the siesta when they discovered they were not allowed to swim unsupervised, and were expected to amuse themselves for a whole two hours while the adults dozed.

'All they want to do is talk, sleep and eat,' Tania said contemptuously. 'No wonder they're so fat.'

'Yeah,' said Bron. 'They're worse than cats.'

'And they spend so much time in the toilet,' said Robbie, breaking into one of his fizzing laughs at the mention of anything lavatorial, 'sitting on their butts.'

'Bums, not butts,' Tania corrected. 'We only say butts with Dad.'

Grown-ups, thought Tania, were gross. She excepted Ellen, who had great clothes, and who had won her admiration by giving her a vial of purple Hard Candy nail varnish, but otherwise – yuk! Hairy, wobbly, smelly and ugly, they were barely tolerable except at bedtime when, for a brief period, her mother was magically transformed into someone intensely desirable and comforting. And why did they have to be so mad at her all the time? Not that she wasn't mad at Robbie, too, for hanging around with Bron. They had insisted on rooming together right away, and Robbie had put up a sign saying, BEWAARE! BOYS ONLY, DETH TO GURLS. Tania was hurt, because, normally, she and Robbie got on pretty well. She was used to being the leader, and having him as her faithful follower. Now he'd switched to Bron. It was that big-boy, little-boy stuff, soooo boring. He'd rather play with Bron or even hang around with the grown-ups, than play any of her games. Well, more fool he. Tania had been congratulated by her teacher in her last report for her 'rich and imaginative take on reality', which was no more than could be expected for one who had already had two poems in the school magazine. Her brother, however, was having none of it.

'But I say butt,' said Robbie, and immediately fell down on to his, laughing.

Polly was not moaning, but here she was again, one day into the holiday, running up and down stairs to check that her husband had enough cool drinks and Nurofen, in between trying to keep the children to some routine. Theo and she were of one mind as to the importance of this, but it was evident after only twenty-four hours that Meenu had a very different attitude. Bron expected to be able to stay up and have dinner with the adults, rather than have tea at six, and he wanted to keep his light on and read. Bron was clearly used to this, but Robbie without a solid twelve hours of sleep was a nightmare. The boys were determined not to be separated, however, and Meenu was no help. In fact, Polly had already had one of those friendly but tense exchanges of opinion on the proper way to bring up a child, a conversation that all mothers dreaded. It was clear her friend thought she was unnecessarily strict and tense, but then Bron wasn't a noisy, obstreperous child. Not that she didn't prefer darling Robbie, who was so much funnier and livelier . . . and perfectly normal. It must be his genes, she thought. Asian children were always more polite and obedient and hard working, and Bron, she had to admit, was a lot easier to have around than her own two.

On the whole, though, she was glad that Guy Weaver would not be joining them for another week, because Guy, especially now he was a celebrity, was someone you really felt you had to be on good form to enjoy. (Polly had never forgotten the way that, after she had had Tania, he had recoiled and said, 'My God, it's going to need plastic surgery isn't it?') She had already moved into Guy's bedroom for the time being, because Theo was so feverish and restless, though she hoped it was only for a couple of nights. This way, she could catch up on sleep, and start to feel less tense. He had rung Theo's mobile a couple of times to check that it was OK to pitch up. Despite his self-assurance he is, Polly thought fondly, still quite humble and insecure underneath.

Polly pottered around the kitchen, letting herself take possession of the house by a hundred small touches, then stopped. The bedroom she was supposed to share with Theo faced out on one side towards the gardens and cultivated groves, but the other room, which would be Guy's, looked down towards the wild wood whose topmost branches were visible from the house, swaying like green clouds. There were other houses dotted around the hillsides, but mostly they were hard to see, due to a general air of having been there so long that each had become part of the landscape. Polly wondered who lived in these houses, whether they were other holiday-makers like themselves, expatriates, or real peasants. It was all so old: the great black beams on the ceilings, the pitted red terracotta tiles on the floor, the whitewashed walls. Black, white and red, the colours of fairy tales. There were strings of onions and garlic hanging in the kitchen, and a bare slab of thick grey marble to prepare food on, rather than the gleaming hygienic expanses of her own kitchen in London.

What Polly liked most was that everything here seemed to be here because it was loved or used. This was the kind of place that somehow made her feel she was young and a student again. She stirred the sauce she was making in a battered enamel pot and wondered if the owner was interested in cooking. There were good recipe books, at least – Anna del Conte, Elizabeth David, nothing fancy or fashionable.

Alone of all the people staying at the Casa Luna, Polly was curious as to the nature and identity of the person or people to whom it belonged. Could he or she be an artist? There were frescoes in the living room and study and bedroom, all done by the same hand. They showed pink and grey towers of medieval hill-towns, rather like those in the background of early Renaissance paintings, and hunting scenes in which hawks pursued doves and hounds sniffed out half-hidden hares in flowery meads. Polly thought them delightful, as did Ellen. But then, why were there so many books? She played her favourite detective game of trying to work out what the owner was like by looking at the bookshelves, but soon gave up because the owner's interests were too diverse. Who on earth read all of Nabokov and also *The Scarlet Pimpernel*? Could the same person really have bought Henry Green and Helen Fielding? At least there *were* books. That was almost the worst thing about Theo's colleagues, you went into their multimillion-pound houses and there were never any bookshelves, just coffee-table tomes, and perhaps one novel that had become fashionable as the result of a ton of hype. How could people live like that? It must be like trying not to breathe. When Polly went to houses like these, she felt as if she was slowly suffocating.

She thought, however, that she would like W. Shade, whoever she or he was. Surely, people who liked the same books liked each other? Surely there was nothing more likely to make you kindred spirits than sharing the joy of entering into an imaginary world? Polly belonged to a reading group, and attending it was the one thing that reminded her that she still had a brain and was not just a kind of domestic appliance for her family's convenience. It wasn't as though she minded being that antiquated thing, a wife and mother, for to tell the truth she gloried in it and thought that people who deprived themselves of their children's childhood were mad. But since she had arrived here she was reminded that she had given up a career, whereas Ellen and Hemani were both forging ahead. They meet people through work, and I do need more friends, she thought, not just other mums I meet at the school gates. On the other hand, I could have been like poor Meenu, and be slaving my guts out as a divorcée. I am a lucky woman. But Polly, as always, kept these thoughts to herself.

Chapter Three

'I long for the simple life,' Betty announced over lunch. 'I always wanted to buy a little place like this, but my husbands could never understand my passion for *la dolce vita*.'

Daniel, who remembered how she had hated staying at his father's house in Martha's Vineyard, was surprised to learn this, but his mother was in a good mood. She had discovered there was a hairdresser in Cortona who, for a ridiculously small sum, would attend to her coiffure at the house. Tuscany, therefore, was not without its compensations. Betty had not washed her own hair for thirty years, and had really been quite concerned that she might have to start doing so. The picture of elegance in camel and navy, she was prepared to be benign.

'This is quite charming,' she said. 'If only poor dear Winkie could have come too, my happiness would be complete.'

Those who had encountered Betty's third son, Winthrop, privately breathed a sigh of relief that this was not the case.

'How clever of you boys to have found this truly *bellissima* cottage. Even with my grandchildren behaving like savages, the views are exceptional.'

'Actually,' said Daniel, 'it was Polly who did it all, Mother.'

'Was it?' said Betty, in a tone poised between incredulity and genuine surprise. 'Well, how convenient for you.' She paused. 'You must find this a great inspiration in your work, Ellen dear.'

'I do,' said Ellen, smiling. 'I adore this landscape. It's so authentic.'

'Of course,' Ivo said, 'it's so good to be in the real countryside where happy peasants toil to provide us with massively subsidised virgin olive oil, lifting their hats to wish one "*buon giorno*". So unlike the hideous British *campagna*, or, for that matter, the American kind, all those endless flat fields of cattle and corn that actually feed people. When I think that our taxes go on supporting this unspoilt way of life, I feel quite delighted.'

It is much harder to be disagreeable when the sun shines.

'Ivo, have you actually ever been to Tuscany before or are you just pretending?' said Ellen. 'Because there are no peasants left, actually.'

'It's all based on what he sees at the movies,' Daniel suggested.

'Yes, the moment somebody English and middle class opens his mouth in the cinema, one simply has to see rows of cypress trees,' said Ivo. 'It's really the only landscape in which one is acceptable, these days, as our dear prime minister has discovered.'

'I didn't know you'd converted to the Left,' said Polly.

'Well, you see, the food is so much better,' said Ivo.

'Just don't let him charm you,' Ellen muttered to Hemani. 'He turns it on like someone flicking a switch. It isn't real.'

'Well, it is while it lasts,' said Hemani. She rather liked Ivo, though she could see he wasn't to be trusted.

'Ivo, you do realise that you don't have to stay in character,' said Polly. 'You're on holiday, you are allowed to be dull occasionally.'

'Oh, I know,' said Ivo. 'But I have to provide a leaven of mischief wherever I go. That's what is expected of me. If people talked about Jews or blacks in the way they talk about journalists they'd be prosecuted for racial hatred.'

'You think that's bad, you should hear lawyer jokes,' said Polly.

'Oh, but everyone is allowed to hate lawyers because you're paid so much more. I was giving a talk to chaps at my old school last month, and one of them said, "If I get a First, I'll be a lawyer like my Dad; if I get a Second, I'll be a banker, and if I get a Third, I'll be a journalist like you."'

'What did you say to that?' asked Polly, not displeased by this ranking.

'Dream on,' said Ivo.

Each morning the light came through the slats of the shutters in ripples, and as it washed towards the inhabitants of the Casa Luna it smoothed away memories of the past. It was for this that they had endured long hours in the grey English winter or freezing American climes, for this that they had waited and planned and worked extra hours. The horrible feelings of stress, tension, anger and frustration that coursed through their veins every day almost unnoticed began to fade.

Not everyone was happy about this. Theo, jerked from an environment in which to leave the office at 3 a.m. was to be accused of doing a half-day, kept feeling that he was missing a breakfast meeting on a Sunday morning. Feverishly, he tossed and turned, tormented by all the unfilled time ahead of him until he could get back to work. He rang his office on his mobile three times a day to check how things were going, though what with the weak signal he had at the Casa Luna and the comparative emptiness of the office in summer, it was hard to get anyone to talk to him. Betty, it was true, came up to see him every morning and afternoon, but that was mostly to lecture him about how he was not swallowing enough vitamins. She herself took so many that it was a wonder she didn't rattle, but then Mother saw any sickness as a sign of weakness, and any sign of weakness as sickness. There had been a time, before his marriage, when this had made them fall out – it was one of the reasons why he'd been glad to be posted to the London office – but even though Mother and Polly didn't get along too well, he knew she was proud of him. He was proud of himself, Theo had to admit. To have made partner by thirty-two and be pulling in one million dollars a year was to have got to the top of the tree. Betty kept urging him to go in for politics next, but Theo had seen enough of that with his half-brother Winthrop's family. He, like Winthrop, had been given the lecture by his stepfather: 'Son, you know why geese always fly in a "V"? Because one goose, yes, one alone is born to lead. Remember, leaders are born, not made.'

Theo had believed this, as far as it went, but not in its more extreme form. This was just as well, because there were rumours that Win, while at boarding school in England, had actually murdered another boy. Theo had been a trainee then, working crazy hours, and the details of it were vague but he knew it had cost a lot of money to get his half-brother out of trouble. There had been a time when Betty had feared that he, too, was going off the rails but he had pulled his life around in time and now he was safe, with Polly and the kids.

I must enjoy this – it's quality time with my family, he kept telling himself sternly. Luckily, he and Polly could talk to each other rationally, unlike so many other couples. It was fortunate they could have separate rooms, at least until Guy arrived. Theo sighed. He didn't know what he'd do when that happened; he was trying not to think of the complications. Some of the dreams he had, of squeezing through narrow sea-caves, desperate to escape before the tide came in, made him think that he must stop taking his medication.

Theo was not alone in his night fevers and restlessness. Each inhabitant of the house had the feeling that something new and strange was surfacing in their private selves. No matter how hard they pretended to be normal, within twenty-four hours, they started to drift away from the quotidian. At present, the sensation was gentle and even pleasant.

'It's odd, just looking doesn't feel like doing nothing,' said Hemani. The olive groves swayed and rippled in the faint breeze, as if invisible beings walked over the furry grasses. The person who cut, with exquisite delicacy, into people's eyeballs with a scalpel for a living seemed infinitely remote.

'It isn't nothing,' said Ivo lazily. 'It's living. What we forget to do for most of the year.'

He was relishing being in the light. Ivo spent about a fortnight of every month stuck in the bowels of a museum, theatre or tiny preview cinema. It was easy enough, once he'd trawled through the enormous glossy folders of rubbish and hype that accompanied each of these excursions, to write the reviews that had made him famous, but he sometimes felt like a troglodyte.

'If only it were,' said Polly. 'If I owned a place like this, I'd never leave it.'

She looked at the vast arc of burning blue and remembered the way everything at home, including the sky, was so pinched.

'Oh, don't talk about leaving already,' said Ellen. 'Let's pretend we're here for ever.'

'Such peace,' said Hemani, drowsily. In the green shade above her head two white doves chuckled and cooed.

Then the children, shrieking, tore past and dive-bombed into the pool, crying one after the other, 'Bombs away!'

'Hush, darlings. Not so loudly,' said Hemani. They ignored her. For them, the only point of being in Italy was to swim as much as possible. Polly and Hemani had of course brought books to read, but that was the last thing a stressed-out schoolgirl needed on holiday, and Robbie had yet to make the jump to enjoying chapter-books. Bron shared his Indian comics, but there was only so often you could read a comic, and after they had all done drawings of the monkey-god Hanuman they became bored again. Nobody was playing with them, and, outside the pool, they had no idea how to play with each other. They lay in bed, wide-awake, listening to the story-tapes, but by the third day they knew every word of *The Jungle Book*, *The Hobbit* and *Tales From Shakespeare* by heart. Anyway, Tania, and Robbie wanted to be active. Within twenty-four hours, they had become almost feral. On the second day they found the body of a dead porcupine, and extracted its long black and white quills to stick into their hair or carry as miniature weapons. They were each bought a paint-kit in Cortona, but used these to decorate themselves and each other, spending hours on anointing their browning limbs with scrolls of green or blue that washed off as soon as they went into the water.

Polly gave up trying to make her children wear anything other than sun-block. It wasn't worth the effort and stress, as she agreed with Hemani. Each felt that if she could run a brush through their hair and shove a toothbrush in their mouths once a day she was doing well. It was the holidays, after all, and if children wanted to run around practically naked then they should. From a distance they looked enchanting, dancing through the flower-beds, running through the wisteria tunnel or climbing among the silvery leaves of olives, their slim figures supple, shining with grease and grace.

Close up, it was another matter. On the very first day, Robbie had scratched his name indelibly on a stone step, Tania had picked half the unripe lemons from the potted trees in the garden and Bron had cut innumerable flowers with short stems as a bouquet for his mother. They forgot to flush lavatories, they stole crisps and, above all, *they just made so much noise*. Incessantly, the three of them bounded around fighting, tumbling, climbing, teasing, questioning, maddening: the sound of their laughter, at once joyous and callous, echoed off the stone walls at all hours.

'It's so like living in one of those nature films by Sir David Attenborough,' Ellen remarked to Hemani. 'Only without the sex,' she added gloomily.

She was lying by the pool in the shade of a white hibiscus tree, attempting to read a chunky pink paperback chronicling the romantic arrangements of four blondes in New York, and it was making her restive.

So far, Daniel had not come into her room. Did that mean they weren't going out together any more, or just that he was tired? Of course, Ellen, as a modern woman, could always go to his, but she knew that this was not the best way forward. She absolutely could not continue the way she was living in New York, where you could (as Ellen pretty much did) have a face like Gwyneth's and a body like Giselle's and *still* not even get a date. Although she would never have admitted it, one reason why she had opened her shop off Bond Street was purely and simply to have an excuse to trawl London for a mate. It was no use looking to British guys, needless to say – they were all said to be gay, or worse, if Ivo was anything to go by – but at home the likelihood of her finding Daniel would have been insurmountable. She sighed. They were so made for each other, it was ridiculous, but so far they had had sex together only three times, which was better than nothing but still not really serious, particularly because she travelled so much. Surely, if he was as mad about her as she was about him, he wouldn't be able to resist? Ellen was sick of guys who expected you to put out even if you had your own Schwab account just because they'd paid for a meal, and yet Daniel didn't seem that kind of man. He was really nice, all through, even when, mindful of his family fortune, she had taken him window-shopping. If he was in love, he wouldn't wait long to get that Harry Winston diamond on her finger. If . . .

'Book no good?' asked Hemani. She herself was re-reading *A Room with a View* and finding it had, in that mysterious way of good novels, altered. When she had first read it as a teenager, she had taken all it said about being on the side of youth, beauty, music and socialism very seriously. Then, she had turned to fiction as a way of mapping out areas of human wisdom and experience that she had not yet encountered. Now, she understood that it was a comedy – a comedy of a very unusual and enchanting kind, but still a comedy. She wondered how she could possibly have missed this before. Was it that good novels, like real people, revealed different aspects of themselves according to the reader's capacity to understand them at the time? Or had she just been stupid with solemnity, like most teenagers? Hemani had grown up in a house full of books, books in both English and Hindi, but she had had less and less time to read during her years of training as a medic. Her parents were highly cultured people, but to them culture was an ornament. They were both doctors, working and living in Kilburn, the suburb of London where she lived also. Hemani, like her middle sister Laili, was the good daughter who had followed in their footsteps, whereas her youngest sister Shirin had been (at least until Hemani's divorce) the black sheep of the family. Hemani did not read as much as she would have liked, for her relaxation was music. Unlike Daniel she did not take this so far as to bring her instrument on holiday. Daniel practised religiously: the Bach *Suite in D Minor* emerged every afternoon just as the rest of the house was trying to have a siesta. Hemani thought it was too mournful, too introspective for their mood at present, but then that was Daniel, whose thoughtfulness irritated her now. She was overjoyed to be reunited with her two girlfriends.

Ellen said petulantly, 'The characters are all just such horrible people.'

'Don't you find that funny?'

'Well, no, because I can't identify with them.'

Hemani said, 'I always laugh at books with horrid people – oh, not horrid like psychopaths, just ridiculous and rude.'

'But you wouldn't want to be with people who were like that in real life, would you?' asked Ellen.

'Well, no, but then neither do they get punished for it in reality. You should see the consultants I work with. If there were any justice they'd all be working as porters, not giving each other merit awards of £150,000 a year. But I want fiction to be a better version of life. Or at least a way of making people more human. Of course, my ex never agreed. He thought it was all style at one end and the balance sheet at the other.'

'He's a publisher, isn't he?' said Ellen.

'Yes,' said Hemani guardedly.

'I think I've even been to his house. Notting Hill, isn't it?'

'Mm.'

Ellen persisted, 'And you're in a flat in Finchley? You didn't get a good lawyer?'

'I thought it more important to stay friends. Besides, it's close to my parents, and I couldn't keep working without my mother's help.'

'You can't stay friends with your exes,' said Ellen. 'Not if you're honest.'

'Well, if you have children together, you at least have to try,' said Hemani. 'Otherwise what are you telling them? That once you loved someone enough to have a child with him, and now you hate his guts?'

Ellen said suddenly, 'I don't think I'll ever marry. I'm not thin enough, or toned enough.'

'Goodness. Really?'

'Really,' said Ellen.

Hemani looked at the woman on the sun-bed beside her, and wondered what, in that case, Ellen must think of the rest of humanity if she herself fell so far short of her ideal. Every movement she made expressed the kind of breeding that the English reserve for their horses. She was perfect, from the top of her blond head to the tips of her pedicured toes. Hemani felt uncomfortably aware of the stubble growing back not only all the way up her legs but also on her forearms. Waxing and threading, she thought, why did I forget? She had inherited her mother's luxuriant tresses, her lustrous, deep-lidded eyes, and the lush curves of a Hindu goddess, but the hairiness was always what she was conscious of.

'But loads of people do get married. I mean, it isn't a sort of beauty contest, you know.'

Ellen, having finished creaming her own flesh, turned to her. She didn't believe in complaining, and was slightly ashamed of her outburst already. I'll have to watch myself here, she thought. She wasn't used to living with other people, only partying with them.

'You'll burn, Meenu. Want some of this? It's really good.'

'Oh, thanks,' said Hemani.

'Here. Turn on to your front, and I'll do your back and shoulders.'

Hemani couldn't help flinching, and wincing, as though Ellen were hurting something tender and raw as she spread the cream over her shoulders, though in fact it was rather pleasant, and smelt of roses. Hemani was painfully reminded that it had been four years since anyone other than her son had touched her, although she herself touched other people in the most intimate places every day of her working life. It was horrible being chaste, even if you got used to it after a while. But she couldn't risk fresh mistakes. Her whole life was work and Bron, and there was no time or energy for other encounters. Even getting to play with the Viner brothers' quartet was often more than she could manage, though her mother was happy to babysit, and was always urging her to go out more. Hemani loved Bron with a passion that she tried to deny because she worried that this would damage him psychologically. She watched her son covertly. He didn't like her being over-protective, and she had to pretend to be indifferent to all that he did, while churning with anxiety. I ought to make more of a fuss of Tania, she thought; after all, I am her godmother, as Polly is Bron's.

Hemani and Polly had been the first of their group of friends to become pregnant, and it had created a bond between them that she sometimes found troublesome. Polly's ideas on child-rearing were different from her own – just how different, the two women had never quite realised, for their children met infrequently. Hemani, always conscious of hygiene, insisted children washed their hands really thoroughly before meals, but otherwise had a relaxed attitude about bedtimes. Bron was used to staying up late and chatting to grown-ups as an equal. Polly seemed not to bother about hygiene, but had fixed ideas about meals and manners: all of which should have made communal life easier, except that it was Bron who was behaving beautifully, and Tania and Robbie who were out of control. Not that Hemani was going to point this out; but it was already starting to annoy everyone else. Why did the house have to run like clockwork? Why was Polly so obsessed by punctuality and by meals? All anyone wanted was a salad and a few bits of mozzarella or salami, not a two- or three-course meal.

Ellen smoothed the cream on to Hemani's back, bending forward. The large platinum-mounted diamond hanging from her neck winked. Daniel and Ivo, both of whom were pretending to read, were mesmerised. Catching sight of this, Hemani felt suddenly despondent. It had seemed like the most wonderful suggestion of Polly's six months ago, in mid-winter, to come out here, but already she was worried. How could she have forgotten that Bron could be such a handful? And then there was her figure. She had spent so much of the past five years desperately working her way up to senior house officer that she was sure her thighs had almost doubled in size. Now she was trying to pretend to her body that she loved it, really, and that its neglect wasn't intentional. It wasn't fooled. It knew that this was only a brief period, that she would forget it again just as a child, having rediscovered a toy and made much of it, would, from one day to the next, lose it.

'Have you tried waxing?' said Ellen.

'My problem is, I can't see the point of body maintenance when I don't have a boyfriend,' said Hemani.

'My problem is,' said Ellen softly, 'I don't want to marry someone who just wants me for my money.'

Hemani thrilled to what was obviously an invitation to confidence from the most glamorous person she knew. Ellen had been a lonely American girl in London when Hemani had first got to know her, through Polly. Now, Ellen was quite famous as well as very rich. The shoe and bag company she had started following her brief stint on *Vogue* had flour-ished. Ellen had appeared in gossip columns, she had been interviewed by glossy magazines and she existed on an altogether higher plane, even, than the Nobles. It was remarkable, really, that she wanted to spend any time with them at all rather than with the famous film stars and models who had made an 'Ellen' the essential bag to carry. But Ellen had told her that these people, delightful though they were, counted as work not relaxation, and that she would far rather holiday with real friends.

'Are you thinking of getting married?' Hemani asked.

Ellen didn't say that she would marry Daniel at once if he asked her, or that she had come out to this holiday at Polly's invitation. Instead, she said meaningfully, 'If I was sure.'

'And, you'd only consider a man from your own background?'

'Well, who else can you trust?'

They were both speaking very softly, as if conscious that the men on the other side of the pool might have some interest in their discussion.

'I don't think what went wrong between Bruce and me was having different backgrounds. My parents think it was, but it wasn't.'

'Yeah,' said Ellen. 'You were what, twenty-four?'

'Almost.'

Ellen groaned. 'A baby, having a baby.'

Hemani blushed.

'I don't think we'd have done it if my mum hadn't discovered some contraceptive pills in my laundry when I went home. You never met Bruce, did you? They got really heavy, insisted on meeting him and treating him like my fiancé. I was so embarrassed. Asian families, you know, they're still very strict. But then I got pregnant, and, well . . . They still think it's shocking. I'm a ruined woman.' She spoke lightly, the bitterness long since gone.

'If I had a daughter, I'd tell her never, on any account, get married before she's thirty. You're too young before then to be smart. Your twenties are just about dating. It's when you're our age that you should start looking,' said Ellen.

'Was that what you came away on holiday for?' Hemani asked. Ellen lifted her head and looked at Hemani over the rounded black rectangles of her sunglasses.

'Sure. Why did you come here?'

Hemani put her own dark glasses on. 'Oh, to see Tuscany, and Polly, of course. And have a rest, you know.'

'Not a chance,' said Ellen; 'especially with Thing One and Thing Two around.'

'And Thing Three,' said Hemani, sighing. She felt mean saying this about Bron, but she did wish he'd be slightly less exuberant. He and Tania were both shrieking at each other, quarrelling over whose legs Robbie should swim through. Perhaps I should have left him with Bruce, she thought. He gets on pretty well with him, after all, and Georgie is as good a stepmother as anyone could wish for. But they had their new baby, and she'd wanted some time with her son.

'Personally,' said Ellen, 'I think vacations are for trying something different. That's always uncomfortable at first, just like a new pair of shoes.'

She looked with some complacency at one of her own creations, its long gold leather straps tumbled on the velvety grass below. As usual, they were exquisite. Even at $500 a pair, they had flown out of her shops in London and New York.

'The problem with that, though, is that you always bring yourself, don't you?' said Hemani.

'Don't you think people change according to their environment?' asked Ellen, who couldn't help hoping that they did. She wasn't too happy with herself, either, come to that. Ever since her father had remarried, she had felt lonely and ill at ease with the life she had been living.

'Well, are you a different person in New York from what you are in London?'

Ellen pondered. 'For me both are work. But yes, I am a little different. I can't wear so much jewellery in England.'

'It is strange, isn't it? I feel somehow,' said Hemani, yawning and turning over, 'as if anything could happen.'

'Like what?'

'Oh, I don't know. Perhaps I'll just fall madly in love, chuck my career and stay here for ever.'

'I wouldn't recommend Ivo.'

'Yes, I gathered that.'

Hemani looked at the men, who, face-down, were having their own muttered conversation across the pool. She wanted to ask Ellen why she hated Ivo, but felt this would be tactless.

'Do you think there's just one person who's right for you?' Ellen said.

'Probably not. But there are loads of wrong ones.'

'I think it is just one. The difficulty is recognising him.'

'You think it isn't always obvious?'

'Not always, no.'

'What's obvious?' asked Polly, joining them. She had brought some long glasses half-filled with fast-melting ice, and a jug of home-made lemonade.

'Oh, Polly, you are a star!' said Hemani guiltily. 'We were talking about how you know it when you've met The One. You know, to marry.'

Polly sighed. Sometimes she felt so old.

'How did you know it was Theo?' asked Ellen. 'Did lights flash and bells ring?'

'Of course, he's so handsome it can't have been hard,' said Hemani. Privately, she thought Theo rather too handsome, like a male model. He was so much of a good thing that in some curious way she never felt he was quite there, quite real. But then Daniel had something of the same quality. Perhaps it was just growing up very rich. Her eyes had almost popped out when she set eyes on Betty, with all her diamonds and couture clothes. She hadn't realised Daniel came from that kind of family, he didn't dress like a rich person and she'd thought, naively, that Theo had made it all. It made her even more wary and uncomfortable with him.

'Goodness,' said Polly vaguely, 'it's a bit like buying a house. You know, there are ones you go into, and they seem fine but there's something about them that you don't like. And then there are others that need lots of work but you think, Yes, I could be happy here.'

'I'd love your life,' said Ellen.

'Would you? But you've got a career.'

'Yes. My brilliant career, designing shoes and bags. It isn't going to make anyone's life better, is it?' said Ellen. She didn't normally think this way, comparing her life to Polly and Hemani's.

'Of course it is,' said Hemani. 'That is, if you can afford them.'

'I must give you a trade discount, next time you come into my shop,' said Ellen.

Robbie sidled up.

'Shall I give you a kiss, Mummy?'

'Yes please,' said Polly.

He nestled up to her, and rested his lips on her neck. Then he blew a loud raspberry. She jumped. He burst into giggles, and ran off.

'Wicked imp,' said Polly. The ice tinkled as she poured the lemonade.

'How about us?' called Ivo, instantly alert. 'Don't we get any?'

'Get some yourself, lazybones!' Ellen called back. 'Honestly, Polly, don't take him any. You used to be such a feminist, and now you're waiting on everyone hand and foot.'

'So what sort of work did Theo need done to him?' Hemani asked, mischievously. 'New wiring, new furnishing or just redecoration?'

'Remarkably little,' said Polly, wondering uneasily whether she had just been disloyal. She hated women who were disloyal to their husbands. 'It's probably me who's changed the most.'

'Yes, that's the problem, isn't it?' said Hemani. 'You think

71

you can stay the same but somehow the woman always accommodates the bloke. And then you've got boring, and they don't love you any more, and you may as well not have bothered.'

Polly rose.

'Love is such a disturbing element,' she said. 'You can never predict it, any more than the rest of the world can assimilate it. You wouldn't think something so beautiful can cause so much unhappiness or pain. People make too much of it altogether.'

Ellen followed Polly's retreating figure with her eyes. Hemani said, guiltily, 'I should go and help too.'

'Relax. Nobody's asking her to do all this.'

'If she didn't, then nothing would get done,' said Hemani. 'And Theo's ill.'

Ellen's voice dropped. 'Do you think everything's OK between them?'

'Why shouldn't it be?'

'Just wondering.'

'Why? Have you heard something?'

'Oh, no, but—'

A shrieking Tania fled past, pursued by Robbie.

'Those kids . . .' said Ellen crossly. 'They're cute to look at, but they're just savages, aren't they?'

'Mm,' said Hemani.

'Hey, kids, show some consideration!' Ellen shouted.

'You suck!' said Robbie. The children disappeared, again, their shrieks and giggles fading.

'Betty's right, their manners are terrible.'

'It's watching *The Simpsons* that does it.'

Hemani yawned, and listened to the doves in the acacia tree overhead. I must try with Tania, she thought.

'We all work too hard, even the children,' she said to Ellen. 'Do you know, they've all done exams this year – even poor little Robbie, to get into the junior school where he's at? You should be pottering about with footballs at six, not revising times tables. It's cruel, and now they need to unwind. Still, they will. This is a magical place, isn't it?'

'It would be if that bozo Ivo wasn't here,' said Ellen. 'I mean, Ivo, what a ridiculous name! How could anyone take a guy seriously who's called that?' She imitated an English accent. 'My name is Sponge, Ivo Sponge, of Her Majesty's Secret Service.'

'Well, you've got some pretty odd ones too,' said Hemani, smiling. 'Dwight, Teddy, Wayne . . .'

'And look at that suit he's wearing. Pink flowers and red hair, puh-leese.'

'A carnivorous plant,' said Hemani, smiling.

'Yeah. So many men, so few with sense. Oh, Meenu,' said Ellen, sighing, 'what is it with me? Do I have horns coming out of my head, or something? All the guys I date seem either mad or bad.'

'They aren't all bad,' said Hemani, anxious for her son. 'I do believe that.'

'Ugh, go away!' said Ellen, sitting up. Bron was running round and round her sun-lounger dripping cold water all over her like a dog, chased by Robbie. 'C'mon, guys, give me a break.'

73

'Put a towel round you, boys,' suggested the practical Hemani. 'You can pretend to be emperors, or priests.'

'I'm Rama, and he's Hanuman,' Bron explained. 'We're fighting the demon Ravana.'

'And monkeys are really wicked,' said Robbie, hardly able to speak for laughter.

Ellen stood up. Hemani noticed that the eyes of both men, now lying on the other side of the pool, immediately followed her.

'I'm going to catch you!' Ellen said archly.

'Nah-nah-nah,' Robbie chanted, and pulled down his swimming trunks to show her his small bare bottom.

Across the pool, the men laughed, a hearty male laughter of solidarity.

'Want any help, Ellen?' said Ivo, in mock concern.

'Frankly, I don't think there's anything you could show me that would impress,' said Ellen, and stalked off to the house.

Tania had discovered a hammock slung between two trees all overcanopied with a rambling rose. She was lying, watching the sky swing backwards and forwards in the faint warm breeze. She had made herself a crown of daisies and was thinking, in a dreamy sort of way, about what she would wear next. Spiderwebs perhaps, all hung about with dew-drops. Or else a dress of rose petals, the creamiest at her neck and the deepest crimson by her feet . . . She was feeling left out. Nobody would play ping-pong with her, and the boys had decided to make a gang that was just boys.

74

She watched a butterfly flutter by, and enjoyed herself repeating these words dreamily. Tania loved playing word games. She would exhaust herself on car journeys unscrambling car number plates to form words, or going through the alphabet to find every word that rhymed with one that occurred to her. She couldn't remember a time when she didn't read, though she did remember when she had learnt to write, her painful pothooks straggling across the page. Tania knew that when she was grown-up she was going to be a poet. She had so many ideas, and the words just wouldn't be quiet. They quivered and thrummed, just out of reach like that horde of midges forming and reforming itself into a pattern that looked like somebody's face, only it melted in the blink of an eye.

'Can I have a go?'

Bron's face appeared above her own.

'Yes,' said Queen Tania, graciously. 'If you pay the price.'

'What is it?'

She pursed up her mouth, and the tiny midge-voices said, Ask him, ask him.

'You have to kiss me.'

Bron looked startled. Then Robbie's mischievous face bobbed up.

'Ow, ow, get off me, little brat!'

Robbie had scrambled up on to the hammock.

'Get off, duh-brain! This is mine.'

'Won't.'

Enraged, Tania kicked him. He thumped her. At once, she transformed into a snarling wolf.

'This is my place, mine.'

'No it's not, it's mine.'

'Selfish shellfish.'

'Fat cow, fat smelly-bottomed cow. No returns!'

'No returns back.'

'Children, children,' called Polly. 'Stop quarrelling or you'll ruin the holiday.'

'It's ruined anyway,' hissed Tania. 'I gave Bron permission, not you.'

'You only say that because you fancy him.'

'No I don't,' said Tania, furious.

'Yes you do, stupid. Your little Indian boyfriend,' said Robbie in a hateful, whiny voice.

'Meenu's my godmother, mine, not yours,' said Tania. 'You don't play with him properly; you just want him to be your henchman.'

The sky, which minutes before had been so clear and blue, was filling up with clouds, and a wind shook down a confetti of pale pink petals.

'Bron is my age, and he should be my friend, not yours.'

'He doesn't like your stupid girlie games,' said Robbie. 'You'd like us to do dancing with you, wouldn't you? Well, we won't.'

'Look,' said Bron, getting up, 'I only wanted to try the hammock.'

'Either play with me or bog off!' said Queen Tania.

'Fine,' said Bron.

He went, glad to be left alone for a while. In his imagination he could see his figure, like that of Rama, gliding through the grasses, sorrowing. Bron examined this figure of himself with a kind of sad satisfaction. He liked Rama, partly because blue skin was groovy, and partly because he just liked him. Rama had had all kinds of bad stuff happen, even though he was a god, and he had still gone on fighting. He was a superhero, really. Some people said that gods didn't exist, but Bron knew they did, inside you. Everyone had a Rama and a Shiva and a Hanuman and a demon Ravana, because everyone had the whole universe inside as well as outside. Only lots of people didn't realise it.

Bron had been five when Dad had finally left, after a series of exchanges in which his parents sounded like angry cobras. They had tried to hide it from him, but Bron had known, even when his grave little face had showed nothing beyond round-eyed surprise. He was frightened, but he understood that they were not in control of their feelings, any more than he was when he stumbled and hurt himself. Where this knowledge came from, he didn't know. Shirin Auntie said it was because he was an old soul, but Laili Auntie said it came from growing up with girls.

'Don't cry, Mummy, I'll look after you,' he often told Hemani, patting her soft hands, and she would hug him and smile again. He loved her so, so much that it made his stomach feel funny. There were many questions Bron himself asked about it all, such as if you got married twice, once as a Christian and once as a Hindu, did you have to get divorced twice too? But remembering the wedding made Mum too sad, so he'd ask about other things instead, like why it took so long for starlight to reach the earth, and whether when you looked at space you were also looking at time. She was always interesting about stuff like that. They would talk about science and germs and things for hours. Dad would come back, Bron was quite sure of that. How could anyone look at Mum and not love her?

But recently, Dad had married again, to Georgie, who was tall and thin like a drink of cold water, who had two children of her own, Cosmo and Flora. They were younger than he was, but he'd been able to handle it; he'd even been quite proud of having a new half-sister because it made him more like everyone else in his class. Practically nobody didn't have a broken home these days, even other Asian kids. Grandma said it was because of mixed marriages, and marrying for love instead of by the old ways, but it was more than that. Nothing was fixed any more. Bron, who loved order and who made meticulous arrangements of all the things he found according to size or colour or function, couldn't understand why people couldn't order and arrange themselves.

Bron sighed, because what made him most uncomfortable of all was the feeling that what Robbie and Tania were angry about was himself. He did try with Tania, partly because Mum was her godmother and so that made them linked, and sometimes, when she wasn't being silly and dressing like a pop-tart, she could be quite fun. She was the one who'd invented the game of getting the grown-ups to stand one behind the other with their legs open for them to swim through. He did love the pool. It was much nicer, this, than the holidays he'd had before – or it would be if only people could be friends. It was odd, he thought: grown-ups were supposed to be able to choose who they went about with, unlike children, but none of these people seemed to really get along. Perhaps that wasn't why they were here; or perhaps, as so often with grown-ups, they simply hadn't noticed yet.

Chapter Four

Ivo was an old hand at house parties, and knew that the trick of enjoying them was to seize pleasure rather than inch gingerly towards it. Immediately commandeering the best sun-bed, he left it only to wander to the fridge for more beer, or some of the children's crisps. The others accepted this behaviour without question, partly because they were too polite to fight but also because themselves were too self-conscious about appearing in their swimming costumes to think about anything else. Both women were careful to put on their sarongs when not in the water, and Daniel immediately began to do lengths, but Ivo remained fully clothed. At a certain point, the temptation of the cool water would become too much and then Ivo, too, would have to hope that his freckled flesh was less flabby than he recalled. Until then, he was going to wait.

'Well, what d'you think?' Ivo said, watching Hemani rub

sun-lotion into Ellen's back. He was making no pretence at reading. 'A little lesbian action there later on?'

'Er – no,' said Daniel, shocked. He towelled himself dry, and lay down on his stomach. At least I don't have hair on my chest, Ivo thought. Daniel was so handsome it made him feel slightly sick, or would have done had his friend shown the slightest sign of being aware of it.

'Ellen's up for anything.'

Daniel knew he was being teased, but said blandly, 'She seems OK to me.'

'She's a user,' said Ivo. Daniel was startled.

'Drugs?'

'People.' This was pretty rich, coming from Ivo, but then it takes one to know one, Daniel thought. He pondered what Ivo had said. On the one hand, it was clearly tainted by malice, an impulse he himself could never understand, and which made him uneasy largely because it suggested a greater complexity of motive than he felt able to deal with, at least beyond the printed page. On the other . . . It was impossible not to see Ellen's beauty and not want to possess it, at least if it were offered him. She was honest about her desires, and he respected that. He would far rather have someone who was honest from the start, but honesty was hard to find. Meenu, for instance, had not lied but neither had she told him the truth about having a son. Was he supposed to know this already? Had her omission ever to mention Bron's existence been one of those stiff-upper-lip British habits that he still kept misunderstanding? He really liked Hemani, he'd thought they were friends, but he'd blown it somehow, because she would hardly talk to him, even here.

'She's got her eye on you, Dan old boy. You'll be hand-cuffed and frog-marched up the aisle if you're not careful.'

Daniel said uneasily, 'Well, we have been seeing each other, but it's not at that stage. You, er, were interested once, weren't you?'

'Nah,' said Ivo, shrugging. 'Ellen's ambitious. I'm just another hack.'

'I wouldn't say that at all,' said Daniel, with the kind of honesty that was too transparent for even Ivo to be suspicious of. 'Right now, I'd say you're probably the best there is in your profession.'

'Journalism isn't a profession,' said Ivo, irritably.

'It isn't?'

'No. A profession is like what you do, or accountancy or law or medicine. You have to pass exams and do a Ph.D. No, what I do is a craft, or a branch of experimental fiction, and I'm by no means the best. Though possibly,' he added modestly, 'I'm one of them. Anyway, I don't earn enough to register on Ellen's radar.'

'Neither do I,' said Daniel firmly. Ivo raised an eyebrow, for it was impossible not to know that Daniel's father, though also an academic, had belonged to the kind of East Coast family that lived off the income of their income. Furthermore, few impoverished academics had a flat in Manhattan as well as one in Kensington. But then, Ivo had never really understood about trust funds and tax havens. Certainly, Daniel, while generous to his friends, didn't splash money about.

'Why do you think she's out here at all?'

'Because Polly asked her, I guess.'

'Come off it! She looks at you the way a tigress looks at a tethered goat.'

'I think that's just her contacts,' said Daniel, flushing. 'She said she was having problems with them.'

'Yeah, sure. Did she ask you to look and see if there was something in them?'

'There wasn't, that I could see.'

'Funny, ' said Ivo. 'There wasn't when I looked, either.'

Ivo knew he was stirring, but then stirring, he thought, was his *raison d'être*. Daniel dropped his voice.

'You sound pretty mad at her.'

'Mad!' said Ivo, loudly. 'Were I not a gent, I'd be hunting for scorpions to drop down her neck. I'd be digging pits full of vipers for her to fall into. I'd be lashing her to her bed and – well, yes, I am just the tiniest bit peeved. But if, despite this—'.

'I'm not in love,' said Daniel quickly. After all, he had only dated her a few times, and for all he knew she had a proper boyfriend in America. All the same, Ellen had presumably wangled her invitation from Polly on the grounds that they were having a genuine affair. He supposed, on the whole, they must be, although it was so difficult to tell.

'You're not? Why not?'

Without thinking, Daniel said, 'Too obvious.'

'Is there such a thing as a woman who's too obvious?' said Ivo.

Daniel pondered. 'Maybe not.'

'That's what I thought,' said Ivo.

A couple crammed into a queen-sized bed instead of a king-sized one cannot sleep, Polly thought as she sweated the two halves of a large purple onion in the kitchen. Why does anyone have queen-sized beds, ever? Why aren't they out-lawed? Who on earth could fit into them, other than dwarves or sex-maniacs limited to the missionary position? Any couple with children needed not just a king-sized bed, but a super-king, six feet across, and a modern life-raft of the *Medusa*. That was one of the things she loved about America: they understood the importance of size, instead of being apologetic and trying to squeeze everything into a tiny space and ending up hating everybody like the British. I do hate the way British people are so full of hate, she thought, savagely, and the way they're so proud of it, too. But then Betty wasn't exactly a shining example of America, either, even if she had produced two remarkably nice sons. It was obvious the big bed should have been theirs, would have been theirs had first one child and then the other not demanded a stop on the motorway when coming from the airport. So they had arrived second at the house they were renting, just as she'd feared. When she saw what her mother-in-law had done, Polly had actually said, 'Oh. Isn't it rather too big for you?' in the sort of tone that most people would know was code for, 'You selfish cow, we need this and you don't.'

But Betty had said, in that bright, irritating voice of hers,

'Well, I was always told that it's the early bird who catches the worm!' and now it was impossible to move her.

Theo, of course, had been far too polite to object, and Polly, though seething, could not very well have fought her mother-in-law single-handed. The truth was, she was afraid of Betty. Her mother-in-law had always made it quite clear that she didn't think Theo had any business marrying her at all. She simply wasn't posh enough, or at least not by New York standards. Polly's parents were academics, just like Daniel's father. They were both distinguished in their fields, and Polly's mother was actually a professor of women's history, and quite famous as a militant feminist. But they were not rich, or titled, and that for Betty was key. In her eyes, somebody who didn't have a trust fund was not worthy of a moment's consideration, and Polly, with her unremarkable face, her floppy brown hair and her flat chest, felt very much like Cinderella, only without the fairy godmother. Theo really must love her, she thought, to have risked the displeasure of both his colleagues (who naturally viewed his marriage as defection) and his mother. Yet Polly had grown weary of waking to find the bed gently juddering with an unmistakable motion when she lay lonely on her side of the mattress.

Had she been of another generation Polly would have done something dramatic like thrown crockery or had an affair, but unfortunately Polly liked the crockery (she had chosen it, after all) and thought infidelity vulgar. Besides, it simply wasn't done to be angry any more. You tried not to draw attention to domestic discontent because that was what your mother's generation had done and the last thing you wanted was to become like your mother. Polly had tried so hard not to become like her mother, who was the most terrible cook and housekeeper, though full of love for her children when she remembered their needs. Consequently, until Polly herself took matters in hand, she and her siblings had actually looked forward to school dinners, and had loved wearing their uniforms. Polly's act of rebellion was to get married young to precisely the kind of man her parents were duty bound to disapprove of, and try to live as conventional a life as possible. She understood this, but she also adored Theo. Who could fail to? He had appeared in her life like the prince in a fairy tale – tall and handsome, rich and smart – and if he had a vile mother, well, that was the price she had to pay.

She looked out of the window above the kitchen sink, checking that Robbie and Tania were still alive. From behind the wire insect-mesh and three iron security bars, Tuscany seemed a long way away. What would it be like to be here alone? She could hardly remember what solitude was like. She had married Theo at the same age that Meenu had married Bruce, but her own marriage had lasted, that was the important thing. She wrenched her eyes from the shimmering outlines of the olive trees and prodded the sauce she was making, then turned over some peppers and aubergines she was blackening under the grill. Polly did wonder why so many of her contemporaries complained about housework, and about the incursions of motherhood on their personal freedom, for dreary as some chores were there was a kind of honour in it. At least while she kept busy she didn't feel too guilty about no longer having a career. Actually, the one good thing about this first week at the Casa Luna was that she and Robbie could have luxurious cuddles in bed together every morning without Theo getting cross.

So far, she hadn't even had a swim. Her activities were confined to the grassy area just beyond the pergola where they had most of their meals, and to the interior of the house.

People kept telling her to relax, but if she didn't get meals on the table by 1 p.m. and 6 p.m. sharp, she knew that her children would become completely impossible. A well-regulated household depended on absolute punctuality, particularly at mealtimes. Polly sighed, trying to chop a carrot. Why did holiday homes never have sharp knives? She must buy a knife sharpener tomorrow.

Why, though, did Theo always insist on these group holidays? It wasn't as if they were short of money, thank goodness, though the recession had eaten into his bonus. Polly was hazy about exactly how much he earned, but it must be close on a million dollars a year, or was that pounds? It was as if he always had to have a sort of mini-court with him wherever they went. Usually, this consisted of his colleagues: pleasant, intense men and women with whom she had nothing in common but whom she smilingly accommodated. Increasingly, these friends of Theo's had children of their own; usually ones that Tania and Robbie could be guaranteed to hate. At least Meenu's son was well brought up, and Robbie adored him. A beautiful boy, Polly thought, but then Indians were generally handsome. His table-manners were exquisite, surprisingly, because she'd been to Meenu's parents' house on occasion and knew they all ate with their fingers. But he knew just how to guide a knife and fork, whereas her two, brought up on the sort of instant food that nannies found easiest to cook, and then (when Polly put her foot down) insisting on having their meals cut up for them, were atrocious.

If only Meenu would stop getting on my nerves, she thought.

She hadn't, after all, spent any serious amount of time with her since they were both unmarried; she had forgotten Meenu's irritating habit of distorting her grave, lovely features and putting on faces that she thought made her funny but which only underlined her insecurity. Nerves, no doubt, but she ought to have grown out of those. Also, she was a lot less well off than they were, which made it awkward about suggesting restaurant meals. Polly was already starting to feel very interested in trying out some local restaurants, but didn't dare suggest it because she knew Meenu would want to pay her way, and as a single parent working as a junior doctor in the NHS she was unlikely to be able to afford much. But the others, well, why weren't they chipping in more? Ivo must be earning a small fortune at the *Tribune*, and he had no family to support. Daniel had his trust fund, and some sort of scholarship while he was in London. Ellen was probably richer than all of them, but so far, apart from giving Polly one of her famous handbags (far too smart to go with Polly's other clothes), had made almost no effort to contribute.

As usual, Polly didn't know how to broach the subject of the supermarket bills. Every year these were supposed to be split between herself and their guests, and every year these bills ended up coming out of her housekeeping account. Theo could never understand why food alone came to more than £1000 a month in London, even without wine or anything special and, somehow, despite all her charge cards, Polly kept finding herself overdrawn. It was horrible having no money of her own, no matter how many times Theo told her that it was their joint income and to come to him for more. She was obsessed by her need for money, and without Marks & Spencer offering her cashback on the charge-card that Theo paid, she didn't know how she'd manage. At least Meenu didn't have to put out her begging bowl with her ex-husband, because of being a doctor. Polly knew she really ought to get a job, now that Robbie was at school full-time, but doing what? The training she had had as a solicitor was now years out of date. The hours that would be involved in catching up made her heart sink. She had done that gardening design course at the Chelsea Physic Garden, which had had the great bonus of introducing her to darling Guy, but not much else. All the same, things couldn't go on like this.

Ivo, of course, was notoriously stingy. It really was too naughty of Daniel to have invited him. Ivo was the hack who took his dry-cleaning with him on assignments abroad, so as to charge it to expenses. The prince of freebies, he was in his element as an arts critic and celebrity interviewer, by all accounts, but she still felt that it wouldn't be safe to leave a five-pound note around when near him.

She rapped her wooden spoon on the side of the pot as if it were a gavel, then jumped when Ivo's voice said, 'Need help?'

'Oh!' Polly turned, flustered. 'That's kind of you. Not really, most of it's done; it's really very simple. I just need a handful of basil, if you could get me some from the garden. Or there's the washing-up, no dishwasher, you know.'

'Don't know what basil looks like.'

Ivo was standing very close to her. His pale skin was speckled with freckles, many of which were beginning to spread and blend with each other into an approximation of a tan.

'Don't you? Oh . . . I thought, seeing your outfit, you must be keen on flowers.'

'I'm saving gardening for when my gonads rattle,' said Ivo. 'This is a beach suit, otherwise known as style, my darling. For those who appreciate that kind of thing.'

'What do you do, then? To relax, I mean.'

'Pretty much what I do for work,' said Ivo. 'Read, watch movies, chase girls. Oh, and shopping. I love clothes.'

'Do you?' said Polly, brightening. 'I love them too. I used to be quite smart you know. Before . . .'

'Ah. I wondered about the bare-faced look.'

'It isn't a statement. I just don't like cosmetics. They seem so dishonest.'

Ivo looked at her shiny face and wondered whether there was an element of duplicity in this. In his experience, people who announced their love of honesty were nearly always far more likely to be embroiled in deceit than those who accepted that lying was as natural as breathing. He felt a quickening of interest.

'Why don't you let someone else cook for a bit?'

Polly pushed her hair out of her face. It flopped back.

'It's my way of relaxing.'

'Ah. You've tried the alternatives?'

'Which particular ones?'

'Drink, drugs, sun, sex . . .'

Polly looked at his bright, mischievous eyes.

'I can't drink, drugs bore me and I burn in the sun,' she said. She felt dull and colourless, sunk in domesticity as in some shapeless enveloping garment. Yet only a few moments ago she had been thinking about how virtuous and good it was. Ivo, she decided irritably, was one of those people who simply by their presence change things for the worse.

'How's Theo?'

'Meenu's been to see him a couple of times, says he just needs fluids and rest.'

'So no sex either.'

Polly blurted, 'You don't, not with children, anyway.'

Ivo began to do the washing-up beside her. He was tall, and she had to admit oddly attractive in his louche way. She could see glints of stubble, like copper filings, on his face. It made her wonder what the rest of him would be like. An erection against a background of red pubic hair would not be enticing, and yet why was it even crossing her mind if not for a certain foxy appeal? She wondered if this was a common reaction to him.

'Well, not entirely, surely, or you wouldn't have had Robbie.'

'Theo and I got drunk. He'd been promoted,' she said, wondering why on earth she was telling him this. She added, 'Aren't these tomatoes magnificent? Why do they never smell like this in England? Are you sure you want to do the dishes?'

'Quite sure. They give me an excuse to flirt with you.'

'I'm not sure that you should,' said Polly anxiously.

'Why not?'

Betty put her head around the corner.

'I'm not interrupting anything, am I?'

'Actually,' said Ivo, 'I was just about to pin Polly to the table and ravish her.'

Betty would have raised an eyebrow had not the nerves to it been frozen.

'I suppose that's an example of the famous Sponge wit? Or at least half of it.'

'But can you tell which half?' returned Ivo. Betty made a small moue of disgust. 'Polly here is wasting her charms on desert airs.'

'Yes, it is rather sultry, isn't it?' said Betty, fanning herself. 'I wonder if you can locate an air-conditioning unit, Polly?'

'I don't think my Italian is good enough,' Polly mumbled.

'I thought you studied in Florence?'

'Only for a couple of months before university.' That was where she had met Ellen, in fact.

'They really ought not to rent to civilised people without air conditioning,' said Betty. 'I'll see if Ellen can talk to someone. She speaks excellent Italian, I know. Where's the number of the agency?'

Polly indicated the pile of papers on the end of the kitchen counter.

'Really, dear, it's no wonder you haven't got your career back together, what with that kind of organisation,' she said. 'When I had my sons, I always had my filing system updated within twenty-four hours of returning from the hospital. And all this laundry! I may as well press Theo's things for him myself.'

'Just Theo's?' said Ivo.

'Oh, Polly can do the rest. She doesn't work.'

Ivo smiled. It was not a nice smile.

'What is it, precisely, that you do, Betty?' he asked.

'I am on the board of a great many charities and conservation societies,' said Betty, with hauteur.

Ivo looked her up and down.

'Of course, you have so much to conserve,' he said.

Betty's eyes narrowed.

'Not as much as you do to lose, I'd say,' she replied, before turning smartly on her kitten heels and going out to the pool.

Ivo and Polly exchanged glances, then laughed.

'The original mother-in-law from hell.'

'I call her the Demon Queen.'

Ivo grinned. 'Does Theo know that?'

Polly shook her head.

'She's all sweetness and light to him, of course, and to Daniel.'

'I'm only doing this for an ulterior motive, you know.'

'Ivo!' said Polly, half-laughing, half-scandalised as he pinned her to the sideboard. It was rather like being kissed by a large, enthusiastic dog. She pushed him away.

'Sorry, sorry,' said Ivo, not looking remotely apologetic. 'There's something about a woman bending over a stove that's the ultimate aphrodisiac; not that you aren't attractive, my darling.'

Polly said, her heart jumping with apprehension, 'That's very flattering, but I am married, Ivo.' Saying these words, she felt, for the second time that day, very old. 'Why don't you try Meenu?'

Ivo laughed.

'Mmm . . . she's a real Asian babe.'

Polly said, 'I'm glad you find her a babe, but she's a very serious person and my oldest friend, and on second thoughts you really shouldn't.'

'Only teasing, my darling, only teasing.'

'Are you ever serious, Ivo?'

'Occasionally, when nobody's watching.'

Theo lay in bed surrounded by white rosettes of crumpled tissues. The room smelt strongly of menthol and eucalyptus, and hot, cross male. An electric fan whirred, but seemed to do no more than stir the thick air. He was very bored. Of course, the shutters had to be kept closed against the sun, so he couldn't even look at the view, and he didn't feel like reading another Tom Clancy novel. He wondered whether a dip in the pool might cool his temperature but when he'd gotten up, the room had spun so vertiginously he'd sunk back on to the hated poly-cotton sheets with relief.

What could be worse than a summer cold? Well, having one in a country with no cable. Ivo had lent him a small radio to listen to the BBC World Service, which Theo had to admit was quality broadcasting; though after Alistair Cooke's *Letter from America* his attention wandered. It was the same problem he always had with British accents, he couldn't believe that they couldn't talk normally. They always sounded completely artificial, like the baddies in movies – although Theo was old enough to remember when English accents had been the acme of desirability. He himself had been in London for ten years now and wanted to go home, but Polly resisted this. She didn't want to bring the children up in New York, and she didn't want to live out in the suburbs. Come to that, he didn't particularly want to commute, either. But he knew that if he stayed too long, something vital to him would die. He'd seen what happened to permanent expatriates.

The reactions of Americans to Britain always tended towards two kinds. (Theo liked dividing everything he came across into two camps: good and bad, Left and Right, man and woman. It was labour-saving and made life much simpler.) There were those who treated it as a hardship posting. They assumed right from the start that all natives were hostile and walked around trigger-happy on adrenalin, waiting to be sneered at for playing baseball in the parks and celebrating Thanksgiving with aggressive enthusiasm. They cooked all-American food and clung to their fellow exiles with a kind of desperation. Unable to make out the mores and customs that they unintentionally offended, they went around with frowning smiles of anxiety. Theo disliked this attitude, but recently he had come to think that they had a point. He had been horrified by just how many Britons actually thought that perfectly innocent colleagues of his, regular guys with degrees and families, deserved to die at the hands of terrorists simply for being American. How could anyone honestly believe this? It still angered and bewildered him. That could have been me, he'd wanted to say to all the smug people in the London media who said his colleagues had had it coming; that could have been any one of us, there were children and cleaners and firemen murdered there as well as lawyers. But the fact was, as far as he could see, to the rest of the world they were no longer the good guys, but bad ones – crude, unthinking, racist and brutal. The America that Theo identified with, the nation of the Pilgrim Fathers, idealists and legislators, simply did not exist.

Then there were those other Americans, towards whom Theo himself felt uneasy contempt. They went around in a perpetual state of apology and humility for being born to the world's most successful capitalist economy, ate only organic, never watched cable, voted Democrat and did their best to talk with a British accent. They became, in other words, Canadians. Theo supposed that they had a valid point of view, but he could not help despising them for being so abject. You had to believe, or you were nobody. Besides, it didn't make you any more popular with the anti-Americans, so what was the point? He worried sometimes that Dan was inclined towards the other camp because he never talked of going back home – but then that could just be Dan, who was always pretty closed in on himself, like all geeks. Theo never really understood his craze for Shakespeare, or music. Why couldn't he care about money, like normal people? He hardly ever drew on his trust fund except to give money to charity, though he had accepted living in Mother's London flat, so he'd probably crack in the end. At least he wasn't a budding candidate for jail, like Winthrop. Theo sighed. The thought of his half-brother, about whom there were some highly unpleasant rumours on Wall Street, had never been satisfactory.

Mother, of course, would never see her third son as the black sheep of the family, but it was not a subject they could discuss anyway. Mother was finally divorcing her fourth husband, and this time it looked as if she might actually come off worse because Bunny, for all his high-society manners, had some pretty sharp lawyers in tow. He hated to think of Betty losing out. Sometimes he thought that Mother was the only one who understood him, deep down. Theo moved restlessly in bed. Oh, if only the mobile would ring! It was recharging now, always providing some electrical fault didn't blow it. You had to unplug everything in a thunderstorm here, according to the Owner's Notes.

'Daddy?'

'Hi, honey.'

Theo was touched to see his daughter sidling into the room, her eyes full of tears.

'I'll be better soon.'

'Daddy, Robbie and Bron are being mean to me.'

Theo sighed. The tears were for herself.

'Sweet-pea, there's nothing I can do while I'm sick.' He blew his nose for emphasis. 'Tell Mom.'

'But she always takes Robbie's side.'

'I'm sure she doesn't.'

'She does, she does!' Tania stamped her foot.

'What's really the matter?' asked Theo, stroking her head. His head felt swimmy with fever again, and he couldn't be sure whether the noise he was hearing was the cicadas or a half-dream he'd slipped into of being on a bicycle and endlessly freewheeling down a hill.

'But I've just told you,' said Tania, lifting her tear-smeared face. 'Bron's mean to me.'

'He's just a little boy.'

'No he isn't, he's three months older than me. Why isn't he playing with me instead of Robbie?'

'I don't know,' Theo said. He felt her light, fragile body resting in his arms like a bird. Theo had not been at all sure about the way he felt when Polly became pregnant, and her slim boyish body had swollen into a form unmistakably female, but as soon as he had heard his daughter's voice, he had fallen in love. Everything about her girlhood was mysterious and beautiful to him. It was not the same with Robbie. He knew what it was like to be a little guy, after all.

'Why doesn't Bron like me?' Tania sobbed.

'I don't know. Boys just want to play with boys sometimes.'

'Did you, when you were little?'

'Well, no, I . . .' Theo checked himself. 'I suppose I did.'

'You don't like his mum, do you?'

'Meenu? Sure I do. She's our friend.'

'She's Mum's friend. Who are your friends, Dad?'

Theo stared at his daughter wildly.

'Why do you ask?'

'I'm your friend, aren't I?' said Tania. 'When are you going to come and play Daddy-and-daughter games with me?'

'Hush, darling,' said Polly, appearing with a tray. 'Daddy needs rest. How are you feeling?' she asked Theo.

She put the tray down on the bed and began to straighten it, automatically collecting the used tissues and putting them in the wastepaper basket.

'Not so good,' said Theo in a weak voice. Actually, he liked it when Polly came up to him and put her hand on his forehead, and treated him like a little boy again. It was this maternal quality that he had yearned for when they had met. Polly was so calm and gentle, she was someone who never made demands, unlike an American wife. She was good, and real, like daily bread. He'd never have got through those manic early years of working twenty-four/seven without her to look after him.

'You must leave Daddy in peace now,' said Polly.

Tania stuck her tongue out at her mother. She was always criticising, never doing anything fun. Not like Dad, who took them swimming at weekends and cycling and who bought them presents. Dad would take her side against the little git Robbie and Bron, beastly horrible Bron who never paid her any attention. Tania saw all the pills that her father was swallowing.

'Can I have some medicine, too?'

'No,' said Polly. She heard her voice go hard. 'Medicine isn't a toy.'

Tania burst into tears.

'Loser! You suck,' she said, and rushed out of the room.

'You're too hard on her, honey,' said Theo.

Polly sighed. Whatever she did was wrong.

'What, so I should let her think she can kill herself with paracetemol?'

'No, but . . . She only wants some attention.'

'All that child gets is attention,' said Polly. 'She's a total drama queen, always screaming and stamping her tiny foot. Those children are behaving so appallingly that they're well on the way to ruining this holiday before it's hardly begun.'

'Honey, chill out,' said Theo. 'They're just kids. I'm going to get up and have a dip to get my fever down. Why don't you swim too?'

But Polly said in a low voice, 'I'm so fed up with their behaviour, Theo. Robbie's too little to understand, but Tania's nine, and she should be helping me more. At her age, I was doing all the cleaning in my mother's house, and the ironing. I don't expect that, but I do expect a bit of table-laying and bed-making from her.'

'She's on vacation. Relax.'

But no matter how many times people told her to do this, Polly couldn't.

Chapter Five

Daniel was swimming. The melting hexagons of light travelling along the tiled bottom of the pool, the fluid,
slow-motion glide of other swimmers above his head
soothed and entranced him. All was muted, lucent, quiet.
When he saw people they were not as they were on land –
vexed, or tense or noisy – but suspended, surrounded by a
halo of swirling, glinting hair, and in a state of grace.
Bubbles issued in cartoon-like streams from their mouths in
place of words, bubbles containing a hundred silvery reflec-
tions that rose and never wounded. Each time he resurfaced
into the heat and hugeness of the world, it came as an
unpleasant shock. It was like being born again, and Daniel
was never so happy with his own existence that this could
be a source of pleasure. At least when doing something
physical he could switch off his mind and inhabit the other
part of himself, the part that was timid like a wild animal
but also at ease. He swam whole lengths, holding his breath

until it was forced from his lungs and he, like air, had to surface.

'Hi,' said Ellen's bright red mouth immediately.

'Hi,' he said, and ducked back down again.

The other reason he enjoyed underwater swimming was that it meant he didn't have to look at the girls. Or at least, not at their faces. Ellen had come to his room the night before. Of course, it was difficult being very quiet, but the whole experience had been so remote and somehow impersonal. Daniel blamed himself for this. There were few people he felt comfortable with. Apart from Clara, the Mexican housekeeper who had effectively brought him up in New York, and of course Polly, he really preferred the company of Beatrice, Rosalind and Cordelia. However, he had come very close to something like trust with Hemani. He didn't, of course, know if she felt the same way, because even after seven years in Britain he couldn't work out people's relationships to him, or even whether they liked him. But until she had become strangely cool towards him, he had really counted her as a friend.

He had been to England as a child, when his father had been on sabbatical there, but had fallen in love with it as a visiting graduate student. It wasn't just the accents, the beauty of the parks and buildings, the irony and all those clichés that Anglophiles such as his father went on about. Even the weather charmed him. Yes, he missed the crisp glories of Harvard in the fall and New York in the spring, and he missed the clarity and certainty of mind that accompanied it. Yet the softness and gentleness of the grey skies suited his own temperament more. Which was not to say that he fitted in at once. People thought him strange for going jogging every day: in Britain, intellectuals were supposed to cocoon their minds in sloth. When he suggested having lunch with his tutorial partner at Oxford, his eyes had widened. It took Daniel a year to understand that lunch, far from being the most casual of invitations, was actually an engagement only arranged between close friends, or else people you were sleeping with, had slept with or might possibly sleep with in the future. Tea was what acquaintances took together, nothing more. It had taken him yet more years to understand the subtle degrees of rudeness with which English people treated each other. When they said things like, 'We must get together some time,' they actually meant they never wanted to see you again. When they asked you to make a date, however, that was serious, and you had to be punctual. The first few times he had turned up ten or fifteen minutes late, he wondered why the reception was so frosty, and why British people, even the nicer ones, would talk to him as if he were handicapped in some way. Eventually, he understood that because Americans didn't expect hostility, they usually tended to be oblivious to these distinctions, which are only worked out with patience and intelligence. Daniel, who was above all a gentle man, realised that the people he had counted as friends probably only accepted him as such years after he had accepted them. He thought that Shakespeare could only have been English, not just because of the language that he so developed and enriched, but because of this subtlety of temperament. There was always a conversation behind the conversation when you talked to English people. That was what made them alternately maddening, snotty, inventive, funny, cruel and great.

Daniel did not mind too much about being classed as an alien, for this was pretty much the way he had felt in America, too. He had a few close friends, scattered for the most part all over the world. Yet he was also lonely, especially once he came to London. Of course, it helped that he didn't have to depend entirely on his salary, but that also cut him off from his less affluent colleagues, who were intimidated by his smart address. To make a friend of someone English, if you hadn't been to school or university together, you had to pursue them so persistently and single-mindedly that it was almost like being a stalker, prepared for seemingly insurmountable prejudice. It was easier by far to stick to other Americans rather than risk the humiliation. Yet Daniel persisted because he understood, in the same part of himself that made him a musician, that his culture and theirs were not so very different, not in the things that really counted. Americans were friendly in a way that usually didn't mean anything, but when a British person accepted you as a friend, you were mates – a relationship as close in some ways as marriage, and in many aspects better. Whatever happened, he would know and like these people for the rest of his life. He didn't understand why so many of his compatriots complained about English people. It was just like learning an instrument: you had to almost give up from pain, tedium and effort and then, suddenly, it was all gone. It had happened with the Viners (although, being half-American, they were probably more open anyway) and it had happened, he thought, with Ivo and Polly. But it had not, so far, with Hemani.

He had met Hemani a year ago through the quartet he played in with Josh and Grub Viner, sons of an old friend of his father's. The Viners were all passionate musicians, and in Grub's case, a professional pianist. When they lost their cellist the Viners invited Daniel to take her place, and so it was that his loneliness as an expatriate was lifted, for despite all the chats in the coffee-room of the British Library and his job at University College he had felt this. Hemani played the violin. To begin with, he had barely noticed her, other than to think that she played well and seemed pleasant. Then he had met her again, at his sister-in-law's. (One of the other strange things about Britain, or at least London, was the incestuousness of life there. Everybody seemed to know everybody else, either from school or university or work. Theo, typically, had parachuted himself right in there.) This time he was struck by the impression of both strength and delicacy that she gave; it did not surprise him to learn that she was an eye surgeon. Naturally, when she accepted an invitation to come to a recital by Brendel, he had thought this was a real date, but of course in Britain you couldn't assume the woman would automatically go to bed with you in return for a meal or a theatre ticket. It was slower here, allowing for each side to retreat gracefully and perhaps even remain friends. The evening had, as far as he could tell, gone well but at her door she had turned and thanked him for a lovely evening in that charming but forbidding way she had.

He had asked her out a few times again, but had never ventured even a goodnight kiss. Daniel had been used all his life to having girls and women make the first move. There were rigid codes of behaviour now, particularly in academic life where more than one colleague of his had been accused of sexual harassment. According to the official guidelines, you had to ask permission to undo each button. Ellen was great, she just laughed at all that stuff, and they had really gotten along so well that he was surprised it hadn't occurred to him to ask her along on holiday.

Now, though, he was mortified. At dinner last night his mother had kept making remarks such as, 'Isn't it extraordinary, Daniel, how much Ellen looks like that girl Theo dated back home? You know, the very pretty blonde who's done so well on Wall Street?'

This remark was obviously intended as much for Polly as for himself, but even so, Daniel felt hideously uncomfortable. Ellen took it in her stride, an aspect of her he couldn't but admire, but Betty ignored Hemani. Too late, he remembered that his mother's idea of being colour blind was to be blind to people of colour. Anyone whose skin was the result of pigmentation rather than a sun-tan simply ceased to exist. Hemani, he could see, was puzzled by Betty's manners. She came from a world in which racial prejudice was so alien as to be almost quaint. Not for the first time, Daniel was mortified by his mother. He longed to do something or say something to make it clear that he didn't for one second share Betty's obnoxious attitudes, but he couldn't think what. The language that flowed so easily when he was seated in front of a word processor or a lectern stumbled on his tongue.

'I don't remember,' he had said, then immediately thought how callous that made him sound.

It should have been such a glorious evening, too. The irritability of the afternoon had receded and everyone was looking forward to another delicious meal, accompanied by the Montepulciano wine that Ivo had unexpectedly produced. The air had taken on a velvety, violet tinge, streaked with orange and gold towards the west, far across the plains. The seven adults sat at the long outdoor table under the pergola of honeysuckle and roses, watching, and the house seemed to watch them from under its swathes of creepers as if pondering what to show next. It was hot, and the stones of the house and terrace seemed to give off even more heat now the sun had set. Slowly, the violet deepened into blue, and from the other side of the hill the clink of church bells sounded. Dogs barked, and the automatic sprinkler system that kept the lawns as soft and verdant as if it were spring rose out of the ground like enchanted fountains, sighing and bending in graceful, silvery fantails. A soft breeze came uphill, as if the earth were exhaling, bringing with it the stony chatter of a waterfall, and a strong scent.

'What is that smell?' said Hemani, sniffing.

Ellen said, 'Sex.'

'No, it's some sort of plant, I'm sure,' said Daniel.

'Well, then it's a plant that smells of sex.'

'What?' asked Tania, pattering out barefoot after her bath. Sex was the children's current obsession. They were always asking Polly about it, then exclaiming, 'Yuk!' at her explanations. 'What smells of sex?'

The adults exchanged glances.

Robbie popped his head between two chairs and said, 'I can't smell anything except Tania's smelly farts.'

'Shut up, pig!'

'It's wild thyme,' said Polly.

'I didn't know time could smell.'

'Not that kind of time,' said Hemani. 'Thyme the herb.'

'Oh, an erb!' said Ellen.

Ivo snorted with laughter, to her bewilderment.

'I love these Transatlantic differences,' he said.

'You say tomahto and we say tomayto,' said Daniel, grinning. 'The Great Vowel Shift.'

'You got it wrong, stupid,' said Robbie.

'I hate you, and I'm not stupid,' said Tania when they laughed, stamping her feet and running into the house. She slammed the french windows. Polly felt a wave of fury as the bang echoed through the house, and for a moment she had the oddest feeling that the house shared her displeasure. She said, 'I'll kill her if she's broken another pane of glass.'

'It's OK,' said Daniel, checking. 'It's fine, nothing's broken. Relax.'

Polly swallowed. 'I don't know why I'm being so horrid to Tania,' she said in a low voice. 'I suppose I feel that she's entering puberty earlier than expected.'

'Well, children are growing up and maturing faster these days,' said Hemani. 'Better nutrition, or hormones in food, who can say? They are so much less innocent.'

'Is Bron?'

Hemani said carefully, 'Sometimes I think he is, but boys do tend to be slower, you know.'

'I so dread going through all the sulks and rows,' said Polly, distracted. 'I thought it'd last longer, somehow . . . I love her being so imaginative and creative, and I dread all that being replaced by, well, boys.'

'Didn't that happen to you, though?' Daniel asked.

Polly flushed.

'Well, not really, no.'

She blamed herself for this, of course. It must be because I've never been pretty, she thought miserably. After all, who could possibly fancy me? Or perhaps he really was just tired from all those late nights at the office.

The swallows swirling around the house suddenly crumpled into bats. Ivo took up a box of matches and began the fiddly job of lighting the big cream candle in its glass jar.

'Ow! Blast, I've burnt my fingers.'

'Let me try.'

'Can I help? Can I?' asked Robbie. He bounded into the house for the bag of tea lights, and placed them carefully around the terrace and down the steps to the garden. Polly observed with pride.

'Why do girls make such a fuss?' said Bron to his mother. He smelt of Pears soap and boy, the two most delicious smells in the world.

She sniffed his hair and said quietly, 'Perhaps she feels left out.'

'But all she wants to do is stupid girl things.'

'Like what?'

Bron blushed. 'Like, you know, girl things.'

Robbie crowed, 'She wants him to do kissing!'

The adults all tried, unsuccessfully, not to laugh. The older boy whirled round on the younger.

'You promised you wouldn't tell!'

'Quite right,' said Ivo. 'A gentleman never tells.'

Ellen looked, and raised an eyebrow.

'Do, do that again,' said Ivo, invitingly.

'My dear, you really shouldn't,' said Betty. 'You've no idea of the problems it will cause your plastic surgeon.'

'Bron, darling,' said Hemani gently, 'I'm sure there are other games you could all play together.'

'No, there aren't, not with girls,' he said. 'That's all they want to do. It's all kissing and dancing with flowers in their hair.'

'I promise you, it isn't.'

'Yes, it is, it is, and it's so stupid. I wish you'd all stop being so stupid.'

Suddenly, tiny needles of pulsing light sprang up. Daniel rubbed his eyes, wondering if they were deceiving him, but one went darting through the air. The cicadas suddenly hushed.

'What are they? What are they?' Ellen whispered.

'They're fairies,' said Robbie, then scowled in case anyone should think him girlie.

'Wicked,' said Bron, impressed.

Tania reappeared behind the darkened glass of the french windows.

'Oh!' she said, darting out. Polly, in the act of rising to take her children to bed, paused.

The three children, Tania in her bell-like nightdress, Robbie in his striped pyjamas, and Bron in plain ones, ran down the shallow stone steps to the flower-beds and bent over the white lilies where the lights were gathering. A cluster of bright, greenish specks swirled around them, settling momentarily on their clothes and limbs. It seemed as if each was suddenly wearing living jewels, blinking on and off.

'Can you catch one?'

'Oh, look, there, it's there! It's floating past your head.'

Bron reached up easily and caught one in his narrow hands, cupping them gently.

'They aren't fairies, are they, Bron?' said Tania, inspecting the tiny light.

'Well,' said Bron, slowly. His dark eyes were enormous in his face. 'I think they're fireflies. I've only ever read about them. We hardly ever get them in England, because it isn't warm enough.'

'They're fairies,' said Robbie stoutly. 'Perhaps one of them will come and take my wobbly tooth. I'm the only person in my class who hasn't lost one, and then I'll get a pound. Or maybe if there's an Italian tooth-fairy, a euro.'

'Fairies don't—' Tania began, but then she peered more closely at the creature Bron was holding. Was it an insect? Surely that was a tiny face, smiling at her? She blinked, and it winked, then floated up, vanished like a needle in the thick fabric of night, to reappear out of reach. Tania gazed after it, open-mouthed. She was absolutely certain that it was a person, and not human. It wasn't pretty, like a Disney fairy, it was like one of the Errol Le Cain pictures in *Sleeping Beauty*, a weird, clever, passionate creature of air and fire.

'Isn't it a bit late for them?' said Polly. 'I thought they came in early summer.'

'It's probably to do with global warming,' said Daniel. 'All the seasons are mixed-up these days.'

'Ye living lamps, by whose dear light, The nightingale does sit so late . . .' said Hemani.

'Marvell. Good stuff,' said Daniel.

She smiled at him, and Ellen felt a spasm of discomfort.

'Do they bite?' asked Bron anxiously. He had more mosquito bites than anyone.

'No. They just glow.'

Ellen said, 'Look, that cypress tree is absolutely full of them. It's as if everything is alive.'

'Everything is alive, stupid,' said Robbie kindly, for it was quite obvious to anyone but a grown-up that this was so.

For a while nobody spoke. The fireflies glittered over flowers and shrubs, so bright they almost seemed to sear the eyes, drifting heatless sparks through the gardens and groves.

'Why do they shine, Mummy?' asked Robbie.

'Because they're looking for a mate.'

'You mean, they want to have sex with each other?'

'Yes.'

The children exchanged glances.

'Do humans do that?'

The adults laughed softly.

'Unfortunately not.'

112

'Sexy fairies,' said Robbie, spluttering.

'Can I take one in a jar to my room?'

If I do, Tania thought, then the boys will have to be nice to me. But perhaps the People will be my friends instead. Already, her imagination was weaving a tapestry of possibilities.

'Yes,' said Polly.

'Will they go on shining?'

'Not if you keep them in a jar, no. They'll die.'

'I don't want them to die,' said Tania at once.

'If you really love something, you have to let it be free,' said Hemani. Tania understood, and sighed.

'Will they sparkle every night?'

'I don't know, darling. Perhaps, for a while.'

'Guys,' said Theo, blowing his nose loudly, 'time for bed.'

The children vanished. The adults began to relax and talk. Ellen took the matches from Ivo, and lit the candles. The fireflies became invisible.

'Well, wasn't that something?'

'We had lightning-bugs all the time when I was a girl,' said Betty. 'They were nothing special.'

Robbie suddenly popped his head up between his mother and Hemani.

'Just one more cuddle?' he said, putting out his arms.

'Back to bed.'

'But I'm scared of the dark.'

He looked at her with huge eyes.

'Oh, all right,' said Polly, unable to resist.

'I love you, Mummy.'

'I love you too.'

Robbie climbed up on to her lap and she buried her nose in his hair. He sighed with contentment, then put his hand on her breast and squeezed it.

'Nice boobies.'

'Hush, darling.'

Robbie looked innocently up at her, and Ivo snickered.

'There's a lad who knows what he wants.'

'Don't, darling, it's rude.'

'Yum-yum,' said her son. 'Yummy Mummy.'

'You're much too easy-going with your children, dear,' Betty told Polly. She gave her grandson a basilisk glare. He hid his face.

Polly said lightly, 'What do you suggest I do, lash them to their beds?'

Hemani said in a sepulchral voice, 'Beat them like gongs.'

'Personally,' said Ivo, 'I've always thought bribery an underrated tactic. Hey, Robbie!'

'Yes?'

'If you go to bed now and stay there, like a good fellow, I promise you I'll buy you a present.'

'What?'

Ellen muttered, 'How about a nice brown paper bag?'

'A toy.'

'Up to how much?' said Robbie, looking very innocent.

'You can have anything you want up to – up to – five euros.'

'Ten,' said Robbie.

'Let's split the difference, and say seven. Any toy up to seven euros, if you go to bed and stay there.'

Robbie flew back into the house, his bare feet skimming the rough tiles. They waited. He did not reappear.

'Well done!' said Hemani.

'Do you think it'll work?'

'Oh, sure – for tonight,' said Theo, blowing his nose and coughing. He felt he was not getting nearly enough sympathy or attention.

'Well, well, Ivo,' said Ellen, mockingly. 'A negotiator. This casts you in a new light.'

'A little baksheesh. Why didn't we think of it?' said Hemani.

'Probably because we attempt to impose other values in our culture,' said Betty. Hemani couldn't ignore the hostility. She felt as though she had been struck in the face.

'Which values do you mean?' said Ivo, amiably. 'The ones which believe that all men are created equal, or the ones that let poor people die if they don't have medical insurance?'

'I'm merely pointing out that you have started a law of diminishing returns,' said Betty. 'Tomorrow he'll demand another bribe. Just how much are you prepared to spend to ensure we're left in peace by my grandson?'

Ivo shrugged. 'Whatever it takes.'

Daniel tried to make up for Betty's remark, but he confined his attentions to asking Hemani if she would like more wine with her food, or more water with her wine. The evening had ended on a sour note, with everyone waiting and waiting for Betty to retire first and then feeling too tired, or too embarrassed, to comfort her victims. Daniel felt obscurely responsible for this, because he had a feeling that it was his presence, rather than Theo's or the children's, that had drawn Betty to invite herself to stay. Sooner or later, she'd come up, once again, with the Marriage Lecture, which only made him more determined to resist the whole idea. He knew he was behaving like a jerk, and it was this sense of failure that had him hiding in the pool the following day. He was by far the best swimmer there, but it gave him no comfort. Ivo swam like a cork in a bottle, bobbing about beamingly; Ellen was athletic yet too correct, Hemani graceful but awkward, Theo splashy and flashy. Polly did not go in at all. Only the children sported, and from time to time they swam beside him, unable to match his speed but tickling his legs like minnows and sending bubbles of silvery laughter up. Their airy unselfconsciousness only added to his self-loathing. He was an asshole, a hairy, lumpen, mole-eyed clod. Of course he should have spoken up. His last girlfriend, Frances, had several times voiced the opinion (fondly at first, then sarcastically) that without his good looks, nobody would ever have spoken to him at all, because he was fundamentally a nerd. Daniel never thought about what he looked like, but if it were true, he was grateful. He thought he probably was pretty boring, because he was slow to speak on any given subject. He had been taught to think before he spoke, and to listen to other people, but they, however, didn't converse so much as express their opinions, like tom-cats squirting all over a garden. As it was, his reserve enhanced people's curiosity – not that he ever noticed this, either, for Daniel was so obtuse about people that even Ivo had on occasion been tempted to kick him. All he knew, as he pulled himself through the water, was that this was probably going to turn out to be the worst holiday of his life.

'It's such a waste,' Ivo lamented. That evening, refreshed by the pool, they had decided to have a walk, and everyone except Polly, Betty and Theo was slowly wandering down the hill in search of kindling for a barbecue. Hemani and Ellen had fallen behind, while the children raced ahead. The path, sunk in a deep mossy lane, was overgrown with scrubby rose bushes and led to the bottom of the garden. Below it there was a steep valley, invisible until now and dense with rustling trees. The olive groves had given way to a dense tangle of oak, chestnut, holly and flowering broom.

'What's a waste?'

'You could pull any number of girls, if you just noticed they existed.'

'But I don't want to pull.'

'That's probably the secret,' said Ivo, gloomily. 'Girls are like cats, they only come on to you if you don't like them.'

'I do like them,' Daniel said, with a faint smile. 'I like them a lot. I'm just not good at talking about whatever it is you're supposed to say to women.'

'Why not?'

'I don't know. Theo's much better at that stuff.'

Theo had all the confidence of the elder brother, and all the domineering sociability, too. He was the golden boy, the one whom older men wished they had as a son and whom younger guys wanted to copy. Daniel, following, was always in his shadow. He took after his father, also a shy man, who never expected to participate in the incessant shimmer and chatter that constituted Betty's life. Daniel, like Theo, had been despatched to prep school as soon as possible, and there his spirit would have shrivelled entirely had he not discovered that he was good at both music and literature. The latter got him into Harvard, and then to Oxford on a scholarship, and from Oxford to his work as a junior research fellow, then lecturer at London University.

He loved his work, but his family were ashamed of him. He was expected to be like Theo, to work until 3 a.m. every day and pull an income of $1 million a year. Dutifully, he did his best, and to nobody's surprise was successful, largely because he was kind to his students and a natural teacher. Had he been happy, he could have married a dozen times over. But the sort of women he encountered were women who were too like Betty. They wanted to talk about things, and things did not particularly interest him. As long as he had somewhere to live, food, clothes and quiet he was not so much content as indifferent.

Ivo, inevitably, teased him about this as they walked through the gardens of the Casa Luna. 'Admit it, your cello case hides an inflatable woman. You spend an awfully long time in your room every afternoon, I notice.'

'No,' said Daniel. 'It is a cello.'

'Right sort of shape,' said Ivo. 'If your tastes run to large curves, that is.'

'They do in music,' said Daniel.

'God, I'm hot. Slow down a bit, can't you?'

The two men paused.

They had come to what seemed like the very end of the garden. The valley, which fell below, was surprisingly deep and green, and in one corner of the wall was a small gap. It led into another sunken lane, quite invisible from above or the sides, as it was overgrown with interarching trees. It was cool, and damp, and invitingly mossy. Ahead of them, running down the hill, the children flickered like little flames.

'Shall we go on?'

'Might as well. If it leads to the wood, we'll get plenty of kindling.'

Flies disturbed from the bracken swarmed around them, but it was a pleasant walk. Flowers grew here that could not survive the more exposed places: arum lily, wild geraniums and fern. Dead leaves the colour of terracotta rustled about their feet, multitudinous as the shades of Vallombrosa, thought Daniel fondly.

'I can hear the sound of water, can't you?'

'Yes. There must be a stream or river still flowing.'

'Careful, this rock's slippery.'

'Shall we – oh damn!'

The sunken path had split into two. The right-hand fork continued down the valley, but the left turned into a high stone wall set with an iron gate wrought in swirling shapes that was padlocked shut with a steel chain.

'Do you think this other path goes all the way to Cortona?' Daniel asked. 'If so, I could jog there. It'd be a good run.'

'Bound to,' said Ivo, who had no intention of finding out.

His affection for Daniel did not include following him in his crazy American taste for early-morning exercise.

Daniel knew this perfectly well, and said, grinning, 'Slob.'

'I wonder where this gate leads to.'

Robbie began to run a stick along the iron-work, making a strange atonal music.

'Come out, come out, wherever you are,' he chanted.

'I don't think anyone's at home,' said Daniel.

'This is where the People live.'

'Who?'

'The shining ones. Tania said so.'

'We can't go any further,' said Daniel.

'I can get in any time.'

Robbie wriggled through the bars, and on to the smooth sward just inside.

'You can't catch me! You can't catch me!'

'Hey,' cried Daniel, alarmed. Bron and Tania appeared, and followed suit, jumping and skipping down the daisy-speckled grasses.

'Whoo-hoo!' Bron's voice floated back.

'Goddammit, there could be snakes.'

'Stop bugging us,' called back Robbie.

'They'll be fine,' said Ivo, mopping his damp face. 'What a strange place. Wonder what's inside; if it's part of the house or separate. Those must be very old.'

Daniel raised his eyes to the gateposts. There were two statues of children on it, one laughing, the other crying. The laughing one had horns, and little furry legs – a faun. It was pointing at the crying child with one hand and clutching its side with the other. Daniel looked at the crying child with anxiety. It was naked, and so defenceless it seemed like a warning.

'I wonder what they are supposed to represent?' he said. The figures disturbed him somehow, and so did the green gloom beyond. He peered at it, and the children's elfin figures flickered in and out of his astigmatic vision.

Ivo resumed his teasing.

'What do you look for in a girl?' he asked. 'I mean, strictly between ourselves.'

Nobody, not even Daniel, could ever believe for a moment that anything you told Ivo was kept private. Nevertheless, he struggled to find an answer.

'Someone kind?'

'Kind?'

'Yes,' said Daniel, defensively. 'Kindness is greatly underrated. I'd place it above beauty, intelligence and charm.'

Polly was kind, he thought.

'But what kind of kind? Someone who always agrees with you? That would be deadly dull.'

'Um,' said Daniel, thinking about past girlfriends. 'Someone who always disagrees with you is kind of tiring.'

'Yes, but you want a bit of spark, don't you? A sense of humour, a bit of spirit?'

'I guess so. But kindness is the most important quality.'

Ivo thought that his friend sounded miserable. He himself had long ago decided never to allow such feelings to enter into his own breast as a matter of principle.

'Personally, I rather enjoy unkindness.'

'Oh?'

'Nothing like a good row to get the juices going,' said Ivo, coarsely.

'I don't like confrontation,' said Daniel, who had never, in fact, confronted anyone.

'Oh, quite, quite, old boy. One doesn't want too much hard work.' Ivo was fanning himself with his hat. 'There's an asbestos quality to Ellen, for example, that would take a blow-torch to get through.'

He probably would see a quarrel as a challenge, Daniel thought. It was true, though, that you didn't want someone like yourself. Look at Ivo and himself, chalk and cheese, extrovert and introvert, and yet somehow they just enjoyed each other's company. Of course, a lot of people enjoyed Ivo, as long as they could forgive his flights of malice. He was simply more interesting than most people, and he knew it.

'What about looks?'

'Well, yes, I guess.' This conversation was making Daniel acutely uncomfortable. Behind him, he could see Hemani, also descending. She lifted her face and was waving with a kind of gallant friendliness. He lifted his own hand. At once, Ellen waved too.

'Funny, isn't it, the way girls always worry about their bums? I mean, I couldn't care less, could you?'

'Nope.'

'Bums,' said Ivo, meditatively, pausing to look back up the hill. The girls had stopped. 'I've seen a few.'

'Uh-huh,' said Daniel. 'The English vice?'

122

'For your information, I seduced the matron of my prep school at thirteen.'

'You did?' said Daniel, startled and rather envious.

'I sometimes wonder whether that isn't the point at which I began to have difficulties, because after that I kept wondering why they didn't all roll over and wave their legs in the air.'

'Sure,' said Daniel. He was sceptical about this story.

'What do you notice most?' Ivo persisted. 'I mean, when you find someone attractive?'

Daniel looked at the statues. They were so spattered with gold and silver lichen it was hard to make out their expressions. Was the child crying or laughing?

'Skin.'

'Yeah, right. You can have a girl with lovely boobs and legs and so on, but if her skin is bad, forget it. Now Ellen, I do have to say, has wonderful skin. Most American girls don't, if you'll excuse me, too much sun or something, but hers . . .'

Daniel thought of Hemani's skin, which was, he realised, very nearly the same shade as the wood of his cello. He found himself grinning a sort of death's head grin, desperate to think of something to say, while Ivo effortlessly monopolised all conversation. Ivo, goddammit, could talk the hind leg off a donkey while Daniel was still putting its hoof in his mouth. At least he hadn't had to talk to Frances, his last proper girlfriend. She had annexed him, in the manner of imperialist Western nations colonising a simpler and more primitive culture. Like many a conquered nation he now felt rather nostalgic for her rule, though profoundly glad to be free of it.

There was no doubt that being in Italy made his sexual itch worse. Being abroad was altogether a bad idea, he realised. The scent of myrtle and lavender, of midsummer roses so deeply crimson their shadows looked black, the tilting rectangles of yellow sunflowers in the plains below – all these were getting to him. You looked at the olive trees and their twisted trunks and silvery branches immediately suggested nymphs frozen in the act of flight; you looked at hills and they were gigantic voluptuaries. And then there were the children, so innocently sensual with an ease he could hardly remember, as completely at home in their bodies as he was wretchedly awkward in his.

Oh, the green leaves, the leaves, the green and blue and shadowy whispers of the wood all starry with daisies and there was a snake, there was, did you see it, Bron? Going up the wall like a trickle of water where those tiny leaves tremble, they're ferns like the fern at home in the bathroom, this is so cool, I can run and run and run on the soft moss and there's a stream, great, just when I needed a drink, oh, cold, it's so cold and cool and I can plunge my hands right down into it and watch them turn white, look, Bron, look, Tania, but not if you're going to make faces at me, it's like glass only moving and singing, the People are singing, can you hear, Bron? Bron?

'Beat you!' said Bron, his face appearing between the bars.

'No you didn't,' said Tania, panting.

124

'Ha-ha, I'll beat you both,' said Robbie. He neighed like a horse.

'And I will beat all three of you with this big stick unless you're through on this side of the gate by the time I count to ten,' said Ivo.

All three wriggled through the gate and vanished back into the gardens above, Robbie still neighing and pawing the ground with his sandalled hoof.

'How much wood do we actually need for this barbecue?' Ivo asked. He wanted to slow down but Daniel was now charging back up on his long legs like the Puritan Work Ethic incarnate.

'A ton,' said Daniel, absently.

'Pity those useless children won't carry any.'

'Aren't you going to get Robbie his bribe?'

'Nah,' said Ivo. 'Tomorrow morning, perhaps. I told him he'd forfeit it if he didn't go to bed tonight, and he tried to raise the price.'

'My nephew is a born capitalist,' said Daniel.

'Born mischief-maker, more like. I dread to think what he'll get up to with Meenu's boy.'

'He seems a nice kid.'

Ivo shuddered.

'There's no such thing.'

Daniel said, his eyes fixed on the stony path ahead, 'You like Hemani?'

'Yes, of course,' said Ivo. 'Lovely girl. Lonely, too. All work and no play.'

'I don't know about that,' said Daniel.

'Does she . . .? Have you . . .?'

'Oh, no, no, no,' said Daniel. 'Nothing like that. We've just played in a quartet, that's all.'

'Well,' said Ivo, 'one has to do something on holiday, apart from eat. Also, it would annoy Ellen.'

'Ah,' said Daniel. He wanted to say that it would also annoy him, except that annoy was the wrong word. It would grieve him if the luminous gravity of her face were disturbed by Ivo.

'You're wondering why Ellen detests me, I suppose,' said Ivo, swishing a stick idly at some wild roses, so that they hissed and recoiled. A tortoise jerked into life, and scrambled away with surprising speed.

'Well, I had gathered you and she don't get along.'

'I humiliated her,' said Ivo, 'quite unintentionally. I was jet-lagged and drunk and, well . . . Now she believes absolutely everything I do and say is false and insincere.'

'Isn't it?'

'No, of course not,' said Ivo, reproachfully.

Chapter Six

The heat intensified. At night the house creaked and whispered, so that they woke to confusion, climbing out of their dreams on the ladder of light cast by the shutters, excited, ashamed, frustrated. During the day each person became more and more enervated, yet also more relaxed. The excessive, insistent heat made everything long to open even when it needed to preserve what little coolness remained. One morning, Polly saw a crimson rose show its heart to the sun, only to fall in a cascade of petals by the end of the day. A siesta had become the only way of coping with the worst of it, although its still pool of inertia made their irritability intensify. A sheen of languor seemed to slick every limb, so that they all moved slowly, idly, passing out on the sofas indoors or the sun-beds by the pool. Daniel, after a long struggle, returned to his cello with desperation, and Ellen listened to the patterns and bars he created around himself, uncomprehending. Hemani, after working the long hours of a hospital doctor, was only too glad to rest, dipping in and out of her book with wistful amusement. Ivo discovered that cold showers merely made matters worse, and was raiding the owner's library. Betty brooded in her eyrie at the top of the external flight of steps. Only the children seemed immune. Quarrelling, chasing, exploring, playing, they disappeared to the bottom of the garden for hours on end, reappearing only when they felt like it.

Like restless sleepers struggling against their condition, the adults tried to regain that sense of energy and curiosity they had had on arrival, just a few days ago. They were in Tuscany, and Tuscany meant culture – otherwise why not spend their holiday in France, so much more cheaply? Guidebooks were opened, maps unfolded and the Owner's Notes were once again consulted. There was Florence, which right at the moment they felt was too far away, and Siena, across the plain. Polly almost succeeded in rousing her children to some enthusiasm by describing the Palio, but Ellen shuddered and said, 'Have you any idea how hot all that red brick becomes?'

'What about Assisi?' said Polly. 'There are the Giottos.'

'I thought they were damaged in the earthquake a while back?' said Daniel.

'But they've mostly been restored,' said Ellen. Her heart sank at the idea of trudging round this tourist hell-hole in a group.

'You remember the story of St Francis, don't you, darlings? The one who was so kind to animals?'

Hemani exchanged glances with her son, who was silently

indignant at Polly's syrupy tone. Beloved Bron, so serious. They shared small smiles.

'Can we meet him?' Robbie asked.

'I'm afraid not. He died hundreds of years ago.'

Giotto was dismissed. In any case, Theo did not feel up to a long drive. He was determined to accompany them. When they saw his prison-pallor beside their own tanned flesh, they all felt very sorry for him, for even his charm looked faded. For the first time, Polly saw how her husband would look when he was old, and she pitied him for he had always taken his golden good looks for granted, and she had basked in their reflected glory. Daniel also felt guilty. I should have spent more time with him when he was bored in bed, he thought. The problem with Theo, though, was that he was incapable of talking to Daniel for two minutes without reminding him that he was the elder brother, the successful one, the star. This wasn't too bad, because the things Theo valued were things he himself did not. Theo had always been the kind of child who was only interested in something if it was expensive and exclusive: to him, the present of a book was the worst in the world, not the best. But it annoyed Daniel that his brother was always trying to elevate himself by making others feel small. Once, he had bumped into Theo and Polly at the Royal Opera House, and Theo had said, with what seemed like genuine surprise, 'Why, Dan, what are *you* doing here?' As if Daniel himself did not know far more about music, and care more, and as if he had walked in on some club meant only for the very rich. Nobody in his family could understand his choice of career. Theo couldn't remark on something Daniel possessed – a shirt perhaps, or a suitcase – without a faint sneer at it for being all that he could afford. He really cared about having a Rolex watch or a designer shirt, whereas Daniel honestly couldn't care less. Their exchanges were always tinged with contempt on one side, and a defensiveness on the other, because deep down, Daniel despised what his brother had done with his life every bit as much.

Still, he had made some effort.

'How're you doing?'

'OK,' said Theo. 'I'll have this bug licked by the end of the week. It's just a lousy way to spend a holiday.'

'Yeah.'

There was a pause.

'I brought my racquet. There are some courts in the town.'

Theo brightened. He loved tennis.

'Sure. Let's book a game. What racquet have you got?'

'The one you gave me, as a matter of fact,' said Daniel.

'That old thing? You should have upgraded it years ago.'

'Uh, I didn't see the need.'

Theo smiled. 'Same old Dan. "Distrust all enterprises that require new clothes", right?'

'Sure.'

'But at some point those old clothes must have been new. Unless you get them second hand. What d'you do, beat them up?'

Daniel grinned. 'Actually, I just wear them when visiting my niece and nephew.'

'Yeah. Guaranteed to give your wardrobe that distressed look.'

Daniel always felt himself becoming quieter and less substantial when Theo was around, knowing that the qualities he had to offer were precisely those which his elder brother (and his younger one too) did not value.

'My brother, the eternal student.'

'There are worse things to be.'

'I've heard all the lawyer jokes. How's everyone downstairs?'

'Great. Just waiting for you to join us,' said Daniel, though even as he said it the guilty, truthful part of him knew perfectly well that as soon as Theo appeared it would be awful. Was it only his imagination, or did a weird sort of resentment pour off his brother's skin like sweat whenever they were together? They could talk on the phone, or email, and get along just great together. Yet as soon as they were in each other's physical presence, it all went wrong. Why should Theo feel like this? He had everything he wanted, didn't he?

Before it became too hot to contemplate anything but cowering in the shade, they set out for Arezzo. There was considerable resistance to this from the children, including Bron.

'Why can't we stay in the pool?'

'Because you can't come to Italy and not see great art,' said Hemani sternly.

'I don't want to see any smelly old art. What's so special about it anyway?'

'Well, there are these wall paintings by someone called Piero della Francesca that are really good.'

'So what?' said Bron, sounding ominously like Tania.

'I don't care what you think, you're coming,' said Theo. He was sick of the Casa Luna, sick of lying about doing nothing, waiting.

Once again, Bron travelled with Robbie and Tania. He knew his mother would mind, but he was determined to show her he was independent, and anyway Robbie was fun. They could sing rude versions of 'This Old Man' and 'Row, Row, Row Your Boat' together and have a blast.

Betty promptly commandeered the seat next to Theo. She climbed in the way she had learnt, long ago, bending, sitting, then swinging her legs over, knees clamped tightly together so that no glimpse of pantyhose should be visible. (Unbelievable, that anyone should wear tights in this heat, thought Polly.) When she emerged from a car, the whole movement was performed in reverse. That was the way to do it, not scrambling in like Polly. This vehicle – a people carrier, she believed it was called – was as graceless as her daughter-in-law. Poor dear Theo reeked of menthol and eucalyptus. She observed with disgust that showers of used tissues fell from his person at every movement, but there was certainly nobody else she would sit with, unless it was Ellen. Yes, Ellen would do very nicely, thought Betty, as long as she would take a few hints.

'I can drive,' said Polly, pushing her fine brown hair off her forehead, where it was sticky with heat and stress.

'No, honey, it's best if you let me negotiate these foreign

roads,' said Theo. Betty grimaced internally. 'These Italian drivers, they're all lunatics.'

'It's hardly any distance,' said Polly; but as always, Theo insisted on driving. Polly sighed. Somehow, he could never accept that she could drive just as well as he could. In fact, he was old-fashioned about most things, so much so that she sometimes felt as if she had slipped into a 1950s sitcom. Their life together was as tranquil as a bowl of cream. Theo didn't like the pushiness and self-obsession of modern American women, the way they always wanted to discuss their complexes. Polly did not believe in discussing complexes either, although she would have welcomed a little more conversation about subjects other than their children. At least she could enjoy the view this way, even if it did mean sitting at the back with Tania. She smiled at her daughter, who scowled in return. Crushed, Polly stared out of the window. What was happening to Tania, her adored daughter? Why was she so angry and grumpy, disappearing for long stretches into the garden? Was it just lack of discipline at bedtime, or was she really entering puberty early, like so many girls these days?

Robbie turned and beamed. She stroked his cheek with a finger, and he put up his little hand to keep it there.

'My bottom tooth is wobbly,' he announced. 'Look.'

'I can't see anything.'

She thought that when he lost his first milk tooth she would go into mourning. They were all there, like little rows of seed pearls; and every one had put a new line on her face, but that was nothing to what his first unmistakable sign of adulthood would do.

'Look, Mum, I can unzip my techno-trousers,' he said.

'Don't lose the bits.'

He took no notice, but began to unzip one leg of his new trousers from Gap to make them into shorts.

'Look!'

'Yes, darling.'

'Seat-belts on, everybody.'

'Man, this car is so cool,' said Bron. 'Like being in a spaceship.'

'Five, four, three, two, one, blast off!' Robbie exclaimed, bouncing excitedly.

'Shut up!' said Tania. 'I've got a headache. Daddy, I want my window open.'

'Wait until the air conditioning kicks in,' said Theo. He, too, had a headache and his nose was red from blowing.

Tania hated the air conditioning. It meant that they weren't allowed any fresh air, and she worried about them running out of oxygen that way, not to mention breathing in Daddy's germs. Tania knew all about germs from her *Nasty Nature* books: you couldn't see them, unless you looked under a microscope, but they were there all the same, waiting to attack. She thought of her body being like a castle under siege, defended by antibodies, which were like warriors, armed with guns to zap them. The germs kept trying to slip past them, on dirty fingers and food and stuff. Other people were even more dangerous, they could give you HIV and AIDS. There had been a lady who had come to talk to them at school about HIV and AIDS, and she'd said you couldn't get it if you were a kid, but that wasn't true because you could, from blood transfusions and maybe even from kissing. Lottie, her best friend, well, the girl who was her best friend sometimes when she wasn't hanging out with horrible Julia, told her that when grown-ups did kissing they did it with tongues, which must be really yucky, like licking snails. Frogs and snails and puppy-dogs' tails, that's what boys were made of. Tania looked at Bron. He didn't look froggy or snaily. He was browner than her, and he was . . . She felt funny, when she saw him, as if her insides had gone like a toffee left out in the sun. What would it be like to kiss him? Tania wondered, as the car began to bump down the hillside. To really, really kiss, with tongues and everything? Grown-ups had disgusting tongues, all bumpy and cracked and covered in slime, but kids' were different. If she could go back to school and tell Lottie that she'd got a boyfriend that she'd kissed with tongues, then she'd be invited to do a sleepover, for sure, but he kept paying attention only to Robbie. Stupid little Robbie, who wasn't playing with her any more. Overcome with fury, Tania suddenly kicked her brother again.

Robbie opened his mouth and for a second, nothing came out. Knowing that a really big scream was coming, Tania stuffed her fingers in her ears. Everyone else jumped, and cowered before the blast of noise.

'SHE KICKED ME, MUM! TANIA KICKED ME!' Scarlet with rage, he turned and thumped her. As she had her fingers in her ears, Tania couldn't for a moment fend him off. 'You nasty, poo-poo snotface girl, I hate you!'

135

Although he was small, he knew how to hit where it hurt. Tania began to cry, too.

'Well, I hate you back,' she said.

'Fart-breath!'

'Pig-snot! No returns.'

'Bum-face! No returns!'

'Quiet or I can't drive,' bellowed Theo.

'I hate you! I hate you all!'

Theo was beside himself. 'Right, That's it No treats! No ice cream for a week!'

Tania continued to shriek. So did Robbie.

Their father racked his aching head for a punishment that might just possibly take effect.

'No pocket money.'

'You don't give it to me anyway, you meanie.'

Overcome with the injustice of her life, Tania's thin chest heaved.

'Everyone else gets pocket money, but we don't.'

Bron looked at her contemptuously, shrugged, then turned to look out of the window. Robbie's sobs subsided, and he crept on to Polly's lap.

Sunk in misery, Tania swore to herself, 'I'll get even with you, I'll make you notice me.'

She would do something – she didn't know what – but it would be something, and soon.

Slowly, the first car ground the gravel beneath its wheels and bounced down the road, leaving clouds of white dust in its wake. The remaining four adults waited for it to clear, then set off as well, the long grasses growing in the middle of the road whispering as they brushed the undercarriage. The sky was too bright to look at, and the shrilling of cicadas seemed to make the silvery olive groves vibrate with sound as well as heat. It was a relief to pass through any patch of shadow.

As before, Ellen sat in front.

'Um, we're not going to Manhattan,' said Hemani, when she saw what Ellen was wearing. She tried to make her voice casual, but somehow it didn't come out like that. Ellen was wearing white Prada, just for a change. Hemani tried to feel faintly superior to all this showing-off, but failed.

'So?' said Ellen. 'Italians appreciate elegance.'

'It isn't just Italians,' said Ivo, with an exaggerated leer. Ellen ignored him.

'God, this road is dire,' she said, as they inched over a sunken boulder. 'You'd think the owner would fix it. Are you sure the car can manage it, Dan?'

'I got it up here,' he said. 'I'll get it down.'

'Perhaps the heaviest of us should get out and walk,' said Ellen, glancing over her shoulder.

'It's the last straw that breaks the camel's back, remember,' said Ivo, with equal pointedness.

The car jiggled from side to side, sliding on some loose chippings, and Hemani found she was clutching Ivo. A moment later, she was firmly detaching his large, damp hands, which had arrived in the most extraordinary places more or less instantaneously. Unabashed, he grinned at her. She found it hard not to laugh because really, there was something almost endearing about his incessant lechery, and he did have an oddly attractive mouth. For a clever man, which Ivo plainly was, to behave like this made her feel as though she was back at university again. If only I'd slept with more people before I got married, she thought. She had been able to ignore her body in England, keeping it wrapped up and subdued, but now it was bleating on and on about needing sex, about dying for it, about not wasting what was left. What was the point of being in a place where every breath of air felt like a caress, if you did nothing about it? Whom would she hurt if she had, just for once, a fling? Ellen obviously wasn't interested in Ivo, and Bron was off with the other children. At least Ivo was flirting.

Her book had fallen out of her bag. Ivo picked it up.

'Aha, *A Room with a View*. The perfect holiday read,' he said. 'Pity people don't write that sort of stuff any more. Peacock, Austen, Forster, Wodehouse, they all understood what we want is fun. Now we're all doomed to improving our minds with multicultural suburbia or Victorian pastiche.'

'Actually, it's a bit more than that, I think,' said Hemani. Despite her shyness, she did not lack for intellectual self-confidence, and felt he shouldn't get away with journalistic licence. 'It is about class, and being true to yourself. I think it's a great novel.'

'Oh, pooh. It's just a light romantic comedy written by a sentimental old poof,' said Ivo.

'Why is it that something that makes people laugh is always dismissed as light?' said Daniel. 'Shakespeare didn't disdain comedy. Nor did Dickens or Mark Twain.'

'Exactly,' said Hemani. 'It's always easy to feel miserable. Something that changes your mood is a kind of magic.'

'Ivo never reads books, do you, Ivo? You just skim them,' said Ellen.

'Well, most aren't worth reading.'

'I thought you used to be a literary editor,' said Daniel.

'You don't think literary editors read, do you?' said Ivo, in horror.

'What do they do?'

'They edit. They take some book frisking about like a dear little lamb and make it into chops. Anyway, I did read this years ago. All about some brawny young bloke who can't help snogging this rather wet girl whenever he sees her, until she succumbs. Really, Forster wanted to shag the bloke himself. There's nothing so pathetic as the way fiction shows up the fantasies of its author.'

'And you would know all about those, of course,' said Ellen.

'I don't see what else they could write, though,' said Hemani. She was enjoying this, it was the kind of conversation she'd had too little of since her divorce.

'By observing what's real and true,' said Ivo. 'The greatest novelists never wrote about love and being abroad, they wrote about the futility of wishing for that.'

'But why are those so futile?' asked Hemani. 'After all, people do fall in love, and do go abroad, and it isn't all disastrous.'

'Ivo takes pride in being a cynic, don't you?' said Daniel.

'Oh, love is all very well in its way, I dare say,' said Ivo, shrugging. 'It just isn't the universal solution to all problems that books and movies make it out to be. It's a sort of glamour—'

'Look, hoopoes!' Hemani said, pointing out of the window.

'What?'

'Those birds with black and white wings, there, flitting down the hillside. I thought you only got them in much hotter countries.'

'Have you ever been back, Meenu?' Ellen asked. Hemani forbore to answer that, for her, it wasn't 'back'.

'I went to Bombay in my gap year before university,' she said. 'It was beautiful, but weird. All these relations I'd never met suddenly appeared out of the woodwork. I think my parents were hoping I'd marry one of them, actually.'

'You mean, you could choose?'

'Oh, yes, of course,' said Hemani, amused. 'My parents aren't that traditional. They only wanted what any parent wants, which was to stop me making mistakes. They had this cousin all lined up for me. But I had to go off and make them, all the same.'

The strangeness of this intrigued the others.

'Bron isn't a mistake,' said Daniel.

'No,' said Hemani, with a smile he glimpsed in the rear-view mirror. He looked at her again, but she was gazing out of the window now, a slight frown between her brows. He knew, suddenly, that she was thinking about her son in the car ahead and worrying about him.

'What was he like, this cousin?' he asked, prompted by curiosity.

'He was OK, a graduate, perfectly nice, but—'

'What was wrong with him?' Ellen asked. 'Not good-looking?'

'No, he was quite handsome, but the thing is, I knew perfectly well what he wanted wasn't me but my passport.'

'Yeah, right,' said Ivo. 'Mmm, that command to let the bearer pass without let or hindrance, dead sexy.'

Hemani giggled.

'That must be strange, looking at a guy and thinking, I've never met you before but I could just marry you,' said Ellen, thoughtfully. 'Kind of empowering.'

'It's just a way of meeting someone. People meet in all sorts of strange ways,' said Hemani. 'It works for some. We all believe in leaving it to chance, falling in love with people you just happen to meet. No wonder it goes wrong so often.'

'An arranged marriage must be simpler, at least,' said Ivo.

'I don't know,' said Daniel. 'Parents are always going to have different values.'

'They want someone who'll bring money and status into the family, whereas you just want someone you won't get bored of screwing,' said Ellen.

There was a small, shocked silence, which Ellen affected not to notice. Ivo snorted. He loved it when Americans affected to be sophisticated; the result was always far worse than innocence.

'It's not just sex that makes a marriage work,' said Hemani. As the only person present who had been married, she felt she had to say something. 'It's all the other things, like trust and intelligence and sharing the same sense of humour.'

'Well, those come into sex, don't they?' said Ellen. 'At least, I've always found they do.'

'I don't know. The arranged marriages I've seen that work, they're more like friends than lovers. I don't think that's enough.'

'Are you saying you shouldn't be friends with your partner?' Daniel asked.

'Whenever I hear someone say that their best friend is their wife, I know they've stopped shagging. Who on earth wants to be friends? Friends are for friendship,' said Ivo. 'A girl is for all the things you couldn't possibly do to a chum.'

'Oh, for God's sake, Ivo, can it!' said Ellen, in a kind of suppressed shriek. 'We all know you'd be much happier living as Cro-Magnon man, clubbing us over the head and dragging us back to your cave, but you might have the tact not to gross us out about it!'

'Did I club you?' Ivo said, in injured tones. 'Did I?'

Ellen gave a loud sigh. 'No, Ivo, I seem to remember that you more or less clubbed yourself.'

The car gave an agonising jolt, scraping its underside on another large ridge of rock, and then they were on to smoother surfaces, sliding past vineyards.

'Love is rubbish,' said Hemani, suddenly fierce. 'Any idiot can fall in love. Ivo's right. It doesn't take any talent, after all, and I don't see why people are always so jolly pleased with themselves when they do it. Mostly what people mean by love is laziness. They don't really love someone, warts and all, they just decide not to notice if they're disgusting.'

'Don't you think that's what love is?' said Daniel. 'The not noticing?'

'How can you not notice?' said Ellen. 'You know, I think that's what's different about our generation? Older people were more accepting of defects, they had to be, but we aren't. We have gyms and plastic surgery and orthodontics, stuff they never dreamt of. How can you censor yourself, if it's possible to get rid of the flaws?'

She looked sideways at Daniel's profile. He was better looking than a lot of male models, his face hard and angular until shadows fell on it, and then she could see gentleness, which was not something she was used to seeing on men's faces. Ellen wondered again whether this was what she really wanted, then decided it was. He wasn't a dude, but hey, what did that matter? Frankly, she didn't want a high-profile marriage like some of her friends in fashion.

What I want, thought Ellen, is what my parents had before Mom died. Perhaps they would have wound up like so many of her friends' parents, divorced and full of bitterness, but Ellen didn't think so. They had been the happiest couple, everyone said so, and that was an almost impossible ideal to live up to. Each time she thought perhaps this was it she realised, but I'll get bored with him. She still had this hope that somehow her own life would be like her parents' had been, full of laughter and interest and adventure. Her face softened, briefly. Then she shook herself. There was no point being unrealistic.

'But those things aren't what somebody is, in themselves,' said Daniel. 'It isn't what's essential.'

He felt foolish and awkward, his discomfort shared by the others. It was one thing to discuss sex, that was intellectually respectable, but love was another matter. What was there new to say about love that hadn't been said before? It was a debased coinage, something beneath the notice of intelligent people: trash.

'But how do you know that you're going to go on loving what's essential?' said Ellen, putting her hand on Daniel's bare thigh. 'You might love somebody for being essentially clever at math, only to find they were fundamentally stupid about everything else. Also, you might get bored with that essential thing. After all, you'd get tired of eating the same food every day, wouldn't you?'

'People always use food as a metaphor for love,' said Ivo in a languid voice. 'It's not helpful, confusing one sort of appetite with another.'

Ellen shrugged. 'Well, you can compare anything to anything I guess.'

Hemani said, 'I don't think that we're all there to be consumed, devoured. To me, love is more like water. You never get tired of drinking water, do you?'

'Personally, I prefer Cristal,' said Ellen irritably, because Daniel had just removed her hand.

'Well at two hundred dollars a bottle, I'm not surprised,' said Ivo.

'And without water, you'd die,' Hemani insisted.

'Plenty of people live without love,' said Daniel.

'Live, yes, in a basic sort of way. But without love, they aren't fully alive.'

Ivo laughed.

'I once told a girl I was mad about that she should marry me because otherwise she'd end up with only a cat to love,' he said.

'She turned you down?'

Ivo shrugged.

'Well, no prizes for guessing that,' said Ellen. 'Your seduction lines are so groovy, baby. Shouldn't we be turning right, here?'

Obediently, Daniel turned.

'Have you been here before, Els?'

'No, I just spotted the sign while Ivo was showing us his club. I haven't been to this part before, I'm usually over in the Marche. That's where most of the factories are.'

'What, no child labour?' said Ivo. 'I thought you fashion people thought you were going to go bankrupt if you didn't blind at least one generation of Third World unfortunates.'

'My designs are made up here, by very highly paid Italians, if you must know,' said Ellen. 'So sorry to disappoint you.'

Ahead, the Nobles' car swished smoothly through the shimmering illusion of water on the road. Irrigation systems lifted arcs of real water to spray maize, or plantations of small trees destined for the garden centres of Europe. They passed a ruined castle, poplar woods and snack bars, lay-bys with lorries.

'Mummy, what are those black ladies doing?'

'What ladies?'

'The ones standing by the road?'

Polly looked, and was appalled.

'Oh,' said Betty, seeing also. 'They are just ladies who need a lift.'

'They're prozzies,' said Bron, ignoring her.

'What are prozzies?' asked Tania.

'Now, I don't think—' began Theo, but Bron interrupted.

'Women who do sex for money.'

'Sex for money, sex for money,' chanted Robbie.

'Ew, gross, do they really?'

'Polly, you really must control your children,' said Betty.

'Let's have a story-tape,' said Polly desperately. 'Here, *Tales from Shakespeare*.'

Tania groaned. 'Oh, Mum. I'm so bored of those.'

'You can't possibly be bored with Shakespeare,' said Polly.

'Well, I am.'

'So am I.'

'The comedies are OK, but the tragedies, puh-leese! All those stupid people killing each other just because they get jealous or have dumb parents. I hate that stuff.'

'But the comedies are also about people who get jealous, or who have stupid parents,' said Polly, sensing an opportunity. 'Why do you think they turn out differently?'

Bron shrugged. 'Just lucky.'

'Is that what you think? Tania?'

'The funny ones have magic,' said Tania, reluctantly.

'They've got jokes,' said Robbie.

'Yes, my angel. Jokes are a big help. And they are lucky,

146

Bron is right. They have good people at the top. The kings decide to help the rest when they're in trouble or being bullied. In the tragedies, they don't, so it all ends badly. Allowing other people to be bullied is almost as bad as being a bully yourself.'

'People can only be bullied if they allow themselves to be,' said Betty. 'You know?'

Several responses to this rose to Polly's lips, and died there, as they always did. Why could she never stand up to her mother-in-law? Was it politeness? The deference due to marriage? She didn't know, but her loathing had become such that she could only laugh about it, privately, on good days.

Theo was busy negotiating a large roundabout. The countryside had petered out, to be replaced by dismal shanties and modern apartment blocks. Above them, the old city rose.

'Can anyone see anywhere to park?'

'No, not yet,' said Theo, peering at the gaps between the road. 'It's as bad as London.'

At last, having driven all the way round the town, Polly spotted a place near the base of the city walls. The others, who had been following faithfully, rejoined them.

'Where's Theo?'

'He's gone ahead with Betty.'

'Ah,' said Daniel, and smiled at his sister-in-law. He was concerned to see her looking dejected. Polly believed in goodness, but Polly's goodness was not the kind that makes people braver, more honest or more active. It was the sort that is modest and efficient, that is closer to charity than love, and that is always anxious.

They were so beautiful, Tania and Bron and Robbie, they did not seem quite human. The light filtering through some pollarded lime trees overhead turned their faces a flickering, mysterious green. As long as they loved her, she didn't care about anything else. After all, not everybody enjoyed food, or books or art, so why shouldn't she be less thrilled by making love than you were supposed to be? She was so lucky, so incredibly lucky, to be living this kind of life when half her girlfriends still had no children, or had, like Meenu, a child but no husband. It always made Polly feel happier to think of Meenu, because Meenu was pretty and clever and strong, yet had lost her husband whereas she had kept hers, despite being none of those things. What would it be like not to have Theo? At times she saw so little of him that Polly felt she could imagine it quite well, but she couldn't, not really, because of the extraordinary amounts of money washing in every month now that Theo was a partner in his law firm. They had always been comfortable, even when he was a junior, thanks to his London allowance but now she could write out the cheques for the school fees and the tennis lessons and the piano lessons and the French lessons, without ever thinking about whether she had the cash. She had a laundry service, a window-cleaner, a handyman, and a Portuguese cleaning lady who came twice a week; she had her hair done whenever she wanted it, and books delivered by Sandoes on the Kings Road. The charges for her Peter Jones card, Waitrose food bills and petrol all came directly out of Theo's account, just as another huge sum went into their pensions. There were holidays like these. All she had to do in return was to take care of Theo and the children and the house, and really, that wasn't so hard. Just because Theo had chosen to go ahead with the Demon Queen didn't mean that he was unfeeling, merely that he wanted some time alone with her.

I hope Robbie will want to be alone with me, sometimes, when he's grown up, she thought, her eyes resting on his slight form. The children were skimming along the steep cobbled roads, so light and airy they seemed not to touch the ground, while the hot and lumpen adults plodded in their wake.

'They look happy together, don't they?' said Hemani.

'Yes,' said Polly.

'I'm sorry Tania and Bron aren't getting on so well as the two boys.'

'Oh, they all rub along,' said Polly. 'You should see some of the children we've had on other holidays. Do you worry about what's going to happen next? To them, I mean?'

'Not right here and now. The loveliest thing about being on holiday is the feeling of irresponsibility. I feel I'm suddenly looking down on my life.'

Which was true, though what she saw was not comforting.

'Do you really?' said Polly wistfully. 'I wish I could.'

'Is Betty getting you down?'

'A bit.'

149

'Yeah, it's a problem, isn't it?' said Ellen. 'For anyone who takes her other son on.'

'Why, were you thinking of it?' asked Hemani, lightly.

'The man who invents a way of harnessing all that infant energy will solve the world's problems,' said Ivo, catching up.

'Why should it be a man?' asked Hemani, descending to flirtation under the guise of feminism.

'You'd have to catch them first,' said Polly, dryly.

'I love it,' said Daniel, following the three figures with his eyes. 'They're a force of nature.'

Ivo stopped and fanned himself with his hat. The women walked on.

'So when's the wedding?' he said.

'What wedding?'

'Why, yours. Once you start finding other people's children anything other than revolting, you start wanting your own, and once you start wanting your own, you're halfway up the aisle. All you have to do now is pop the question.'

'I think what I most need to find is a long cool drink,' said Daniel. Really, Ivo did presume too far.

Every café and bar was crammed with other foreigners, flushed and limp in shorts or floppy dresses, all with the same expressions of wary incuriosity. Penned behind dusty hedges in pots or by makeshift fences they looked, Daniel thought, like human cattle. He was embarrassed, and thoughtful. What had Ivo meant? Of course he wasn't thinking of getting married.

'Do you think *you*'ll marry?' he asked Ivo, suddenly.

Ivo said, with unusual soberness, 'I don't know. I don't want to be some saddo bachelor, trying to pretend I'm still a teenager, do you?'

'No. But people, friends, basically want you to stay single, don't they? When I split up with Frances, you said, "Welcome back."'

'That was because we all loathed her,' said Ivo. 'It's a pain when your mates go out with someone you don't like, because you inevitably lose touch. It's only people like Hemani who want to please their parents, the rest of us have to please our friends, or else live in a social desert.'

'Well, she didn't, did she? Meenu, I mean.'

'I suspect there's a will of iron under that luscious exterior.'

'You seem to think that about all women.'

'Yeah. Basically, terrifying.'

'Uh-huh. You're interested?'

'Well, you have to do something on holiday, don't you? And I bet she'd be hot stuff.'

'I wouldn't know about that.'

They kept to the shadows, and eventually found the church where the famous frescoes were housed. It was a relief to enter its cool, dim interior. Ivo automatically approached the font, dipped his fingers in the water and crossed himself. So did Ellen. For a moment they looked at each other, in mutual surprise, until Ellen shrugged and turned away.

'So, where are these great paintings?'

'At the far end, look. Where they make you pay to get in.'

Once again, they were herded, and eventually were allowed into the small, dimly lit chapel.

'Why's that man got a sword through his head?' Robbie asked.

'He's in a battle.'

'Why isn't he screaming?'

'He's probably had injections in his face, like Grandma,' said Tania. 'Does it hurt having them, Grandma?'

'*Il faut souffrir pour être belle*, as the French say.'

'What?'

'One must suffer to be beautiful.'

'But you—' Robbie began.

Polly, anticipating disaster, interrupted brightly, 'What about putting on one of these personal stereo things? That'll tell you all about the paintings.'

All the children assented enthusiastically to this. Any technology was better than art.

Only Bron, who was good at art, was intrigued, particularly by the battle scene. There was a man in a white chef's hat blowing a trumpet, and somebody else in a brown helmet shouting from a rearing horse. It was all swords and lances, no archers, Bron noted. Rama would have done it better.

How beautiful the faces are, thought Hemani. She wondered whether people really looked like that when getting a sword in the head. She had not been dignified or restrained during the times of conflict in her own life, she knew, though she very much wished she had. Remembering some of the exchanges she had had with Bruce, she felt a wince of anguish. Even now, years afterwards, she found herself holding her breath when driving down certain streets. She wondered whether it was the same for everyone, that the map of the world became overlaid by another kind of map, of where this or that betrayal had occurred. It was always the horrible times she remembered, now, never the good ones. At least she had never come to Italy with her ex. She was glad of this, because it meant that she was doing something new, without him, at last.

'It's really an early version of cinema,' Ivo said. 'Think about it: when there was nothing else to see, churches were the greatest show in town.'

'Featuring the Oscar-winning Jesus and his mother Mary,' said Ellen. 'Supported by . . . who are these guys, anyway?'

Suddenly, in a carillon of tiny tunes, Theo's mobile exploded into noise.

'Theo Noble? Oh, hi there, hi! No, not at all.'

His voice dropped to the crooning, seductive note men only ever seemed to use to mobiles. Talking, he walked slowly out of the church.

Ellen said irritably, 'Doesn't he know to turn it to vibrate?'

'Oh, but he wouldn't hear it then,' said Polly.

Ellen said impatiently, 'You put it in your breast pocket.'

'Why not your knickers?' said Ivo.

Ellen rolled her eyes.

'Ivo, do you ever not think about sex?'

'Only when I have to.'

'I hate this place, ' said Tania plaintively. 'I want to go home.'

'To London?'

'No. The house with the pool.'

Chapter Seven

Squatting on the floor, looking uncommonly like her grandmother, Tania was writing:

> *RULES FOR MY ROOM.*
>
> *(None of this applies if (see exceptions below.))*
>
> *You will obey me, even if I tell you to dance.*
> *You will bog off if I say so!*
> *You won't snoop.*
> *You will enter only with a permit signed by me.*
>
> *OBEY ME OR DIE!!!*
>
> *Exceptions: floods, fire, terrorists or The Simpsons.*

She sucked a lock of hair. That should show them. Those boys would be wild to know what she was up to now. The mirrors on her embroidered T-shirt flashed and winked.

Mum had bought it for her when she was still being nice instead of horrid and grumpy all the time. Tania really did think that Mum hated her these days. She was always bugging her about something, like her table-manners and other boring stuff and trying to stop her wearing make-up, like she was a Victorian. Even if she had Pre-Minstrel Tension it was no excuse. As if Tania wasn't suffering agonies of boredom, as if Tania had anything to read or anyone to play with, when the People went away. All the stories warned how unpredictable magic was, and they were true. Sometimes she thought she was all alone, and then suddenly she'd spot one of them, buzzing about as a bumblebee or a fly, or even a mosquito. They could appear out of a cloud of dust, and disappear just when a game was getting interesting. Then she was thrown back on her own resources. She was fed up with painting and fed up with poetry, which after all didn't just happen every day. Tania was writing a poem about an owl this week, after hearing one hooting at night outside her bedroom window. Recently, she had discovered that the lines didn't all have to rhyme with each other, that she could make patterns of different endings. Very excited, she had written in a kind of frenzy:

The Hunting Owl.

A feathered creature is the owl
All other birds despise.
It is a most peculiar fowl,
With glowing amber eyes.

She liked that. Tania always sided with predators, and particularly those that were ganged up on by others. It was like the girls at school, afraid of the games she liked to invent. Sometimes they'd play them for a bit, but mostly they just wanted to have fairy doll's house tea parties at break times. Tania loathed dolls with a passion, just as she loathed pink and ballet. (Clothes and make-up were different, for they were part of the mysterious world of teenagers that she could see was infinitely desirable.) What she loved was nature.

Grimly, she continued,

> *His screech is nastier than a howl,*
> *Mice from their nests he'll prise.*

She thought of Robbie, cowering before her when she flew into one of her rages. She was furious at the way he and Bron continued to ignore her. How dared they? It made her feel as if she didn't exist. It was all Bron's fault. Without him, she and her brother would be best friends again.

What rhymed with howl? Tania went through the alphabet, hearing the happy splashes from the pool. She had stroked an owl once, on her birthday. The Animal Man had brought it, along with a ten-foot-long python and an armadillo and a fruit bat.

> *His plumage softer than a towel,*
> *A silent ghost, he flies.*

It could end there, but she could feel it wasn't enough. 'He really is a frightful fowl?' No. 'His head is full of feathers foul.' That made him sound stupid, as stupid as she felt. Increasingly, all three children found it impossible to sleep. It was too hot, and despite the green coils like snakes that were supposed to drive the mosquitoes away, there were insects.

> His head is covered by a cowl,
> At night he haunts the skies.
> His taste is vile, his nest is foul,
> He'll vanish at sunrise.

Suddenly, her bad mood had gone. It was good enough to go into the book Meenu had given her for Christmas, a lovely Indian book with an orange and green and gold silk cover like a sari, bound with a golden cord. Tania only put the poems that she knew were good in it. She wrote the poem out again carefully on another sheet of paper, then took it downstairs, expecting praise. But none of the grown-ups seemed at all interested or impressed; not even Dad. He was on his mobile again, talking to the office about some boring old law stuff. Tania made faces of fury. They were supposed not to be working, but they didn't act like that. Mum said absently, 'Very good, darling' but only glanced at it. Ivo actually warned her against becoming a poet, saying that when he had worked on a newspaper he had been sent dozens every day, all written in green ink by lunatics. Mean old Meenu said she didn't read poetry.

Uncle Dan was playing chess against Bron and Robbie again. Grandma swatted her away like a fly. The mortification that swiftly follows any act of creation was new to her, and she had no defences against it except rage. They were all stupid, stupid, even Ellen who just wanted to get all lovey-dovey with Uncle Dan. They gave presents to Robbie for being naughty, and none to her. Who wanted to come and live in this nasty hot house anyway? It would serve them all right if she made a poison.

She stomped upstairs again. Oh, she was so bored! It would be ages before things were ready. A number of mixtures were ranged on the deep window-ledge, fermenting in tumblers. She had painted them with stripes and blobs of colour, to make them look more magical. The People approved of that, and urged her to add honey in tiny excitable voices. Tania stirred the contents, and peered at one mush of leaves and flowers in the little china teapot she had found in her room. She was brewing potions, and the best would go into her new purple glass bottle that she had bought in Cortona. Everyone was into potions at school, but hers were real, not from kits with stupid Harry Potter on. She collected all the ingredients herself, from the garden and the woods below. Tania had found a large piece of cloth in a kitchen drawer. It had pictures of herbs and flowers, and underneath, some faded, curly writing in English about the powers each one had. This cloth had become very important to her; had she been a little younger she would have taken it to bed with her at night.

The house creaked and sang to Tania. She could see its

People if she let her mind slide. The grown-ups thought they were insects, they never noticed anything. Of course she knew the Tooth Fairy didn't exist, and neither did Father Christmas, it was just grown-ups trying to trick kids and keep them like Robbie, but Tania saw the glitter of the eyes that watched what everyone did. Ever since, she had started to rescue sodden bumblebees and half-drowned moths from the pool, cupping them gently in her hands. They liked her for that.

She could smell the individual jars over the tang of drying chlorine on her hair and skin. A couple, like the ones made with lavender and rose petals, were really nice but others were frothing and going a sort of yucky yellowish brown. She really ought to have some eye of toad and foot of newt, but all she wanted was to give them a taste of their own medicine.

Medicine! Why hadn't she thought of that? Tania wondered whether it would be allowed. So far, the People and the cloth had only told her about plants, but Dad wouldn't miss any of his, and there were bound to be a few pills, particularly in Grandma's sponge-bag. After all, Grandma was a witch, Mum had told her once. A wicked one, no doubt, because she seemed to make people so cross. She was always asking Dad why he didn't bring the family to America more often, saying that she'd even pay for the tickets – as if Dad couldn't pay for them himself, as Mum had remarked afterwards. Dad made a lot of money. In fact, they were quite rich, which was odd because they didn't have a lot of servants. Tania knew this was something that made Mum and Dad quarrel sometimes, along with the subject of living in America, because Dad did want to go back, whereas Mum absolutely did not. Tania could understand, sort of. New York was great to have fun in, and to buy stuff, but it was busy and noisy and only had one big park. In any case, she couldn't see why Daddy couldn't work in New York and catch the plane back. He was always catching planes, and never there except at the weekends, and sometimes not even then, so what was the big deal?

Downstairs, the ancient record player was blasting out music, the Mozart one called Cosy. Mum loved opera, but it gave Tania a headache most of the time. It was always about love, and people getting mixed up, which sounded dumb because how could you not know the people you loved? You just loved them. Grown-ups were supposed to be wiser and cleverer than children but they thought too much, it was like thinking about breathing, a sure way to turn blue and fall down dead.

Tania stirred her jars of potion, then remembered about the medicines. Snooping about in other people's rooms made her feel so excited that it was worth doing even if she didn't find anything. She tip-toed down the corridor. Its long white walls looked almost blue, the shutters drawn and sharp rays of brilliant light slicing through the air at intervals where they weren't quite closed. They were full of tiny, dancing specks of gold. Tania put out her hand. She could see them, but she couldn't touch them, the beautiful tiny People with glittering wings and eyes. Slowly, Tania held out her skirt,

161

and twirled. All around her, the shining specks swirled and twirled too, dancing with her, and then all the specks sang, their voices high as a mosquito's whine, telling her what to do next.

'Children! Lunch-time! Children! Wash your hands!' Polly called, from below.

'Honey, please,' said Theo, wincing. He couldn't stand it when his wife got that note in her voice, so strident and unlike her usual soft tones. Just now Theo was tense, because at any moment the call might come to jump on a plane to Frankfurt as all the pieces of his deal were coming into place at last, and he could really do with some quiet. 'They can't hear even when you shout.'

Hemani rolled her eyes. It was true, Polly was driving everyone round the bend with her insistence on military precision about meals, but she hated Theo's bossiness too. Now that he was up again, it was increasingly frequent. At least, while it's just Bron and me, I don't have to put up with what a man wants, she thought. We can just get on with our lives. Men are never happy unless showing off and having their egos massaged, and I just don't have the time for that. At least, that was what she'd thought before this holiday, but here time was so strange. It was like being in a dream: certain parts of the day, such as the afternoon, lasted for ever, whereas others, like the morning, were over in a flash.

'I'll lay the table outside, shall I?'

'Yes please,' said Polly absently.

Hemani collected a tray of plates and cutlery, and walked out.

'I must say, your friend Hermione does seem to have a strange taste in clothes,' said Betty.

'Hermione? Oh, you mean Hemani.'

'Whatever,' said Betty. She was blending up another one of her mushy drinks.

'I think her taste is rather wonderful, myself,' said Polly, coming close to defiance. 'I love those bright colours, don't you, Ellen?'

'They're perfect on her,' Ellen said diplomatically. 'I couldn't wear them, of course.'

'Ellen, dear,' said Betty, 'would you go and call Danny in?'

'Sure,' said Ellen. 'I think he's by the pool.'

She went out into the brilliance and noise of the garden. The heat struck her like a blow. She saw specks moving before her eyes, as though she were about to faint. The shrilling of the cicadas wound her suddenly to such a pitch of misery and hopelessness that a lump rose in her throat, as hard as stale bread.

Ellen didn't know if it was just English house parties, or if it was people with kids, but so far her vacation was not a success. Perhaps I should have gone to the Hamptons, she thought, where I could have had a good time by the sea, at least. She was trying hard to be brave and optimistic, but this was no fun. What sort of person had sex only once a week? What was the point of both of them being here otherwise? True, he hadn't invited her, but she had really thought when Polly asked that it had come from him, indirectly, or she wouldn't have risked humiliating herself. The trouble was, you could never tell what was going on. For such a brainy guy, he was hopeless at understanding that there was more to life than study. He was always jogging or swimming or reading or playing his cello, and although she had actually bought a pair of brand-new trainers so as to join him on his jogs to Cortona, so far she had always overslept. Ellen was normally an early riser but at the Casa Luna she couldn't get to sleep until it was nearly dawn because first, it was too hot and second, she kept thinking that maybe tonight he'd sneak into her room. She'd even get up and go to the bathroom to let him know that she was awake, but he didn't get the hint.

Gloomily, Ellen thought how much easier it must have been before. In the old days, before AIDS and sexual harassment, it was easy – you just did it. Of course, that was before she had realised that, basically, it was finding a soul-mate that mattered. It was no good looking when you were in your early twenties, anyway, that was when you had to lay down experiences like fine wine to savour when you were old and boring. Still, it had been great. Now that she was in her thirties, the whole dating game was as formal as a waltz. You never rang him, you waited to be rung. You had to let the man do the chasing, which meant that you got sex-maniacs like Ivo Sponge clogging up your in-box, rather than the kind of well-bred East Coast banker she was predestined for. Maybe she should never have gone to bed with Daniel before the third date, but living as she did in two continents it was that much harder to judge whether his feelings were involved.

Now, Ellen wished she had rented her own car, so that at least she could get away. It wasn't impossible even now, but she'd have to go all the way into Perugia to get one, and the thought of travelling in the heat undid her. They could go shopping together, which would do a lot for her morale, but dropping hints about this didn't seem to work. Daniel didn't anticipate. Sex with him was like trying to teach someone how to do a three-point turn: up a bit, left a bit, back a bit; she thought she'd expire with impatience. Daniel was the kind of guy who, left to himself, would still be figuring out the moral implications of the wheel. Yet he was the one for her, she knew. He had sent her flowers each time they'd slept together in London. That was the sort of nice, old-fashioned chivalry she really appreciated, that told her more about his feelings than anything else. She loved him, she really did. He was one of those nice, solid, straight-arrow guys her father would approve of.

Of course, he was never going to rock, like that Brazilian photographer she had dated, or, for that matter, the cute Italian count with the amazing tongue, but the point was, Daniel was eligible. Plus, he was a nice guy. Plus, he was seriously gorgeous, like Clark Kent in *Superman*. That was a rare combination. Ellen knew she had to be level-headed about this. There just weren't any heterosexual men available for marriage in New York, and she wasn't prepared to wait until she was so desperate that she'd relocate to somewhere like Seattle. Dan might be an academic but he was from the right kind of family and, even if he wasn't Catholic, he was someone who would fit in. In fact, having a professor for a husband might be kind of interesting. Ellen paused to view the landscape with unseeing eyes, imagining the way the media would portray them as a couple – the Egghead and the Airhead, perhaps – not that she would remind anyone that she had gone to Sarah Lawrence before the Parsons School of Design. Everyone assumed you were intellectually challenged if you worked in fashion.

But how to detach him from the appalling Ivo? Whenever she tried to get Danny to open up, Ivo watched with such a sardonic expression that somehow she didn't dare be more bold. After all, she wasn't really so tough that she could take much more rejection, or so confident that she could risk that many knocks to her pride. She had asked one evening if Danny might lend her his book when he'd finished it. It looked serious but also vaguely romantic, and she wanted to show him that she could share his interests even if she didn't share his passion for classical music.

Now she was having a perfectly miserable time reading about German women being raped by Soviet soldiers. It was awful, and it had already given her one nightmare, because her family had been German, originally, and even though her grandfather had come to America long before the homeland had been tainted with incomprehensible evil she felt the echo of shame. Of course her family, cultivated and liberal, would never have been caught up in Nazism, but it could so easily have happened. At least *Berlin, The Downfall* had been good for squashing a large bug later. The number and variety of insects in the Casa Luna were seriously gross. Ellen tossed her gilt-blond hair, and wandered through the arch, admiring the way her embroidered slippers looked against the smooth green turf. The bushes hummed with bees, so many flowers, she supposed Polly would know their names. Polly seemed to know everything about houses and gardens, knowledge that Ellen respected without feeling it at all necessary to learn. After all, what were housekeepers and gardeners for? Still, Betty had a vast garden at her place in Rhode Island, so she supposed it was something she'd better get acquainted with.

She caught sight of Daniel, still churning up and down in the pool, and suppressed a flash of irritation. Ellen had tried going into the pool too but the only person who immediately joined her self-conscious frolics was Ivo, who had committed the ultimate crime of splashing her.

Ellen called, 'Lunch, guys.'

'Great. I'll go change,' said Daniel, hauling himself out of the pool. She watched the water stream down his chest and legs. He'd said that he had to swim every day in order to keep a back problem under control. She hadn't known whether to be impressed or depressed by this apparent lack of vanity. It was as if there was no connection between the great packaging and what went on inside, which was partly what intrigued her. Even when they were most intimate, there was a kind of detachment about him, as if his mind was someplace else. She saw Ivo intercepting her glance, and glared at him.

'Hey, kids, lunch!' called Ellen, hearing a ribbon of laughter winding through the woods below. Daniel padded past, dripping.

'So what?' came Robbie's high, defiant yell.

'Where are you?'

'We're hiding!'

Giggles rippled and trilled from the silver leaves all around.

'Can't catch me, can't catch me!'

'Suit yourself,' said Ellen archly. She turned, and saw Ivo still lying on his sun-bed.

'Are you coming or not?'

Ivo tipped his hat over his eyes.

'Too much pasta, my darling, not good for the old waist-line.'

Ellen glared at him.

'Like, I could care.'

Ivo's mouth said, 'Well, you used to.'

'Did I? I can't remember.'

Ivo tilted up his absurd hat, and looked at her, a glance as direct as a blow.

'Don't lie. It makes you ugly.'

Ellen flushed.

'I don't care if I look ugly to you, and you know what? You look ugly to me. You're greedy and mean and selfish and lecherous, and it was stupid of me to have ever been fooled by you. I don't know why you're here, but I really wish you weren't.'

'I'm here because I was asked to come on holiday by a friend,' said Ivo in a surprised voice.

'The great British Sponge Fleet sails again,' said Ellen.

'Yes, what's so bad about that?'

'Because really good things aren't offered, and they aren't free,' said Ellen. 'They have to be won. And, Ivo, you don't have the balls to win anything.'

She turned, and walked up the steps.

'Oh, don't I?' Ivo muttered, to her retreating back. He picked up his book, stared at it, sighed, put it down. 'Oh, fuck, fuck, fuck,' he said softly, and walked off.

Bron, who had been listening intently, swung down from the tree.

'He fancies her.'

Robbie spluttered and snorted, 'He said a bad word.'

'He does, too,' Bron said, intrigued.

'So what? Grown-ups are weirdos anyway but when they're in love, they spend all day doing stupid babyish things like kissing and lying on top of each other and even showing each other their bottoms.'

'Yeah.'

'That's really gross.'

'Someone told me that they even put their willies in girls' mouths and do wees in them,' said Bron. 'But I asked Mum, and she said that it was rubbish.'

Robbie didn't want to think of Ivo doing something like this, for Ivo had recently bought him a supersoaker gun and they had had a great game in the pool. If he preferred to show his bottom to Ellen rather than play squirting, then Robbie felt very sorry for him.

'Yuk,' Robbie said.

'Yeah, but that love stuff is important, you know,' said Bron, slowly, thinking of Hemani.

'Why?'

A confusion of images and memories shuddered through Bron's mind: his mother weeping, his father's new baby, the feelings of sadness and absence that he couldn't even put a name to but which drew him as the sea is drawn by the moon. He said, finally, 'It costs a lot of money when it goes wrong.'

'Oh.'

Robbie wasn't too worried because as long as he had his pocket money saved up they were rich.

'It made my mum very sad when Dad left us.'

Robbie thought about this. He couldn't imagine his mum being sad. She was just there, like the sun. She did get tired, sometimes, and cross. He didn't like it when that happened, because she shouted at him and her face went red and funny-looking.

'Shall we play something?'

Around them, the insect voices rose in a shrill, commanding shimmer. Robbie listened, grinning.

'OK.'

'We could play match-making, you know,' said Bron.

'How?'

'Well . . .' Bron was uncertain. How did families arrange a marriage? For there could be no love without marriage, that was clear. He thought of what his grandmother and aunties had talked about.

'Do they need to show each other their bottoms?' asked Robbie, exploding with laughter.

'We should put them together,' Bron said, trying to puzzle it out.

The insect-voices thrummed. Robbie listened.

'Not yet,' he said. 'Let's play some more.'

Betty watched the other guests shovelling down lunch, then supper, then breakfast the following day with deep distaste. In a small cell, locked away in her brain, she remembered that she too adored food and this memory made her even angrier with Polly for cooking it so well and in such abundance. She sipped her drink and watched them getting flecks of sauce or milk on their clothes, the grease spreading and blotching round their mouths. This heat was really becoming intolerable. Under the pergola it was quite shady, with a pair of lime trees trained to shield them from the worst of the noon-day glare, but one couldn't even lift a glass without perspiring.

She considered her sons. They were fine grown men, full of the strength and vigour that ebbed daily from her own limbs, no matter how many pills she took or laps she swam. For Betty, too, used the pool – before her abominable grandchildren began horsing around with that coloured boy. She was the last person in the world to be racist, but all the same she was a little surprised by Theo's choice of friends. Not that she was anything like as worried about him as she had been, given that he had settled down ... If only Danny would do the same. Betty could see that Ellen was absolutely mad about him, and it wasn't surprising seeing that he resembled his father so much. All Betty's husbands had been good-looking, and all of them had been a disappointment to her, but none quite so much as Daniel's father. He had been the real love of her life, if she could count any of them as such. He had been the one who could have run for office if only he'd bothered. But he hadn't. He'd preferred the quieter waters of Harvard, and all those dismal faculty meetings, and parties at which people discussed the number of angels dancing on a pin. It looked like Danny would turn out the same way, unless he could be diverted.

Betty thought about Ellen. Her family was not political, but they were an impeccable choice. She had met Ellen's father several times on the charity circuit and had even considered making a play for him herself until that Terri woman had gotten hold of him. It was a nuisance about Bunny because, however useless, a husband was always preferable to a walker. Now, though, it looked as if he was going to cost her a bunch of money instead of the other way round. On the whole, Betty thought she should take more control of her children's lives. At least Theo was coming home soon, and he was the son she hoped most from. Meanwhile, there was her second son.

Really, Ellen ought to have Danny tied up in knots by now. Modern girls just didn't seem to learn the art of getting a gentleman to propose. Betty had kept her ears open for any sounds of nocturnal activity, and she approved of the way Ellen was obviously playing it cool. All the same, you could overplay your hand on that one.

She had already summoned Daniel for a discussion about his future on the balcony at the top of the external flight of steps that she had requisitioned as her own. It was thickly shaded, and commanded the best view of the gardens below. He had been deep in practising one of his dreary pieces of Bach – how she regretted ever letting him get hooked on music! – but put down his bow when she said, 'Danny, I want to have a serious conversation with you.'

Betty did not so much converse as hand down a smaller tablet of stone. Daniel pushed this irreverent thought away and looked suitably eager for what he knew would be coming: the bi-annual Marriage Lecture.

'You're thirty-two, Danny, and—'

'Actually, Mother, I'm thirty-three,' said Daniel mildly. He hated being called 'Danny' so much it made him feel slightly ill. He wished Ellen had not picked up this habit, a presumption of an intimacy that repulsed him every time she used it. It never occurred to him to tell her this. He did not want to hurt her feelings. He did not want to hurt the feelings of anyone, if he could help it.

'As I was saying, you're quite old enough now to think about settling down.'

'I have thought about it. I just haven't done it.'

'Why not? You know my only wish is to see you happy.'

Betty placed her hand, with its long red-painted nails, on his arm and looked up at him with that mixture of flirtation and pathos she had employed ever since his voice had broken. Daniel swallowed.

'I know,' he said. The internal struggle between the two

sides of his nature always became worse in her company, and he became more than usually tongue-tied.

'It's my fault, I suppose,' said Betty, angling her strong, beautiful face with its taut skin away from the light. 'Mothers can never win. I traumatised you with all those terrible divorces. You know, I suppose, that even Bunny and I have called it a day? Believe me, dear, if I could have made them work I would have. I simply had rotten luck each time. But just because I've been unlucky doesn't mean that you will. Marriage and parenthood are the two greatest achievements in any life. If you only knew the joy children can bring! I always count those early years—' Her voice broke off and she suddenly said with her usual asperity, 'Tania! Robbie! What do you think you're doing?'

Betty's grandchildren froze in the act of attempting to tear each other's hair out. Robbie opened his mouth to scream, met Betty's implacable gaze, and quailed. Their hands dropped nervelessly to their sides. Daniel, who knew all too well what it was like to arouse her displeasure, smiled at them weakly. They didn't even notice. At that moment the large lumps of ivory hanging round Betty's neck looked just like skulls, and the glass in her hand was a lightning-bolt. Robbie and Tania gave a terrified squeal, and fled.

'As I was saying,' said Betty, resuming, 'one of life's greatest pleasures. I suggest you turn your attention to it. Remember, your trust fund is still under my control. I believe you would find it uncomfortable to live on a British academic's salary.'

This was all too true. Daniel knew how poorly the academic life paid on this side of the Atlantic: the brain-drain was all the other way. People thought he was crazy to have stayed on and accepted the University College lectureship, at half the salary he could have obtained back in the US of A. Sometimes, he only had to think of the nightmare of applying for a job through the MLA and the horror of jostling for attention among thousands of other graduate job-seekers all trying to get hired to remind himself of how much he loathed the pushiness expected of him. Of course, there were other Americans who felt just as he did, and who managed to survive it, but they were different. He didn't mind being a permanent exile.

'What about this girl, Ellen? You are, I take it, *à deux*? What about her?'

Daniel swallowed. It was hard having Mother interfere in this way, it was one of the reasons why he (and he suspected Theo) had wanted to come to England in the first place.

'I've been seeing her.'

'Well, what about that? Why don't you marry Ellen? You do want children, I take it?'

'Sure I do,' said Daniel. It was true, too: despite their outbursts, he was fond of his niece and nephew, although he found Bron more congenial company. They had found an old chess-board and played against each other pretty well until Robbie had insisted on dragging his friend off to the pool again. Still, Daniel had found himself thinking, really for the first time, how good it would be to be with a kid like that. 'But it's, you know, pretty casual.'

175

Betty leant forward.

'Danny, is there anything you want to tell me? In confidence? A mother knows how to keep her children's secrets, you know.'

He stared at her, then realised what she meant.

'Oh – no, Mother.' Relieved, he gave her one of his rare smiles. 'There's nothing like that.'

'I'm glad to hear it. So, what's the problem?'

'The problem?'

Betty sighed. For a Harvard graduate, her son could be remarkably obtuse.

'Why don't you marry her?'

Daniel rubbed his nose wearily.

'I do wish you'd concentrate,' said Betty.

'Oh, uh, I do. Some of the time. But, you know, I – well, marriage is a very personal thing.'

'You aren't getting any younger, honey. Even Prince Charles was married by your age.'

Yes, and look what happened to him, Daniel wanted to retort.

'I would so like to see you give me grandchildren,' said Betty. 'And Ellen is the sweetest girl. A real beauty. Didn't she do modelling for a while, before taking to design?'

'I don't know,' said Daniel. 'It's not something we've discussed.'

'What do the young discuss these days, I wonder?'

'Well,' said Daniel, wondering this himself, 'work, I guess.'

Betty made a faint grimace.

176

'So unromantic. At least promise me—'

From around the corner, there came the sound of gravel crunching beneath car wheels, and two short toots of a horn.

'Now, I wonder who that can be?'

Below them, the three children had already gone to investigate, racing through the garden.

'Guy, Guy, Uncle Guy!' came childish voices.

'Is there another guest arriving?' Betty asked, in a tone of deep disapprobation.

'Sounds like it,' said Daniel.

'A relation of Polly's?'

'A family friend, I think, if he's the Guy, or guy, I've met before. He's very nice. A gardener.'

'A gardener?' Betty's voice dropped several degrees. 'Really! That kind of person should not be mixing with our family.'

Daniel shrugged hopelessly. He wondered whether he should tell Betty that Guy Weaver was and was not 'that kind of person', but that would sound as if he were correcting her, or worse, criticising. He heard Guy's voice saying, 'Hello, chicken,' and then he joined the general rush to the front door because really, he couldn't bear Betty any longer, even if she was his own mother.

Chapter Eight

With the arrival of Guy Weaver, something in the house changed. Perhaps, thought Polly, we simply needed a change of the human menu, or perhaps it was an event in what had become at once monotonous and chaotic. What had seemed like a short span of time was now stretching out in her imagination to the crack of doom. If they all managed to make it through the fortnight without open warfare, it would be a miracle.

Polly had moved from worrying about whether her guests were enjoying themselves to feeling increasingly resentful that none of them seemed the slightest bit concerned about her own well-being. Wasn't she owed something, as the hostess? Weren't they supposed to be real friends? She didn't expect it from the men, but she had hoped for a lot more from her own sex. With every hour, she felt censure rise in her throat like bile. Ellen was useless, utterly useless. All she did was loll about looking decorative, while Polly, who had barely the time or energy to put on mascara, ran herself ragged looking after the needs of the house and children. It was as if meals appeared on the tables by magic, and the laundry did itself. Whereas it was all Polly, running round like a hamster in a wheel, just as she had feared, doing twice as much housework as at home with half as much help. Needless to say, the promised cleaner had not materialised, despite three calls to the Italian Dream offices, and although people kept telling her to put her feet up, the fact was that you just couldn't in a hot country. The moment so much as a Rice Krispie was left on the floor, troops of ants invaded the kitchen. And then, their rooms were so messy. Hardly anyone had bothered to unpack, but were living out of their suitcases, and throwing dirty clothes all over the floor. When Polly had taken to patrolling the corridor with a basket and calling, 'Laundry-time! Does anyone have any laundry?' Ivo had called her, not entirely jokingly she felt, 'the Oberhygieneführer'. All of which made her even crosser.

Her anger was particularly intense towards Meenu. She had forgotten, when she had shared a flat with them, just how messy her friends could be. Ellen, of course, was used to living in houses with hot and cold running Filipinas to keep everything immaculate, but the same could not be said of Meenu.

Underneath some of her anger was a consciousness of having been particularly kind to her old friend. It had been one thing when she was married to Bruce, and living the glamorous life of a publisher's wife. Polly had enjoyed meeting authors and agents and people in the arts at Bruce and

Meenu's house in Notting Hill. Now, though, Meenu was both those dreaded things, a divorced women and a single mother. Most of their mutual friends had dropped her (as Hemani had not failed to notice). Yet Polly had continued to invite her to dinner parties, both out of genuine affection and out of a pleasant sense of her own generosity. This generosity was now being severely taxed, she felt, by Meenu's lack of corresponding helpfulness. Perhaps she was tired, but then so was Polly. It was exhausting being a full-time wife and mother; nobody realised that it was a real job, at least if you did it properly and conscientiously, as Polly did.

Meenu was a doctor, so how could she bear to live in the utter chaos of her room? Why did she never do more than lay the table? Weren't Hindus supposed to be particularly clean people? Although she herself was as poised and immaculate as ever, she didn't seem to give a damn about Bron's dirty long nails, or even about his teeth. Polly seriously doubted that Bron was even brushing his once a day, and her rule about allowing the children only one fizzy drink a week had long since been undermined by the stacks of Fanta and Coke.

'I know, it's messy, but kids need to have a break. Besides, it'll build up his antibodies to get filthy now and then,' Hemani said when Polly had suggested, in her brightest and most friendly tones, that she lend her a pair of nail-clippers.

But Bron could barely see out of that long fringe of his, and what was worse, Robbie was completely under his spell and determined to copy what he did. When Polly tried to keep his appearance under control, he wriggled like a fish and bit her. He and Tania quarrelled the whole time, and whenever Polly tried to suggest to the latter that as the elder she should be gentler or more patient, Tania would turn on her and scream, 'I hate you! I hate you! You're all against me, and I'll get my own back on you, you wait!'

Then she would run off to disappear in the garden below, terrifying Polly in case she'd been bitten by a snake or scorpion. She was utterly fearless, like Robbie, and climbed trees or jumped off walls without the slightest regard for her own safety, particularly when angry. Polly grew sick of the sound of her own voice, calling for her daughter, only to have her reappear close by, complaining that she was never allowed any peace.

Tania was in disgrace with the other adults, all of whom seemed to have decided that she was too spoilt and unpleasant to be worth bothering with, which of course made matters worse. Polly suffered both for herself and on Tania's behalf, for she knew that underneath her daughter was a lovely child. Poor Tania, she couldn't see this about herself, though.

'I have horrible Bugs Bunny teeth,' she sobbed the night before Guy arrived, 'and a fat stomach.'

'You don't, you don't,' Polly said, almost crying with pity and love. 'Your big teeth just need to come through properly.'

Tania lifted her tear-streaked face and cried, 'I need braces and liposuction, and you know it!'

Polly was horrified.

'Where on earth do you get such an idea? If you need braces, you'll get them at twelve, but the last thing you need is plastic surgery.'

'Other girls are having it,' said Tania defiantly.

'Who? Where?'

'In America.'

'Listen to me,' said Polly fiercely. 'There may be girls silly enough to want to turn themselves into Barbie dolls, and parents idiotic enough to allow it, but you are absolutely perfect. Do you hear? Absolutely perfect. Don't ever let anyone tell you otherwise. I wish to goodness that I had your—'

She stared at her daughter's huge eyes, swimming with tears, at the thick dark lashes, the spotless skin, the lustrous hair and long smooth limbs. Neither child nor adolescent, she seemed some other kind of creature entirely, one who mimicked femininity as a kind of game or protective colouring rather than knew instinctively what it was. Tania, her mother realised with astonishment, was *camp*.

'You only say that because you're my mum,' said Tania.

'I don't! I don't!' said Polly, but Tania turned her face to the wall of her room and wept.

Polly told Theo about this later, her voice shaking with fury. He, too, was disturbed.

'It's having Meenu and that bloody boy of hers,' said Polly. 'She wasn't like this before.'

'Honey, she was interested in make-up and stuff ever since she was in first grade. I don't think you can blame the boy.'

'Well, what else can it be?'

Theo thought. He came up with the male solution to all female woes. 'Maybe I should take her shopping,' he suggested.

Polly's face cleared. 'Oh darling, I'm sure she'd love that. It's been days since we've gone into Cortona.'

'I don't know why we bother with that supermarket in Camucia,' Theo said.

Because it's cheaper, Polly thought, but she said, 'Guy's arriving tomorrow. You could take him, too.'

'Sure, that's a great idea.'

Now Guy was here, smiling the huge friendly grin that made him the pin-up of housewives from Aberdeen to Zennor. The British guests, who had all at some time watched him on TV, were at once determined to behave as normal and completely fascinated.

'How long, I wonder, before he strips his shirt off?' Ivo muttered to Hemani. She giggled, for it had been rumoured that Guy Weaver had it written into his contract that he had to display his upper torso at least once in every programme.

'Hi, Guy,' said Theo.

'Hi, guys,' he said, then advanced on the other guests with outstretched hand.

'Ivo Sponge,' said Ivo.

'Ivo, Guy Weaver, pleased to meet you,' he said. 'Now, I know you,' he said to Hemani. 'You're Minnie, aren't you?'

Polly shared her friend's embarrassment, for she had had

them both over to dinner at least three times, hoping to make a match of them, but it had never worked.

'My friends call me Meenu,' said Hemani.

'Meenu, of course,' said Guy.

'Ellen von Berg.'

'Oh, but I know *you*,' said Guy, in far warmer tones than he'd used a moment ago. 'You design shoes, don't you? Now, why don't you do a range for men?'

Ellen was immediately charmed.

'I've been thinking along those lines, as a matter of fact, Guy, but I'm not sure the market is—'

'We've met before, too,' said Ivo.

'It doesn't matter; that often happens to me,' said Guy.

'Yes, at some TV shindig,' Ivo insisted, suddenly looking, Hemani thought, like a large ginger tom squaring up for a fight.

'You in the business too?' said Guy, with a sudden braying laugh. They all jumped, and stared, unable to believe such an odd noise could have come from him.

'Tangentially,' said Ivo.

'Ivo's a critic,' said Ellen. 'He graduated from tearing wings off butterflies to incinerating movie stars over the slow fuel of his prose.'

Guy ignored this, for the children had arrived. He swept Tania into his arms, crying, 'Who's this gorgeous girl then?'

For the first time in weeks, Tania gave one of her beaming smiles and, quite unprompted, kissed him. She was holding the purple glass bottle in her hand.

'Uncle Guy, I've been making these potions, come and see—'

'Now, Tania, I don't think Guy is ready to be bombarded,' said Theo.

Robbie and Bron skidded to a halt, tumbling over and laughing.

'Guy, Guy, Uncle Guy!'

'Hello young fellers. I know our Robbie, but who's your pal? Tania's boyfriend, are you?'

'I'm Bron,' said Bron, formally.

'Pleased to meet you, Master Bron. Now, what have I got in my bags for you?'

'Presents! Presents!'

He rummaged around, and brought out two packages. 'Oh, and there might just be something for you, too, Bron, that is, if you're allowed sweets.'

Shrieking with joy, the children disappeared back into the garden. He turned and said in a conspiratorial whisper, to the remaining audience, 'I just had a feeling there might be another little one staying here.'

'You're too kind,' said Polly.

'Eh, well, got none of my own to spoil,' Guy said. 'Don't suppose there's a beer in the house? I'm thirsting and bursting, I am.'

'Just juice and wine, but we can get you some this afternoon,' said Polly. 'The loo's over there.'

She hoped that the children had remembered to flush.

'Don't worry, I'll get it myself,' said Guy. 'Besides, who needs alcohol with a view like this? Hello there.'

185

'Hi,' said Daniel, shaking his hand. 'I'm Theo's brother. You probably don't remember me.'

Guy gave his braying laugh again. It was such an extraordinary sound, so full of melancholy, that the contrast with his happy smiling face made them laugh, again.

'Of course, how could I forget?'

He went off and urinated loudly. On his return, he said, 'Now, then, did someone mention a pool?'

'There is a pool,' said Polly. 'We'll show you.'

She made to take his arm, but Guy was already moving towards the french windows, pulling off his T-shirt as he walked.

'This is champion, Pol old girl,' he said. 'Lead on!'

Ivo and Hemani exchanged glances, then burst into peals of laughter.

'He's a terrible ass, isn't he?' she said. 'I never watch – what's his programme called?'

'*One Man and His Roots*?' said Ivo. '*Roots and Shoots? Real Gardening*? There are so many. He must have worked on that accent for years. I don't believe anyone still says *champion*, do they? Look at him, trotting about and stroking those leaves. He's Polly's Mellors, I bet.'

'Well, he was sweet to Bron, however odd he is. Did you notice the tufts on top of his ears? Weird.'

'Celebrities are just like real people, only more grotesque.'

'He'll be happy here,' said Hemani, thoughtfully.

'So why aren't you?' Ivo asked, seeing her down-turned head, its dark feathers like those of a blackbird.

She was expressionless for a moment, then said, 'Of

186

course I am. I'm just a little . . . tired, that's all. The heat, you know, and the insects.'

'Human or otherwise?'

'There's a beetle in my room, and I can hear it chewing its way through the beams every night,' she said. 'It makes a nasty ticking noise.'

'Death-watch beetle,' said Ivo, in sepulchral tones. 'One day you'll wake up to find the roof has snapped and come down around you.'

'Well, it's quite possible. There's a fine film of sawdust on my pillow each night.'

'You know what the solution is?'

'No, what?'

'Move out of your room and into mine. There aren't any beetles there, I assure you.'

'You're offering to swap?' said Hemani, deliberately mis-understanding his offer. 'But what if the beam collapsed on you? I wouldn't want you on my conscience.'

'A conscience,' said Ivo. 'What a very old-fashioned thing to bring on a holiday.'

'Do you think?'

'I had you down as progressive,' said Ivo. He touched her short dark hair.

They were both leaning against the back of the white sofas in the half-gloom of the living room. Hemani's eyes followed a heavy, glistening fly as it blundered noisily from the windows to the large stone fireplace, streaked with the soot of past conflagrations. The whole of her skin was crawling with heat, or desire, or both. When there would be so little difference between being clothed and unclothed, when she was practically undressed already, what was the point in refusing what she was being offered?

She said, 'A conscience isn't something you can assume and dispose of at will.'

'Are you perhaps religious?'

'No,' said Hemani. 'At least, not in the way you mean. It's more . . .' She stopped and shrugged.

'You wear white knickers,' said Ivo, to whom the gauzy garments jerking on the laundry line had been a source of idle speculation.

'I beg your pardon?'

'Well, it's pretty clear which are Polly's,' he said. 'Polly's have those dreadful sprigs of flowers that Englishwomen seem to feel might be appealing, even when distinctly past girlhood, and Ellen's, well, Ellen's pure Victoria's Secret. You advertise the fact that you're living like a nun.'

Hemani was more embarrassed by this than she would have thought possible. This was what she had dreaded about communal living, only when she had shared a flat with Polly and Ellen they had all respected each other's privacy.

'I wear white, if you must know, because they're cheapest.'

'And because you don't expect anyone else to see them, only they have, and now you're found out.'

Hemani glared at him.

'I wasn't expecting to be subjected to this sort of vulgar scrutiny, if you must know,' she said.

'Why not?' asked Ivo, suddenly stepping into the space that had separated them. Before Hemani quite knew how he'd done it, he was kissing her, and her body, like the stupid idiot that it was, had responded. She forgot to keep her teeth clamped shut, and opened her mouth to his. A jolt of energy swayed backwards and forwards between the two of them, as each struggled for mastery: Ivo over Hemani, Hemani over herself. It was a question of wills, and Ivo was just discovering that he had underestimated Hemani when there was a clatter from behind them.

They sprang apart. Bron, who had been chasing a butterfly, was staring at them, and behind him was—

'Uh, sorry,' said Daniel, stooping apologetically. 'I was – I mean . . .'

He looked horrified. Beside him, Ellen burst into loud laughter.

'Well,' she said. 'I knew Ivo had some fast moves, but I didn't think you'd fall for them, Meenu.'

Bron darted away, back into the garden.

'Nothing to be sorry about, dear boy,' said Ivo.

'Don't,' said Hemani, her face hot. 'I was just leaving anyway.'

She turned and ran, up the stairs to her room. It was only when she arrived there that she wondered why she felt so much angrier with Daniel than with Ivo.

'My!' said Guy, floating on his back and looking up at the sky. He was wearing black Spandex shorts that showed off his muscular buttocks to a degree that was faintly troubling.

'Look at that long line of cypress trees along the hill opposite, you couldn't do better than that! If I'd known you lot were living it up while I was toiling away in rainy old England, I'd have come out sooner. Pity I can only stay for three days.'

'Three days!' said Polly. 'Oh no, we were hoping for a whole week.'

'Sorry, love, I'm a busy man.'

'What is it you do?' asked Betty, who had descended to witness this extraordinary creature, and was treating him to her bridled ferocity of manner.

'I'm a humble servant of the soil,' said Guy. 'Me, I'm a gardener. No threat to anyone, gardeners. Completely harmless.'

He beamed at Betty.

'Oh?' she said. 'I've always thought that gardening was overflowing with the seven deadly sins. Covetousness, envy, greed – don't gardeners always want a plant that isn't theirs? Don't they envy someone else who has it? And aren't they angry when they can't get a piece of it too?'

Guy's smile remained as innocent and cheery as it always did, but there was, Polly thought, something else going on that she couldn't quite understand.

'No lust, though, Betty,' she said, trying to make light of her mother-in-law's hostility.

'No?' said Betty. 'Did nobody tell you about the birds and the bees, then?'

'Guy's really a TV star,' said Polly. 'We met when I did that course, you know, at the Chelsea Physic Garden, and then he got talent-spotted.'

'I'd never say that,' said Guy.

'Cable?'

'No, national, but what I really would like,' said Guy, 'instead of blowing my own trumpet, is to do a bit of exploring. Now, you're probably sick of the place, but does anyone want to come to Cortona and show me the sights?'

Once again, Theo, Betty, Polly, Ivo, Ellen and Dan were walking into Cortona. The three children, lured by the prospect of ice creams, were frolicking ahead, visiting the primitive playground before racing to the small formal garden at the foot of the shallow stone amphitheatre where a huge open-air cinema screen had been erected. Here, old men read newspapers, parents watched their young take their first steps or ride their new bicycles with anxious pride, and a number of dogs were enjoying a brief walk before the mid-day heat became too much for their owners.

'Mmm, nice,' said Guy, surveying this.

'Not a thing you'd have on your programme, I take it?' said Ivo.

'Well, I do love a bit of kitsch, when all's said and done, particularly because Tuscany is so tasteful. That style of planting, red salvias, pink begonias and orange marigolds, well, it may be a bit colourful for some but it gives a lot of pleasure to ordinary people, and that's what it's all about.'

'It's lovely because it's here,' said Polly. 'I never like this kind of thing in England.'

They entered the Via Nazionale, where small shopkeepers sat outside on wicker chairs, gossiping and fanning themselves, or drinking a pre-prandial coffee made in one of the many cafés that lined the street. The relief of being out of direct sunlight was considerable. They visited the Palazzo Casali to see the Etruscan bronzes, and the beautiful portrait of *Motherhood* by Severini, which made the children giggle because it showed a woman suckling a child. They visited the Museo Diocesano housing the famous *Annunciation* by Fra Angelico, with its pink, blue and gold glory of drapery and wings counterbalanced by a tiny picture of the weeping, naked Adam and Eve being expelled into the wilderness from Paradise by the self-same angel brandishing a sword. Polly, observing this, felt a vague sense of dread. They had less than a week left.

Guy commented loudly on all that they passed and saw. He had, thought Ivo, the sort of innocent egoism that was almost appealing, except that intermixed with this was the kind of vanity that clearly made him calculate his effect on others. At all times he had to be at the centre of attention. The children gambolled around him, shooting off the spinning figures he had brought them.

'They're wonderful toys,' said Ellen, looking at them with a professional eye.

'Yes; but they're not as pretty as the real thing,' said Tania, breathlessly.

'What do you mean, real? They look pretty real to me, honey,' said Theo.

'Yes, but they're not—' said Tania, then stopped.

Theo said indulgently, 'Is it some game you're playing about fairies? Tania has such a strong imagination, you know, we sometimes worry about it.'

Tania scowled at him, but Guy said, 'I've never seen what's so wrong about that. You can go too far harping on about exams and learning, but imagination and enthusiasm count for far more in real life. After all, I left school with only two O levels, like poor old Princess Di, and it was imagination and enthusiasm that saw me through. Besides, I believe in fairies.'

'Do you?' said Robbie, his face upturned. 'Have you seen them?'

'Many a time, at the bottom of the garden,' said Guy, gravely, but the laughter of the other adults revealed this to be one of those tiresome grown-up jokes.

'He is a piece of work, isn't he?' murmured Ellen. 'Look how he's cosying up to Polly. I haven't seen her this animated for years.'

'Are you saying she and he . . .?'

Ivo watched them with speculation in his eyes.

'Don't tell me, you made a lunge at her, too?'

'I don't see that you should care,' Ivo retorted. 'She's far too virtuous.'

The group ahead had stopped in front of a shop displaying rolls of exquisite wrapping paper. Theo emerged with a *Herald Tribune*, and Ivo felt the pang of pure lust for a newspaper, any newspaper, which all journalists feel when on holiday.

'Wonder if they've got the *Telegraph*,' he muttered. 'Though I'd even settle for the *Mirror* here.'

Daniel was examining a roll that had staves of music on it, a faint smile on his lips. As always, Ellen felt a rush of anxiety and resentment, for music was a world from which she was absolutely excluded.

'You know what? Sometimes I think that we'd all be a lot happier forgetting about sex. It just doesn't last long enough to support all the expectations we place on it,' Ellen said vehemently. 'I mean, why don't we base compatibility on shared pleasure in food, say, or particular movies, or even sunsets? Why this insistence on fooling around?'

She looked at Daniel, who was striding ahead again, chatting to the others. If it weren't for all the admiring glances and whistles she was getting from passing Italian men, she really would have thought she needed a total make-over. Their footsteps echoed on the stony street, punctuated by the steely waterfalls of metal shutters and grilles being rolled down for the siesta. The buzz and hum of people increased in the happy anticipation of lunch.

'Things not so great in that department?' Ivo enquired.

Ellen said, 'That's none of your business.'

'Oh, I don't know about—' Ivo began, but Daniel had turned back to them.

'What do you think about going out for lunch?'

'Oh, yes!' said Ellen, instantly brightening.

'Excellent idea,' said Ivo, brightening also. 'I might even be able to put it on expenses.'

'Guy thinks Polly has been doing far too much work, and I agree, and so we should give her a break,' said Daniel.

'Has he tried having a meal with the children around?' asked Ivo dubiously.

'He's suggesting a couple of places outdoors. There's La

Grotta, which is good but low-key, and the Loggetta, which is swankier, both off the main square.'

Ellen surged forward, tucking her hand under his arm possessively.

'Why don't we check them both out?' she said. She was relieved to be there without Hemani, but did not wonder why this was so, except that ever since she'd seen her friend kissing Ivo she had felt angry.

Daniel smiled down at her.

'Sure. Mother?'

'Whatever you prefer,' said Betty, too pleased to see them behaving like a couple to object.

La Grotta turned out to be in a narrow, sunlit courtyard just by the café in Piazza della Repubblica. It had an old iron pump in the middle, surrounded by pots of ferns, and a handful of tables under umbrellas. The Loggetta was in a street above the square, under an arched and pillared canopy. The smell of sizzling steak from its more modest rival decided them.

'The Loggetta's more the kind of place for a romantic dinner,' said Polly, gazing up at where waiters in crisp black and white were performing a kind of dance of the one napkin. 'Not that I wouldn't love that one evening, if somebody were willing to babysit.'

'Mum, we're not babies any more,' said Robbie, indignant.

'No, indeed you aren't,' said Guy. 'Great big chap like you could probably travel the world alone.'

Robbie considered.

'Well, I'd miss my mum,' he said.

'Ah, that's the problem with all of us,' said Guy, his twinkly grin directed at Betty. 'We always miss our mums.'

Betty looked hard at him. 'Well, that's always good to hear,' she said sceptically.

'Oh, yes,' said Guy, launching into reminiscence, 'I remember my mum, God rest her soul—'

'God,' muttered Ivo to Daniel. 'Are we going to have to put up with this song and dance for the rest of the holiday? I'm not sure I'll be able to stand it.'

'You seemed to be standing it just fine recently,' said Daniel, stiffly.

'Well, one has to do something to pass the time, old boy.'

'Hemani isn't anybody's pastime.'

'What's a pastime?' asked Bron, who had gravitated towards them, as bored by Guy's monologue as any adult.

'More like a present-time,' said Ivo, snickering. 'A lovely bundle of sense and sensibility wrapped up in—'

'You might have the sensitivity not to talk like that right here and now,' said Daniel, and there was a coldness in his eyes that Ivo had never seen before.

'It's harmless dalliance.'

'Is it?' said Daniel. 'You have a great capacity for mischief, my friend. So long as it's confined to people who are big enough to look after themselves, that's not always a bad thing. But there are others who just aren't that tough. I'm not sure I would be, I can bet you she isn't, either.'

'She's too sensible to take someone like me seriously,' said Ivo. 'Most women are, alas. I'm just the good time had by all, as Ellen may have told you.'

'Hemani may not take you all that seriously,' said Daniel, 'but she does take herself so. That's why she could get hurt.'

'That's so typically American,' said Ivo. 'An English person who takes themselves seriously is just asking to be taken down a peg or two, because everyone will agree they're the most frightful bore otherwise. Whereas you lot all boost each other from the cradle. Then you all wind up in therapy because somehow, you don't get to be president and it must be your parents' fault.'

Daniel pushed his gold-rimmed spectacles up his nose, and flushed with anger. Ivo had never got under his skin in this way before, and he felt a wave of pure dislike course through him, followed by distress.

'That's the biggest load of bull I've ever heard, even from you, Ivo. I could reply by listing all your nation's many failings, including that of having so conclusively lost sight of any worthwhile ideals that you're all doomed to mediocrity for ever, but I'm not going to fall for that one. All I'm trying to say is, don't play any of your games with her.'

'By the sound of things that's not all you've fallen for,' said Ivo. He, too, was furious. He forgot how fond he was of Daniel, how much he respected him personally and intellectually, and only wanted to lash out.

'Don't be absurd.'

'Oh, Ivo can always be relied on for absurdity, even if he can't be relied on for anything else,' said Ellen.

'I'm glad you can rely on me for something, even if it's only buffoonery,' said Ivo, now pale and tense.

Polly turned and called, 'Are you going to stand there, or are you going to order?'

'You go ahead. Don't wait for me,' said Daniel.

He turned, and walked rapidly out of the courtyard.

Alone in the Casa Luna, Hemani, who had pleaded a bad headache, now gave way to the luxury of tears. It was a luxury, too, after the effort of keeping up a serene face in front not only of the other adults but more importantly of Bron. He hated it when she got upset, hated it with the white-hot passion of a child, for it is only children who rail against fate, adults having trained themselves above all to distance themselves from feeling. She spent so much energy pretending to be cheerful and jolly, she hardly realised how draining it was.

She was angry with herself for not going with Bron and the others to Cortona, because she needed a break from the countryside, just like the rest of them, but she needed some time alone even more. Ivo's kiss, and her response to it, alarmed her deeply. She felt that she was poised on the edge of a diving board with no certainty of being able to execute anything but a belly flop if she launched herself off it. It was obvious to her that, if not the monster Ellen liked to depict, Ivo was a slippery man. He simply wanted to have a holiday fling. Half of herself, the rebellious side, thought this was not such a bad idea. He wasn't heart-stoppingly handsome, like Daniel, but he was attractive: she could imagine that he would be enthusiastic and uninhibited in bed, which would rather suit her, as she was far too cautious and romantic by nature. All those Bollywood films, she thought ruefully, for a surprisingly large part of her cherished the idea of people singing songs and chasing each other round trees as an expression of passion. Also, Ivo was funny, which was more than could be said for Daniel.

Hemani was disappointed in Daniel, there was no getting away from it. She had thought that he was a serious person, someone who would need serious courtship. She had been badly hurt by her ex-husband, and had made it a rule that she had to know someone for at least a year before even contemplating a kiss such as the one Ivo had stolen. She expected Daniel to respect this. True, she hadn't told him about Bron, but surely nobody got to their early thirties without trailing quite a bit of heartbreak. He himself had mentioned a long affair with somebody called Frances back at Harvard, which she gathered had ended badly. She had kept her wedding ring (largely out of distaste for being mistaken for an unmarried mother), but told him she was divorced. Their conversation had been studiously impersonal apart from this. He had never asked if she had any children, and this, as much as anything, had convinced her that he saw her as a friend, not a possible partner. Well, he was Ellen's now, so it shouldn't matter to her. All she had to do was decide whether or not to have an affair with Ivo.

She paced up and down the inside of the house, because the outside, with all its blaze of light and colour and insect noise, was too distracting. Here, she was able to be calmer. She noticed the smell of beeswax and ancient plaster-dust. The blue shadows on the rough, whitewashed walls, the reflected light on the white-painted tiles between the black beams, laid out like staves of music, with small clots of house-spiders for quavers here and there. The pitted, uneven floor tiles whose rose-coloured rectangles, laid in a herringbone pattern, invited the mind to wander.

But my mind mustn't wander, thought Hemani, massaging her temples, where pain was gathering. I need to make a decision. She tried lying down on one of the long linen-covered sofas and putting a cushion under her neck, but the fabric felt slippery and sticky, glazed with a faint sheen of dirt. She wandered into the kitchen, and ran her wrists under the large brass taps of the butler's sink. The water sang as it came out. It was strange being here alone; there was a faint, continual humming noise that she'd never noticed before, some piece of old machinery, perhaps, although it was more musical than that. A bowl of tomatoes ripened even further in a deep stone window-sill, combining their scent with that of a pot of basil. It smelt so delicious, so wholly good and fresh and alive that she paused in her pacings. Was she being idiotic to get so upset about a kiss? Was she being as silly as Lucy Honeychurch, without the excuse of being an Edwardian maiden? Plenty of people kissed, and it didn't mean a thing. Plenty of people had sex with people whose names they didn't even know, and didn't seem the worse off for it. It was her upbringing, and its insistence on modesty and decorum, that was causing her distress. Much as she adored her parents, she cursed this. Ivo was a modern man, for all his style of dress and absurd, P. G. Wodehouse affectations, and Ellen had warned her he was notorious for this kind of thing. He couldn't be blamed for trying to get lucky with the only unattached female in the place; it was her own naivety that was causing this, her inexperience. She had only ever had sex with two men, one of them her ex-husband, and they were also the only ones who had ever kissed her. So no wonder I'm shocked and confused, she thought, because in my limited experience one thing leads inexorably to the other, and I'm not at all sure that would be a good idea.

At this point, she burst into tears again, hardly knowing why she did so. It's this confounded place, she thought; it invites sensuality. Living, eating and even sleeping outdoors, with the warm breeze caressing your skin; swimming and going around with hardly any clothes on; picking furry, juicy golden apricots and thin-skinned cherries off trees as if in the garden of Eden – it was no wonder she was beguiled and caught off-balance. You tried to shut it all out, and it refused to stay, any more than the butterflies, bees and bluebottles flying in and out of the slatted oblongs of light, vibrant with life. And she was going to go upstairs to her room, and start packing all of it away into memory, because she couldn't afford another mistake. Explaining to Bron wouldn't be easy, he was deliriously happy here, but she could see no other solution.

Her feet had carried her halfway up the stairs when she stopped. Was that the sound of a car parking?

Oh, no, she thought, blowing her nose and catching sight of her dishevelled reflection in the shuttered window. Surely they can't have finished lunch so soon? It was not all of them, as she had feared, only Daniel, in his baggy T-shirt and shorts, blinking in the dark dazzle of the interior.

'Hi,' he said awkwardly. 'I left something behind.'

He immediately cursed himself for such a lame excuse. It was reasonable to be worried about her. They were friends, and she really didn't look well, her face bruised with shadows like carelessly handled fruit. It moved him as Ellen's vitamin-enriched healthiness somehow did not.

Daniel said, 'Are you, uh, OK?'

'What? Oh, yes. I'm just . . .'

She looked down at him, and hot salt welled up in her throat again. She put a hand up to her eyes to conceal this, for it humiliated her that he should see her defenceless.

'You look terrible,' he said, his concern overcoming his diffidence. 'You should be lying down.'

'Yes, I should, I was just – I was just going . . .'

To her horror, the pain, which had been gathering its force, now pounced and shook her in its teeth.

He sprang up the stairs, taking them three at a time, his long legs carrying him faster than she would have thought possible, to catch her as she swayed.

'Do you have a headache?'

'Migraine,' she said, for how else to explain the sudden flashes of light, and the tiny faces within them that filled her vision?

'I get them too,' he said, with great kindness, although his voice, his presence, only made it worse. She longed, more fervently than she would have thought possible, for him to go away.

202

'I've got some tablets, but I think I'm going to—'

She made a rush for the nearest bathroom as her whole body convulsed, and vomited into the toilet bowl. It lasted until there was nothing but bile, and strands of wet, malodorous fringe clamped to her head like iron. The pain was still hanging over her like a knife, and the faces – narrow, pointed, gleefully tormenting – still swam blotchily past.

'Come,' said Daniel, 'I've closed the shutters in your room up tight.'

I must pack, she thought, hardly daring to move in case the pain should descend again, but the idea of folding clothes and reducing the mess in her room was too much. The rasp of insects outside was like sandpaper on her eyes, on the raw flayed creature she had suddenly become. Through slitted eyes, she saw that Daniel had, as promised, blocked out all light but that now coming through the open door, even looping the bedspread over a curtain pole. She fell forward into the throbbing darkness, and lay pinioned beneath it.

Chapter Nine

By the time the others – well-fed, relaxed, revived – returned, Daniel had thought up a good excuse for his sudden flight and phoned his brother's mobile. He told Theo that he had discovered Hemani in the grip of a migraine, and that everyone needed to be quiet when they came back. Given that the insects were making more noise than anyone it was largely a gesture of concern, but it was also a gesture that Ellen, at least, took seriously.

Ellen decided that pro-action was required here. The next day she got up early, and instead of having breakfast put on white shorts and a singlet. All four men looked up when she came in, and if only Ivo and Guy whistled, she was still satisfied by the attention Daniel gave her. She danced a little jig on her toes, stretching her arms and flexing her bust, ostensibly to warm up.

'There are people who'd pay good money to see you do that,' said Ivo.

'Aye,' said Guy; and at last, Daniel said, 'The run up to the top of the hill is pretty good, though I've been going to Cortona.'

'If you catch me, you can have me!' she cried mischievously, springing off like a deer.

She pounded up the hill, the loose, white shingle hardly disturbed by her light prints, the drops of her sweat instantly absorbed by the dust. There were rock-roses in mauve and carmine splashes of brilliant colour tumbling over boulders the size of elephants, darting bright-green lizards, olive groves interplanted with some sort of long grassy crop, and, as she ran higher, increasing patches of gorse and scrub oak. At one bend in the road she could look down upon the Casa Luna, its tiles like the scales of a red mullet, all gilded and silvered by the same lichens that spattered the rocks and trees. The colour and texture of these delighted her, and she began to ponder how she could replicate them in shoes and bags – perhaps with devoré velvet, or suede? The pleasure of this took her mind off the strain of the ascent. She had begun designing shoes purely because she could never find any she thought beautiful, and although she had rivals (Emma Hope in London and Jimmy Choo everywhere) it was this passion that underlay her competitiveness. Now, as she jogged alone, it was her work that preoccupied her rather than the people in the house below.

Ellen had managed to get through her life so far without the kind of anguished introspection many people are prone to. She had had her fill of anguish when her mother died, leaving her to navigate her adolescence alone, borrowing other people's personalities and styles instead of developing her own. Ironically, this was partly what made her so successful in the fashion world, where everything is transient. Ellen loved her work – not the showing-off and the partying but the way it fulfilled her creativity, and the practical wish to make things. For underneath the shallow, sarcastic manner she had adopted was someone simpler and nicer, someone she had almost forgotten until recently. Because she did not make a habit of examining her thoughts and behaviour she had no idea that it was this person that was making her irritable. She only knew that she felt a sense of relief at getting away from the rest of the household.

The woods below were completely invisible, lost in the precipitous hillside. Without the terracing, she thought, there would be no possibility of growing food in such a terrain. The earth would just slide straight down. This combination of practicality and beauty was what made the landscape so special. There were other countries that had cypress and olive, others that enjoyed the abundance of flowers and birds, but none had this quality of being simultaneously beautiful and useful. Though now, sadly, it was increasingly just for beauty. The groves she jogged past were, she could see, slowly being strangled by brambles and overgrown by scrub oak. In places, great boulders had slipped and tumbled, or walls been torn down in an attempt to make the land more accessible to tractors. The groves that still looked neat and well-tilled probably belonged not to farmers but to foreigners, for whom the production of virgin olive oil was a hobby, the rest being largely imported from poorer countries such as Spain and Greece.

Ellen had reached the top of the hill, or at least as far as it was possible to go without being shredded by a million brambles. These weren't really hills, they were mountains, but so fertile where cultivated that their true size wasn't immediately apparent. Her whites were no longer crisp, but it was worth it, for the view was glorious. There were more houses dotted around than she would have suspected, the grand old villas and odd castle standing out whereas the old farmhouses melted into the hills from which their stones had been dug. Down below on the part of the vast Val di Chiana plain, the rectangles of sunflowers and rape glowed with enamelled brilliance in the sun, and fine arcs of an irrigation system crossed and recrossed, keeping the crops green while those on the hillsides burnt ochre and umber. The lush roses and dreamy verdancy of the gardens around the Casa Luna seemed unreal, in this dry, fierce landscape. Up here, the sounds the swallows made were like scissors ripping through paper.

A hot wind gusted up the hillside. Ellen spread her arms like sails to catch it, lifting her face to the sun. Whatever else happened, it was good to be here in the pure, clean air instead of in the busy cities where she made her living. It was places like these that reminded her who she really was, and what she cared about. She remembered her mother, and the holidays they had had together on the Italian coast, before the cancer that destroyed her. Those had been such good times, and Italy had always been associated in her mind with pleasure and happiness ever since. If only, she thought, I could say, my husband proposed to me in Italy.

Perhaps she'd come to the wrong place at the wrong time. Todi was brimming with people she knew, and the houses round there had proper showers instead of the dribbling limescaled one in the bathroom she shared with Daniel, Ivo and the rest. She grimaced, for she wasn't used to sharing. At least her room, like all the bedrooms, had its own faucet so that she was spared having to queue to brush her teeth. She could have done with not having to put on make-up by peering at herself in the speckled antique mirror angled over her marble-topped chest of drawers, but it was really the toilet facilities that annoyed her the most. Worst of all were the hand-written notices demanding that you placed used toilet paper in a bin, rather than flushing, like any civilised person, because paper blocked the drains. Even if Polly was the only person who ever saw the contents, when tying them up to put in a larger liner of rubbish, the very idea made Ellen shudder. She bet nobody in Todi had to do such a primitive thing.

Sighing, she jogged back down again. Tomorrow she must bring a bottle of water. There could be something very sexy about sharing water, as long as it wasn't with Ivo. Ellen wrinkled her nose, thinking of that. He was the sort who'd slobber all over the neck of a bottle and drool saliva into its contents . . . She wondered whether she had been unwise to issue the challenge to all of them at large, because Guy looked at least as fit as she was. Still, he was so obviously Polly's. She'd never have thought it of her old friend, though

208

knowing Polly there was probably nothing doing. Strange, she mused, that both my London girlfriends are so hung-up about guys, whereas I've been quite the opposite. It was different now, of course. As soon as a girl turned thirty she had to get serious about who she dated, which was kind of a pity because it meant passing up on so much fun. Ellen could not help sighing to herself. As she approached the house, a familiar figure came into sight, plodding up the road she was coming down. It was, predictably, Ivo.

She slowed, jogging on the spot, and said, 'The view's great up top, I recommend it.'

'Don't think I'll make it,' he said.

'Danny could,' she taunted.

'I'm sure. Still, there are other things.'

'Such as?'

'I brought some water.'

Ellen looked longingly at the bottle he took out of his pocket.

'Take it.'

'How do I know you haven't slipped something into it?'

Ivo looked at her, and raised his eyebrows.

'I'm really not that bad, you know. Check – the seal isn't broken.'

She grabbed the bottle.

'What do I have to do in return?'

'A blow-job would be nice.'

Disgusted, she turned away.

'Joke, that was a joke,' he called after her retreating figure.

'You don't need me when your sense of humour sucks,' she called back. All the same, she couldn't help grinning, even when the unmistakable wails of Robbie rose to greet her from below.

Nasty bee, beastly bee, DEATH TO BEES, I wasn't doing anything to it and it just flew down on to my arm so I could be an island while it had a drink and then it stung me, DEATH TO BEES, bloody fucking hell poo-poo bees, I didn't do anything it was mean Daddy's fault, it's ALL YOUR FAULT, I hate you, I hate you, I want my mummy, 'Ow-ow-ow,' roared Robbie.

Tears streamed down his face and the sound of his piercing screams reverberated off the ancient stones and made flocks of birds fly up in alarm. Hemani, lying still as stone on her bed, would have shrieked too had she been able. Even the beetles gnawing the beam above her head were momentarily silenced.

'Hush, now,' said Polly, clasping him to her bosom, and half weeping at the sight of his poor arm, the bloodless circle of poison surrounded by a rapidly swelling red lump. 'Let me put some Savlon on it. It didn't mean to hurt you—'

'It did, it did,' howled Robbie. 'I saw its nasty face, it looked at me with its mean eyes and then it jabbed me with its spear, it meant to do it, it meant to—'

'Now, son, bees don't think, it was just an instinct,' said Theo.

'Well, that's a great comfort to him,' said Polly angrily.

'Hang on a tick,' said Guy, who had run into the house,

and who now brought out a white plastic tube. 'This thing here is for sucking stings out. I always bring one, because as a gardener I never know when I'm going to encounter an angry wasp or bee, but if you'll hold him still, Pol, I can just – that's it – gotcha!'

Miraculously, Robbie's shrieks subsided.

'I–hate–bees,' he sobbed, limp and damp on his mother's lap. She stroked his cheeks, silvered with tears, and dropped kisses on his head.

'Yeah, I know. But to him you were a great big giant about to hurt him. And he died, giving you that sting,' said Guy, in his warm, soothing voice.

'It meant to hurt me,' Robbie insisted. 'It said I was being naughty.'

'Now, I don't think bees notice things like that,' said Theo.

'You didn't hear it, stupid,' said Robbie.

'Where the bee sucks, there suck I,' murmured Daniel, absently.

'You know, I used to have a poster of that, with all the "s"s as "f"s in my first year at Cambridge,' said Ivo, collapsing on to a steamer chair.

'Why?' asked Tania. 'Oh, I get it, so you could say a bad word. Daddy, Ivo—'

Later, Polly went up to check on Hemani. There was nothing much she could do, beyond bringing her fresh cold hand-towels to put across her eyes, and giving her Nurofen. I've spent at least half my holiday nursing people, she thought wryly.

211

Hemani lay like a statue in bed, pinned under the weight of her pain. Polly looked at her and wondered what had brought it on. Ellen had confided, whispering and snickering, that she had walked in on her kissing Ivo, and it was a well-known allergic reaction to him. Polly couldn't help laughing too, though she wished that Ellen would let up a bit. She was so contemptuous of him, and seemed unaware of what an unpleasant light it cast on her.

'I don't see the point in that kind of talk,' said Guy, after Polly told him what Ellen had said.

'No,' Polly agreed.

'Of course, I get that sort of stuff all the time. People are jealous of my success. You know, it's the worst thing about living in Britain, the tall poppy syndrome they call it. First you get built up, then, when they think you're going to get too big for your boots, they come along and chop you down. As if I'd be such an ass as to believe my own publicity.'

He laughed, and Polly couldn't help wondering why, if fame meant so little to him, he was always going on about it.

'Not that I let being voted TV personality of the year go to my head, you know, but it is so refreshing to be here with perfectly ordinary members of the public,' said Guy. 'I take my friendships very seriously. Of course, it is nice that Ellen is also well known, and of course Betty too, I wouldn't like to spend time with total non-entities.'

'Oh,' said Polly blankly, 'that's nice to know.'

One result of Hemani being temporarily absent was that everyone else felt free to suggest going out more. The excuse was that this would give her more peace and quiet in which to recover, but the fact was they were all longing for the sight and sound of other people. By the evening, a visit to a pizzeria in the valley had been suggested and accepted. There were several, but the best, according to the Owner's Notes, was at a place near Ossaia.

'It's where the bones of those killed in the war between Hannibal and the Roman Army lie,' Polly read.

Once again, she wondered about W. Shade, the lucky owner. It must be wonderful to live here all year round, or almost all year, she thought. But perhaps he or she only had it as a holiday home. It was pretty spartan, on the whole, though the old vinyl recordings of classical music had been of their best, a decade or more ago. Polly sighed, as the climax to *Turandot* rose into 'Nessun Dorma', which in this particular context was all too appropriate. Its romantic certainty made tears well up in her eyes, for how could anyone know that they'd win? Now that Guy had arrived, she and Theo were back to sharing the tiny double bed. As usual, nothing was happening in it. Every evening, they would each read for a few minutes, and then Theo would say, 'Lights out.' As soon as the room was dark, he'd turn over and go to sleep. Polly had tried to prevent this, but her husband never seemed to notice. She would fall asleep hugging her pillow, waking up in the night clinging to the edge of the mattress, or being bruised by his whale-like turnings and thrashings, or convulsing from half-remembered dreams.

Robbie was furious, because it meant there wasn't enough

room for the three of them. He'd creep into their room at dawn, and wind his arms around her, covering her with passionate kisses. Then, when she returned them, he'd wriggle, giggling, into the crack between Polly and Theo and begin his daily campaign to force them further apart. Theo's stern, muffled tones said, 'Hey! Stop that!'

'Yes, stop it, darling,' said Polly, but without conviction. The fact was, she revelled in her son's cuddles. Furthermore, given that she found herself being pushed to the edge of their bed every night, she couldn't muster much sympathy. If only Theo had the balls to stand up to his mother, neither of us would be suffering like this, she thought.

Guy, though, was great. He got Theo to play ping-pong with the children. They all enjoyed this, though Tania was still very intent on her potions. Polly had thrown some of them out because she really couldn't let the child clutter up her room in such a way and had been rewarded with a monumental sulk.

'Bubble, bubble, toil and trouble,' muttered Tania in her room. 'Fire burn and cauldron bubble.' She had done that poem in year three for Hallowe'en, and it had come back to her in patches as she stirred. Of course, she didn't have eye of newt and toe of frog, but she had found some blue pills in Grandma's toilet bag with the word VIAGRA written on them, and these, when crushed up, had made the People get very excited. She'd added some Pepsi, too, and some rosemary, although she worried it might have been lavender by mistake because it was hard to tell the difference.

The glass jar she was holding over a candle flame was going nicely smoky, but it was getting awfully hot. Quickly, she removed it, then poured the contents into the little china teapot to cool it down. There'd be just enough to fill her purple glass bottle.

'What are you doing?' asked Robbie, barging in as always.

'None of your beeswax.'

'Are you having a tea party?'

'No, I'm not,' she said crossly. 'I'm doing magic.'

'Really?'

'Yes. But you can only join in if you and Bron are nice to me again.'

'OK,' said Robbie. 'What does it do?'

'I'll tell you later,' said Tania.

'D'you want some help with that?' asked Ivo, seeing Polly cleaning out the fridge.

'Oh, yes,' she said, surprised. She hoped he was not going to use this as an excuse to attempt to kiss her again.

'Don't you ever stop? I mean, is it a sort of hobby for you, all this housekeeping?'

'Well, not exactly. Everything goes off a lot faster than at home. And there are ants,' she said. 'I do have a cleaner at home, of course.'

'I'm glad to hear it. But you are making the rest of us feel guilty, my darling. Won't you come out and have a swim?'

Polly thought longingly of the pool. Then she thought

how it would feel to wear a bathing costume in front of her mother-in-law.

'Maybe later.'

'How's Meenu?'

'She seems slightly better, though not enough to come to the pizzeria.'

'Ah.'

Polly was longing to learn whether her match-making plans had succeeded.

'You seem to have taken my advice, I notice.'

Ivo shrugged. He wasn't going to examine his own motives too closely, but he was glad to be getting away from the house again.

It was cheering to be dressing a little more carefully and formally, and to think of being with other people, too. There was a sudden rush for the ironing-board, and the children submitted to having their hair washed and brushed without complaint, delighted by the idea of having fast food instead of home-cooked meals.

'I really miss chicken nuggets,' Bron admitted to Tania. He had gone up to visit his mother, bringing a cold wet towel to put across her eyes. She had thanked him in a whisper, assuring him she'd be better the next day, but he was starting to feel homesick.

'Yes, and fish fingers. And Mum's chips are never the same as McCain's,' she added.

The sun was streaking the sky the colour of a peach by the time the two cars left, bumping slowly down the road. Brambles squeaked against the sides, as if reluctant to let them go. The cypress turned a darker shade of black, like cooling metal. Through the open windows came the sudden pungent smell of fig leaves.

'You know, I'm coming round to this country,' said Ivo, from the back seat of Daniel's car. 'It may be the most terrible cliché, but it does have real quality.'

Ellen, sitting beside him, did not bother to turn.

'That's such a relief.'

Betty, who had decided that she had better travel with her younger son this time, said in her dry voice, 'It does have exceptional leather goods. And art – one mustn't forget the art.'

'Oh, no, one must never forget the art. Such a good investment,' said Ivo, mocking.

'Well, I've certainly found it so,' said Betty, 'but then I only collect Impressionists.'

There would have been a time when Ivo would have been impressed by this, but he was used to rich Americans by now. Daniel flushed. He hated being reminded of all the cold cash waiting to snare him if he did what Betty wanted. Even seeing her next to him was enough to intimidate: the huge sapphire earrings and matching ring on her claw-like hand, the torque of heavy gold round her neck, the designer clothes, the helmet of expertly tinted hair. This would be what his wife could turn into, if he married. And yet, he must marry; Mother was right. If only Ellen were strong enough not to succumb to the habits and mores of a caste. She was clever, and strong, and had her own business; she had been the first girlfriend he had had who didn't seem to drag him off shopping all the time, and yet – Daniel stared at the road ahead, and wondered if he was crazy to think that something might exist in life as it did on the page.

'Mum, I am so not a tomato pizza sort of person,' said Tania. 'I want a white pizza with ham and that's that.'

'All right, darling.'

Polly wondered how long her daughter was going to speak in this frightful Valley Girl argot. All Tania's friends spoke this way, and when Polly was less stressed-out she found it quite funny to hear their posh little voices turn nouns into verbs and drawl about assignments and sleep-overs.

'What would you like, Bron?' she asked, feeling sorry for the boy. He was more withdrawn than usual, his fine features pensive. 'Are you worrying about your mother? I'm sure she'll be better by tomorrow.'

He looked at her but didn't say anything. Of course he was worried about her. He had seen her and Ivo kissing, and he didn't know what to think. One minute he thought Ivo was in love with Ellen, the next he was in love with his mum. This sex business was pretty confusing, and now Bron wished he hadn't always shut his eyes during the snogging parts of James Bond videos because then he might have a better idea of what it was all about.

Bron had gone in to see Hemani three times a day, bringing her the hand-towels soaked in ice-cold water to try and help soothe her poor head. She was hardly ever sick, except with migraines, and those, he noticed, came when she was feeling particularly stressed, and trying not to let him see this. She'd had a bad one when Dad's new baby had been born, though he believed her when she said she wasn't jealous, or in love with him still. *She's probably worrying about me, that's all,* he thought.

All around them, other families were drifting in to sit at the round, white-draped tables. Some were tourists like themselves, pointedly ignoring each other, but most were Italians, out for an evening meal.

'I can never understand how they manage to keep it so cheap, here,' said Ellen. 'I mean, has anyone tried to get a decent meal in France recently? The food is vile, no matter what you pay. They've just lost it.'

'It's not as posh as Tuscany, is it?' said Guy.

'I've always thought France over-rated,' said Ivo. 'There's nothing they do that the Italians don't do better – apart from literature, of course. But it's become this great democratic holiday destination because it's cheaper, closer and most people can manage a few words of the lingo. Whereas Tuscany really pisses people off, somehow. You only have to say the word for every Left-wing impulse to rise up and boo.'

'Except when they're following round Tony Blair on expenses, of course,' said Polly.

'Oh, no, that makes it worse. That's why he's started going to Cumbria, not Umbria, poor sod.'

The children, turbo-charged by Fanta, ran about on the fine grass of the garden that had been made between the pizzeria and the road. They could see the lights of Cortona tumbling down the hillside above them, and bats crumpling through the deep blue skies.

'The moon's got fatter,' said Robbie, stopping to pant behind a bushy magnolia. The others, an unspoken truce declared, also stopped to stare up.

'It'll be full by tomorrow,' said Bron.

A cricket burst into noisy song beside them.

'My potion is ready to be used,' said Tania, excitedly. 'It needs moonlight to work.'

'Smelly old potions,' said Robbie. 'Bet they don't do anything.'

'Bet they do.'

'What do they do, then?'

Tania pulled a horrible face.

'Are they real potions?' asked Bron, interested. 'I mean, made to a scientific recipe?'

Tania hesitated.

'I'm following instructions,' she said.

'What do they do?'

Tania reddened.

'It makes people, you know . . .'

'What?'

She said in a hurried whisper, 'Want to have sex.'

Robbie burst into squeals of laughter, but Bron did not.

'I've heard of something like that,' he said.

'Yes, but this is different, it's not only that,' said Tania, passionately. 'It's different, you'll see. They'll fall instantly in love.'

The innocent intensity with which she had written her poems had transferred itself to the potion, and she knew that a single drop of what she had brewed would take effect, as mere words had failed to do. Bron and Robbie believed her at once.

'Are you going to try it out on one of them?' Bron asked.

Tania looked at him.

'Maybe.'

'Who?'

Tania shook her head. The truth was, she hadn't decided, and it wasn't her decision anyway. She could see the People hovering around the great white globe of the pizzeria's light, dancing so thickly and madly that it seemed somebody else must notice them – only they didn't.

'Try it on Ivo,' said Bron, suddenly. He had made up his mind. It wasn't fair that Dad should have Georgie, and a new baby, and Mum have nobody except him, however much he loved her. 'It's not dangerous, is it?'

The luminous halo round the garden light intensified. An incessant shower of innumerable tiny forms arrived from all sides, pulsing the answer.

'Nah,' said Tania. She liked the idea of using Ivo as her first experiment. He'd really annoyed her, bribing Robbie with presents and never giving her anything.

The subject was forgotten as the pizzas arrived. They were thin and hot and utterly delicious. Even Betty, who was picking her way through a plate of grilled vegetables, looked less discontented.

'Things OK, Mother?' Theo asked anxiously.

'Fine. Strange, isn't it, that we have to come to a place like this to get decent cooking?' she said.

'Are you offering to take over, Betty?' asked Polly, in her quiet voice.

'Me? Oh no. I leave that kind of thing for my staff, when I have company.'

And how often was that? thought Daniel guiltily. Who but a bored and lonely woman would go to all the trouble of living with people it was plain she didn't like or respect, simply because her sons did? Betty would ring him at least three times a week, unless he rang her, and always say, 'Hello? Daniel?'

Then, when he had confirmed that it was indeed he, she would say in that wounded but determinedly cheerful tone, 'I was just wondering whether you were happy – as happy as you ever can be, of course.'

Daniel never knew what to say to this, except to assure his mother that he was fine. She had never been so concerned about his morale when he was at prep school, so he deduced that what she was really trying to tell him was that *she* was unhappy. He wondered whether she did this to Theo, too, and suspected that on the nights when he wasn't being made to feel guilty, Theo was, though perhaps as Mother took his job more seriously than his own, she might respect his office hours.

He saw Ellen watching him anxiously. She was so pretty, and talented, and Upper East Side and he was being mean to her, too. Ellen was the kind of girl he was programmed, by birth and education, to dream of marrying, so why shouldn't he? She was tall and thin and blonde, she embodied the grace of America's own aristocracy but she was also funny

222

and smart. Ivo loathed her, it was true, and had warned him against her. But then, it was mutual, they obviously hadn't got along since some failed pass of Ivo's, so he was just going to have to accept the fact. Of course, if he did marry Ellen, it would probably mean giving up his job in London, and the life he'd made there away from his family. That would signify the destruction of all that he'd built up over the past seven years, although his publishing record probably would be good enough to help him get a job at NYU or Columbia. Daniel thought of re-entering the heated, aggressively ambitious world of American academia again and shuddered. But there was always going to be some price to pay.

Ellen touched his leg under the table, and he found himself squeezing her hand. She smiled radiantly, understanding this to be a promise. Betty, noting it, turned her hooded eyes to her grandchildren's inability to cut up their own pizza without half of it slopping over the plate on to the tablecloth.

'No, Robbie, you must use your index finger to guide the knife,' she said to her grandson, who hadn't the slightest idea what an index finger was. Daniel watched sympathetically. Anyone would think that his and Theo's table-manners had been different, but the fact was, any graces they possessed came from a poor Mexican woman who had had to leave her own children behind in order to earn the money to feed them. At all costs he would never cause his own children to need such sacrifice – assuming he ever had them. He knew Theo loved his, for when Tania was born his brother had said, with a rare show of emotion, 'I've suddenly realised what it's all about, all the long hours and hard work: it's for them.'

Daniel drank; they all drank. Somehow, nearly a dozen bottles of rough white wine were consumed. By the time they drove back along the long straight road from Ossaia (having become slightly lost and confused) the adults were laughing and whooping at each bump. The children sat primly in their seats, wide-awake and mystified as to all the noise and silliness that adults could indulge in.

'Don't forget about the potion,' Bron whispered to Tania.

'I won't,' she whispered back, and Robbie giggled.

'They'll like that,' he said, and she wondered whether he, too, could see the People.

'Oh, stop, stop,' cried Polly suddenly, as they were swerving up the worst bend of the hillside.

Obediently, Theo stepped on the brake. She pointed, and there, in the beam of the headlights, disappearing into the thick shrubs above a tumble-down terrace, were a mass of squirming greyish brown buttocks.

'What are they?' he asked, mystified.

'Wild boar,' said Guy.

They were all slightly breathless with the excitement that comes from seeing wild animals in their natural habitat. The energy of those hindquarters pumping and jostling into the night was thrilling, thought Polly, and also revolting, like coming upon something almost human having sex in the open air.

'They looked greasy,' said Tania.

''Spect they are. Pigs are full of fat.'

'Not wild ones that run around the hills,' said Guy. 'They're lean, mean, eating machines. They go up on their hind trotters and pull down grapes in vineyards. It used to be a test of your manhood in medieval times, killing one.'

'Why?' asked Robbie.

'Because the only way you could do it was to go down on one knee and get your spear right in through its mouth. A pig's hide is so thick and tough, see, it's like armour. Just imagine how much courage that took, waiting while something with foot-long tusks and a body the size of a large, heavy dog ran at you.'

The children wriggled with excitement. This was what they loved about Guy: he told them interesting things instead of asking questions about school. The other grown-ups yawned.

'Uncle Guy?'

'Yes, chick?'

'Why don't you have any children?'

'Tania, don't ask personal questions,' said Polly sharply.

'I just don't,' said Guy.

'But don't most grown-ups want children?' Tania asked.

'Why,' said Polly, amused by the incredulity in her daughter's voice, 'do you find that so hard to believe? Some do and some don't.'

'You wanted us, though, didn't you?'

'Yes,' Polly said, 'I did.'

Theo was wrestling with the steering wheel.

'Didn't you want us, Dad?' asked Tania.

'Don't ask Daddy questions when he's driving,' said Theo, through gritted teeth.

'Of course he did,' said Polly brightly. 'That's why we got married, darlings.'

The car drew up with a rattle of gravel, and then Daniel's car followed suit.

'Did you see the wild boar?' Tania demanded.

'What?'

She repeated her question, but none of them had.

'They never notice anything,' Robbie whispered.

'Well . . .' said Bron. 'Are you really going to do it, then?'

'Yes,' said Tania recklessly.

'When? Now?'

'What are you three buzzing over?' Polly asked. 'It's far too late for you to be up. Off you go.'

They went, pursuing the darkness, and were tucked up in bed in less than the usual time.

'I wonder if poor Meenu's any better. Now Guy's here, it'd be nice to do some expeditions,' said Polly. 'Don't you think?'

After Theo had grunted politely, and gone up to take the first shower, Polly wandered into the garden to be alone with it for a while. She didn't mind the faint sting of mosquito bites that accompanied this; it was just bliss to be out in the gentle night air. Bliss, too, to be alone. Polly sat down on a shallow stone step and watched a shooting star streak across the sky, like a small tear in a piece of black velvet. The night was so full of stars it was hard to believe this was the same sky that glowed above her roof in London. You hardly ever saw the stars in London . . .

Perhaps Theo was right to want to move them all to the States. She'd be able to see the stars there, if they lived outside New York. He couldn't conceive of his kids being brought up anywhere but the Great Good Place. When she thought of some of the gentle leafy suburbs in Connecticut, where children could cycle up and down and people just had so much space in what they called, with that lovely American diffidence, their yards, it was tempting. If not as tempting as the fantasy of staying here, of course. But how could I? Polly thought. There were the children's schools, and Theo's job, and all the myriad chores of daily life that would catch up with her the moment she stepped back on to British soil. It was only people like W. Shade who could enjoy such luxuries, even if he or she had to let other people enjoy them too, by renting out this house.

One by one, the yellow lights of the Casa Luna went out, and then there were no more sounds, but for the cheeping of the crickets and the sighing of the wind in the olive groves and the woods beneath.

Chapter Ten

The lights had gone out, as Polly had seen, but not everyone was in their proper places. Tania jumped out of bed, and gave her potion a stir. At last, she was going to repay some of these lumpen, unjust adults for the slights and insults heaped upon her during the holiday. Ivo deserved what was coming. She poured half the mixture into her own glass, and added mineral water to it. It looked pretty normal, at least by moonlight.

She knocked on the boys' door. They were still wide awake. Moonlight flooded their room, too, for Polly had forgotten to close their shutters, and looking into its watery beams Tania could see the People swirling.

'Hi, guys,' she said, thrilling to her own words.

'Hi.'

Tania said, conscious of her importance, 'I've got it. The potion.'

'Great!'

Bron's enthusiasm increased her confidence.

'But listen, Robbie's the one who has to give it to Ivo.'

'Why?' asked Robbie suspiciously.

'No, it's just that he'll be nicer to you than to me,' said Tania. 'You never look as if you're doing something bad even when you are.'

Robbie's appearance was a considerable advantage, and he knew it. He flapped his hands briefly, and shivered with excitement.

'OK,' he said. 'What do you want me to do?'

Robbie was growing up, Tania thought, even if he still hadn't lost any baby teeth. She explained, and he nodded, then, carefully carrying the glass with the potion, slipped into the adult wing of the house, and pattered down the corridor.

It's long, long, longer than it is in daytime, thought Robbie, and there are creepy shadows at the end and in the ceiling where monsters probably are, but the floor's like a river, it carries me along in the moonlight though all the doors are dark and all the same and I can't tell which is that man's room, I'll just follow the wondrous butterfly floating, swooping and sailing the air, past the moon that bobs up there—

Robbie gasped, but Ellen gave a small shriek, for the last thing she had expected was to see anybody else, least of all a child standing outside her door.

'What the – what are you doing?'

Robbie forgot his instructions and stood, mutely. He raised his pointed little chin and looked so perfectly innocent and so perfectly angelic that Ellen said in a softer voice, 'Bad dream?'

In answer, Robbie lifted the glass. Its contents caught the moonlight, and threw strange lights on the wall behind Ellen, lights that were almost, but not quite, rainbows.

Ellen paused. She couldn't just leave this whiny little kid – he might wake everyone up.

'I'm sure it's just fine.'

'Yes,' said Robbie, looking up at her with his huge brilliant eyes.

Ellen, who was very thirsty, swallowed a mouthful, and suddenly Robbie remembered.

'No! No, stop!'

Ellen took no notice. She was standing quite still in the moonlight, swaying, with a weird look on her face, her eyes half closed.

He tugged at her and said, in a shrill voice, 'You shouldn't have done that.'

Ivo's tousled head appeared in the next doorway.

'What is it? Hush, there's a good fellow, you'll wake—'

He saw Ellen, and suddenly she opened her eyes and saw him.

'Ivo?' she said, and Robbie thought her voice had gone funny too. He grabbed the glass from her hands and said, 'She's drunk—'

'I can see that,' said Ivo, waving away the glass that Robbie was now trying to push into his hand. 'Go away, now. The loo is the other door, remember?'

'OK,' said Robbie, and as he found he did need the toilet, he trotted into the bathroom, putting the glass down by the basin as he did so. Carefully, he lifted the seat and released a tinkling stream, then flushed, washed and scampered back to bed.

'Did you do it?' hissed Tania's voice.

'Yes,' Robbie said yawning.

'And?' asked Bron.

'You'll see,' said Robbie, and fell instantly asleep.

'Typical,' said Tania. 'I bet he's got it wrong.'

'That's so like a girl,' said Bron, equally withering. 'I bet nothing's happened.'

'I bet it has,' said Tania, stoutly. 'I bet they're doing love-stuff now.'

But when she peeped into the corridor, it was empty.

'Ivo,' said Ellen, in a slurred voice. 'Ivo, c'here.'

'I am here,' said Ivo, panting. Ellen was draping herself all over him. She was almost as tall as he was, and surprisingly heavy. 'Come on, I know you've had a bit too much, but – ow, Ellen, no!'

'I want you, Ivo,' said Ellen. 'I need you.'

'How I wish I could believe this was *in vino veritas*, but right now you need me like a hole in the head,' said Ivo irritably. 'Which is what you're going to feel you have when you wake up tomorrow morning. Come on, old girl, one foot in front of the other.'

Ellen suddenly burst into noisy sobs.

'I know I'm getting old,' she said, tears running down her face. 'Oh Ivo, save me! I'm thirty-three, and I don't want watching *Friends* on video and having candle-lit baths as my greatest sensual pleasure!'

Ivo, exhausted by trying to manoeuvre her into place, sat down on the edge of the bed, and mopped his forehead with his pyjama sleeve.

'Ellen, I'm sure there's much, much more to your life than watching *Friends*, although I can think of no greater sensual pleasure than watching you take candle-lit baths, and frankly age cannot wither you nor custom stale your et cetera, but do, do, get back to bed.'

Without warning, Ellen fell, as if pole-axed, on top of him.

'Take me, Ivo, take me!' she said. 'I want you so much. Look!'

Ivo, trying to catch his breath, averted his eyes as she tried to rip off the delicate silk nightdress she had put on to seduce Daniel. One of her breasts slipped out, like a puppy's head. Ivo gave a muffled groan.

'Isn't this what you've always wanted?'

Ivo tried and failed to sit up. He, too, was rather drunk. He wondered whether this was actually happening or whether, as so often in his dreams, she would suddenly turn into a bouquet of flowers.

'Ellen, really, there's only so much flesh can stand, and you'd hate me even more if I—'

Ellen began to yowl. She was running her hands up and down her body and writhing.

'That really isn't such a good idea, you know . . .'

She gave a wriggle, and suddenly he was lying on top of her, her legs wrapped round his waist.

'Take me! Take me!'

'This really is not fair,' Ivo said, appalled, amused and hopelessly aroused. 'I seem suddenly to have wandered into an Austin Powers movie – oh God, this is too much – you—'

Somebody knocked on the door.

'Ellen?' said Daniel's voice hesitantly. 'Are you OK in there?'

'No,' wailed Ellen. 'I need help – I need—'

'Cover yourself up, you ninny,' said Ivo, but it was too late. Daniel burst in just as Ellen had succeeded in tearing the front of her nightdress open while lying beneath Ivo.

'Danny!' said Ellen, in a tragic voice, then hiccuped.

'This isn't what it looks like, it really isn't what it looks like. She's out of her skull with drink,' said Ivo nervously.

Daniel was standing there bare-chested, looking very angry, and for the first time really Ivo realised how big he was when not stooping in his apologetic, scholarly way. He wondered whether he was going to get hit, because Daniel's fist was curling and uncurling into a ball, just the way people did in really bad movies, only this was all too real. Ivo hadn't been punched since he was in infant school, and he didn't like the memory of what that had felt like.

'So I guess you thought you'd take advantage?'

'No – no – quite the opposite,' said Ivo, almost wringing his hands but finding they were needed to keep up his pyjamas. 'Ask her, she'll tell you. Ellen? Ellen!'

Ellen, though, had fallen asleep with her thumb in her mouth. Her blond hair streamed across the pillow. The two men stared at her lying spreadeagled across the bed, and then Ivo moved. Daniel bristled, and made to stop him, but Ivo simply drew the sheet up to cover her.

'Silly idiot. There,' he said. 'Look, on my word of honour, nothing happened.'

'I don't believe you know what honour means,' said Daniel.

Ivo shrugged. 'You know, you're probably right. I wouldn't dream of quarrelling with a Shakespeare scholar at any rate. But I promise you, I was only trying to get her back to bed, not join her there. I don't particularly go in for shagging girls when they're blotto. She probably won't remember a thing tomorrow.'

'Let's hope so,' said Daniel. 'Because if her account is any different to yours, I can promise you that this particular freebie is over.'

Tania scanned Ivo's face eagerly the next morning at breakfast for signs of passion, but could only see him looking rather more sheepish and rumpled than usual.

'Loser,' she hissed at Robbie. He threw his bowl of Branflakes at her, missed, and the next moment there was milk all over the terrace floor. Polly shut her eyes, and suppressed the scream that was already rising up in her throat.

'Am not.'

'Are.'

'Am not.'

He paused for a moment, then, 'Muu-um!' he wailed. 'Tania's being nasty to me again.'

'Tania. It's our last few days here, you might *try* to be

nicer,' said Polly, too busy mopping up the floor to notice Ellen come in.

She sat down at the table and said, 'Hi.'

Tania saw the blood tint beneath her tan, like a piece of fruit ripening suddenly.

'How are you feeling?' Daniel asked, with heavy emphasis.

'Um,' said Ellen, in a muffled voice. 'Er . . . not so good. I've a hell of a hangover.'

'Coffee?' asked Ivo.

'Yeah.'

'I'll pour,' said Daniel.

'Be my guest,' said Ivo.

Ivo and Daniel exchanged glances, and the children, normally as unaware of adult moods as adults were of theirs, watched curiously. There was something odd going on, for sure. Uncle Dan and Ivo were looking at each other the way Bron had seen two stegosauruses look at each other in *Walking with Dinosaurs*, only without the frilly bits round their necks, and he was just wondering whether they'd start to stamp and fight, and what the voice of Kenneth Branagh would have to say if they did, when his own mother came out. She was walking in a daze, like she usually did after a migraine, and when Ivo called out, 'Hello there, Hemani. Better at last?' she suddenly stopped, and stared at him.

'Mum?' said Bron, jumping up. 'Shall I fetch you some breakfast?'

'What?'

'Would you like a juice? Or some more ice water?'

'I've just had some,' said Hemani in a wondering, sleepy voice, quite unlike her usual one. 'In the bathroom.'

Robbie looked up, as something rose in his mind, then remembered he was biting his piece of toast into a pistol, and the memory sank back, flickering a little then lying quiet.

'We've planned a trip to one of the islands on Lake Trasimeno, today,' said Polly briskly. 'No more lolling about, I think. And we really ought to fit Florence in, the day after. There suddenly doesn't seem to be any time, does there?'

'Good idea,' said Ivo. 'A bit more activity. Just what we need.'

'That sounds most unlike you, Ivo,' said Hemani, with an intimate little laugh.

'I have hidden shallows,' he said in a nervous, jocular tone. She was giving him a soft look which somehow he didn't think was quite natural. 'Even shallower than the ones you already know about, that is,' he said to Ellen, before she could add her observations. But Ellen, too, was looking at him in a most peculiar way.

'Oh, Ivo, I've never thought you shallow,' she said sorrowfully. 'That's only an affectation. Everyone knows how brilliant you are, really.'

'Yeah, right,' he said.

'But it's true,' Ellen cried. 'Most people only buy *Manhattan* to read what you write. You're practically a god – your editor told me he's terrified you'll ask for a raise.'

'A pay rise?' said Ivo, now frankly incredulous. 'Ellen, this is a bit much over breakfast. Can't you wait until my coffee has sunk in before your next round?'

Ellen's eyes filled. 'Why do you always assume the worst about me?'

'Ellen, honey, I know you've every reason to feel sore at Ivo—'

'No, she doesn't,' said Hemani. 'She has absolutely no justification for it at all. It was all a drunken mistake.'

'How do you know?' asked Daniel, puzzled. 'You were asleep, weren't you?'

'She told me,' said Hemani passionately, 'and, really, if you want to know I think Ivo's behaved like a real gent, taking the flak he has from her.'

'You promised you wouldn't tell,' said Ellen angrily.

'That was before I saw you being horrible to him all the time.'

'Now then, now then, what are we doing today?' said Guy, bouncing into the kitchen and rubbing his hands.

'We're going to have a picnic on an island on the lake,' said Polly. 'That is, if Theo wakes up before noon.'

Her husband had been asleep when she had got back to the house, and remained so all morning, despite her best efforts. She felt like the princess in the fairy tale, who finds her true love only to be unable to rouse him. Was she so unattractive that he simply couldn't be bothered, or was he, as he claimed, drained by hard work? Or perhaps he's having an affair, she thought despairingly. Only, when would he have the time?

'Oh, good, a picnic. I love a bit of a picnic,' said Guy, bouncing into the pergola. 'Anything I can do to help?'

Ivo groaned. 'I'm not sure if I can stand all this bright-eyed and bushy-tailed stuff. What do they feed them on at Channel 4?' he muttered. Both Hemani and Ellen laughed hysterically.

Guy's ears twitched, and then he let out his braying laugh.

'Oh, very funny, very funny. I suppose you're hungover? I stick to Coke, meself. Never been able to take the hard stuff.'

'It's only wine,' said Hemani, though her own head was aching too.

Polly said brightly, 'Bless you. Why don't you take the children to pick some salad stuff and fruit from the garden?'

'I knew Robbie would get it wrong,' said Tania, as they followed Guy between the buzzing grey spires of lavender. Already the heat was suffocating. The slim, flickering leaves of the orchard gave scant relief.

'It was your idea,' said Bron.

'Yes, but I never thought he'd give the potion to the wrong person. Two wrong people,' said Tania.

'If it's truly that,' said Bron.

'What else could it be? Ellen's in love with Uncle Dan, not Ivo. I was planning on being their bridesmaid,' Tania added in a mortified voice. 'Now he's got your mum and Ellen all sexy about him.'

'I don't think it's sexy exactly,' said Bron, in an uneasy voice. He didn't think he should be discussing this sort of stuff with a girl. 'There haven't been any bottoms yet, just lots of shouting.'

'That's what sex does,' said Tania. 'Like in *The Simpsons*.'

'Well, anyway, you've got to give them the antidote.'

'The what?'

'The thing that'll make the potion stop.'

Tania looked dubious.

'I think it just has to wear off. It won't hurt them, it's all natural and stuff.'

Bron was less convinced. Of course, Nature was always being called upon as a sort of powerful but kindly force in advertisements. If a shampoo had natural ingredients in it, it was supposed to be especially good at cleaning your hair, and if a breakfast cereal was full of natural goodness, it was supposed to be better for your digestion than the nice, choc-olately sort, to make up for the way it was full of bits of grit. In fact, Bron wasn't sure that Nature was really on the side of Man at all. For one thing, Mum had told him that boys and men might be an accident of genes, and people were really all supposed to be female, and for another, well, there were things like toadstools and snakes and deadly night-shade.

'Um, Tania, what exactly did you put in the potion?'

Tania shrugged. 'I just followed instructions,' she replied, not saying whose. Bron might be the coolest boy she'd ever seen but she knew he wouldn't be able to see the People.

Bron listened. The angry adult sounds from above had stopped, and meanwhile the funny man they called Uncle Guy had filled a basket with fruit. Robbie had climbed up into the trees to find the best peaches and plums, and now they were picking tomatoes. Bron put out his hand and picked one too. It was warm from the sun, and slightly split, and it smelt strong and almost peppery. When he bit into it, it tasted so brimfull of sweet, juicy, slightly runny tomato-ness that he thought Nature must be OK, really, even if it was never going to be ketchup.

'That's the best taste in the world, isn't it?' said Guy, kindly. He bit into one too. 'Champion. Funny plant, the tomato. People call it a vegetable, but it's really a fruit. Some say it's the one that heroes fought over in Greek myth, but what I find interesting is, the meaner you treat it the more delicious its fruit becomes.'

'Why?'

'Makes the taste all watery, if you turn a hose on. In this hot sun without any cover, it gets more and more concentrated.'

The children pattered back behind him as he returned to the house, pausing every now and again to tie up some fallen creeper or dead-head a flower.

'Ah, isn't that lovely,' he murmured, bending over a red rose. 'The most odious of plants.'

'Don't you mean odorous?' asked Bron.

'Odious, odorous, a rose by any other name would smell as sweet,' said Guy.

'Uncle Guy?' asked Tania, skipping along beside him.

'Yes, chicken?'

'Why are your ears so furry at the top?'

'Don't know. They just are.'

'Is that why you haven't got married?'

Guy paused. 'Well, I'll tell you something.' He put his face close to hers and whispered, 'I'm not really the marrying kind, see.'

'Oh.' She patted his hand sympathetically. Poor Uncle Guy, not to be able to marry because of his ears. Tania had often discussed marriage with Mum, who was very firm on how it should be central to Tania's life when she was grown-up, whatever Nana told her to the contrary. Nana, who was Mum's mum, had strange ideas about something called feminism which Polly said was about never doing chores in the house like washing and ironing, and about girls being cleverer than boys and not having babies too soon. Secretly, Tania thought this all sounded pretty sensible, except that she did want to be a bridesmaid.

Theo was talking into his mobile.

'Right. Right. And have you an update on that report? Sure. Fine. I'll see you at seventeen hundred hours.'

He flipped the mobile closed, a look of pure relief on his face.

'Sorry, folks, that was the office. Something's come up with the deal. If I catch the ten o'clock express-train to Rome, I can be in Frankfurt by five this afternoon, so let's move it.'

'Oh!' said Polly. 'When will you be back?'

'Tomorrow, the next day, depends how it goes. You'll be able to cope, won't you?'

'Course. I always do,' said Polly.

'Bad luck,' said Hemani. 'Not much of a holiday for you, this, is it? Listen, when he gets back you must let me babysit. It's ludicrous that you haven't had any time off together yet.'

Polly tried to look grateful, but her heart was very low. It was mortifying seeing Theo, who had been so slow as to be almost comatose, suddenly not just shaven but walking about with a spring in his step.

Betty was clucking and clacking about, whisking shirts off the line and getting in everybody's way while ironing them, saying, 'If only I had some of my lavender spray! Conchita always uses that on my linen, and it makes such a difference. Oh, dear, and your boxer shorts, you can't possibly send your husband to work in unpressed boxer shorts, Polly.'

Tania cried out in dismay seeing her father's squashy black leather bags in the hall.

'Why are you going? You're supposed to be on holiday with us!'

'It's only a day, sweetheart,' said Theo, hugging her. He never loved his children so much as when he was saying goodbye to them. 'You're giving me a ride to the station.'

'But we haven't played tennis or bicycled,' said Robbie, remembering these rash promises.

'We will when I get back,' said Theo impatiently. He went over to Polly, and gave her a long embrace – the sort he only ever gave in public, she thought sadly, even as she hugged him back.

'Ah, bless,' said Ivo.

'Tell you what,' said Daniel, 'I could do a knockabout on the court with you kids, if you like. Tomorrow?'

'It's always tomorrow and tomorrow and tomorrow with grown-ups,' said Tania, bitterly. 'Why not today?'

'We're going to an island today.'

'Listen, I promise I'll give you all a knockabout tomorrow,' said Daniel.

He was feeling oddly at a loss this morning. Something had changed; he couldn't quite put a finger on it, but it seemed as if Ivo had been telling the truth last night. Ellen, far from spitting like a wildcat every time Ivo came near, seemed disposed to overlook the whole incident, which was most unlike her. In fact, she seemed pretty mad at himself, Daniel thought, for intervening. Perhaps she was just embarrassed. He had expected her to come to his room last night, but clearly she'd been too drunk to do so. Yet in that case, why had Ivo been there?

Hemani, though, had said that Ivo was blameless, so perhaps she had been there earlier. Daniel's head hurt too, in the relentless heat. It was oppressively hot, now, not that lovely clear heat they had enjoyed before, and they had to have the windows up and the air conditioning on as soon as they got into the car. Even the swallows or swifts seemed stunned into submission, confining their swoops to the morning and evening. The hills were burnished the colour of metal, the long grasses between the olives a pale gold, the trees pewter. No breeze stirred. The view across the plain to the distant peak of Mount Amiata had vanished in a dull haze, and as he bumped the car slowly down the chalky road in the wake of the larger car, Daniel thought for the first time that he would be glad to get back to London.

Beside him, Hemani stirred restlessly and sighed. Ellen had insisted she sit in the front seat, because of dear Meenu having recently recovered from her migraine, while she and Ivo sat in the back. Daniel had thought this kind of her, but Hemani, oddly, did not seem to appreciate it. She kept turning her head to talk to them on the back seat.

'. . . used to think Polly had an easy life, but now I'm not so sure.'

'Oh, the life of an executive wife isn't so hard, but you have to be born to it,' said Ellen.

'Most of the girls I was at Spence with have married guys just like Theo. I'm not saying Polly isn't a great person, but she's just so British about some things. It's really kind of a boring life, just kids and entertaining and doing charity work, and running a couple of houses or so.'

'Whereas you, of course, have more fun spending your daddy's money and running a couple of shops,' said Ivo.

'Sure I have fun,' said Ellen. 'Is there any crime in that? But I work hard for it, and, for your information I'm not spending my daddy's money. He encouraged me and backed my first collection, but after that it was all me. And I paid him back every cent.'

'You were lucky to have a daddy to borrow from at all,' said Hemani, and an acid note crept into her voice that Daniel had never heard before. 'I had to borrow from my bank to complete my training, and I've only recently paid it off.'

244

'And that's to work as a doctor?' said Ellen, incredulous.

'Yes.'

'The British health-care system really sucks.'

'At least we don't ask people if they've insurance when they need emergency treatment. You never get to see that bit in *ER*.'

Hemani had not felt as angry and upset as this since her divorce. She knew what was causing it. She had woken out of the stuporous sleep that always followed the tail-end of a migraine with one decision clear in her mind: she was jolly well going to sleep with Ivo. So what if it had no future? Who could tell, anyway? If she didn't take what chances she was offered, as a single parent, she'd never have sex again. Hemani had come down to breakfast intending to make it clear to Ivo that she was ready and waiting, only to find bloody Ellen all over him. Was she trying to make Daniel jealous?

'Lovely day,' said Ivo, in a slightly strangled voice. He was finding the drive down less enjoyable than usual, because at every jolt Ellen was cosying up to him in a most extraordinary manner. During one particularly violent thrust, he found she had stuck the tip of her tongue in his ear, and just now he was appalled to find her hands busily engaged with the zip of his trousers.

'What the fuck do you think you're doing?' he hissed, seizing her wrists.

'Oh, Ivo, don't be coy. You've never been so before,' Ellen murmured, casting him a glance so sluttish that he immediately shrank into his corner of the car, blushing violently.

245

'I . . . read any good books lately, Hemani?' he asked, seeing her head swing round to look at him.

'I still haven't finished *A Room with a View*,' she said, 'but I do see what you meant about all the kissing.'

She shot him a long, intense glance.

'Oh! Quite,' said Ivo. He caught sight of Daniel's quizzical gaze in the mirror. 'All that love business. Always makes a novel second-rate.'

'Most great works of fiction have been very much to do with love,' said Daniel. 'Even Shakespeare, as I recall.'

'Ah, the Bard,' said Ivo uncomfortably. 'Well, I haven't read as much of him as you have, old boy, but he probably just did that for the masses, didn't he? I mean, today he'd be writing scripts for *EastEnders*. Or Hollywood.'

'I don't doubt that he needed to earn his crust just like any other writer,' said Daniel, 'but nobody can pretend to know his mind. It's like God's in that story of Borges, so infinitely various—'

'Oh, come on,' said Ivo. 'There's nothing original about his mind, just the way he writes. Of course he had to do all that love-stuff, just like any other hack. They just aren't a patch on the history plays, that's all. I read history at Cambridge on the strength of them.'

'I think he wrote what he wanted,' said Daniel; 'and why should love be so disprized as a subject?'

'What else pervades our waking lives, and even our dreams, too?' said Hemani.

'Well, I'd have thought work does, just for a start,' said Ivo, 'and war and money.'

246

'Oh Ivo,' said Ellen, 'I've worked all my adult life, and I've never yet had a single dream about it. Has anyone? School, yes, but not work. And as for war . . . well, when was the last time you were involved in a war, anyone? It just doesn't enter into Western life these days. I've probably come closer to the horror of war than any of you, recently, and it doesn't fill my subconscious. You know what? It's just a testosterone fantasy. And I never dream about money – what's the point, when money is a sort of dream itself? Whereas love – well, I know all that stuff about it being a thing apart for guys and a woman's whole existence, but that's just an attitude. Guys pretend it doesn't matter so much, because they're afraid of its power.'

They watched Theo alight at Terontola station to catch the express to Rome. He kissed Polly through the car window, waved to his children and strode off to the ticket office.

'Poor Polly. It must be hard, in the middle of a holiday,' said Hemani.

'Yeah, they have a great marriage,' said Ellen. 'Now, that's love, wouldn't you say?'

'It's all biology,' said Ivo, keeping what Polly had told him about her sex-life as a confession. 'If it weren't for two thousand years of the Christian tradition we wouldn't think of pretending otherwise.'

'Well, I'm not from that tradition,' said Hemani, 'and I believe in love. Love isn't just sex, Ivo, you know that as well as I do.'

'I do?'

'Yes, of course you do. It's about realising that life is bigger than you are. Why is that bad or wrong?'

'That's exactly what makes it so rubbishy as a subject for art,' said Ivo. 'Anyone who's read *Madame Bovary* ought to know what that tripe leads to. Debt, vulgarity, suicide. Romance is the true opiate of the masses. We'd all be much better off without it.'

'I feel I should point out that technically, romance is not the same thing as love,' said Daniel.

Ivo snorted. 'Well, anything that elevates love above the level of lust is romance. The only good love stories are sad ones, for that reason, though personally I don't feel a shred of pity for anyone who buggers up their life for a delusion.'

'Why should love be a delusion?' said Hemani. 'What about its real power to transform your life?'

'Delusion,' said Ivo. 'People's lives *are* commonplace.'

'You may see them as so,' said Daniel. 'I don't. Shakespeare didn't.'

'Oh, Shakespeare,' said Ivo wearily. 'He was writing about kings and wizards and people who were the opposite of ordinary. Even his fools are the fools of a genius, so of course his lovers speak and act the way a genius would. It's still all poetry and moonshine. Nobody would ever fall in love if they hadn't read about it or seen it at the movies.'

'In that case,' said Daniel, 'isn't it the greatest creation of all?'

'Love isn't just that. It's about a kind of wildness—' Hemani said, and then stopped, for she had not even thought she knew all these things until she said them. 'Haven't you

248

ever felt that? That there's something in you that is more than what you are?'

Ivo said vehemently, 'No, of course not. Or at least, if I have, it was always an illusion.'

Daniel quoted,

> '*Tell me where is fancy bred,*
> *Or in the heart or in the head?*
> *It is engender'd in the eyes—*'

'I don't think so,' retorted Hemani. 'I know all about eyes, after all.'

'Yes, I don't know how you can bear to do what you do,' said Ellen. 'It's bad enough for most people just putting contact lenses in.'

'I don't think he meant the eye in that literal sense,' said Daniel. 'He meant in the sense of the inner eye, the imagination. I did my doctorate on Shakespeare and eyes,' he added apologetically, for he never expected anyone to be interested in his work.

'And what conclusions did you draw?' asked Hemani.

'Well, he was probably short-sighted, because the things he describes are what you notice close-up, not far away,' said Daniel, unconsciously touching his spectacles.

Ellen said, 'You spent three years just working that out?'

Ivo burst out laughing. 'You know, it's the remarkable thing about academics: they look at Shakespeare and always see their own faces in him.'

Daniel flushed.

'If that's true, then we're the better for it,' he said. 'After all, we have what he lacked – the scholarship, the original ideas – and he has the passion and the poetry.'

'I can't say I've noticed academics being exactly lacking in passion,' said Ivo, 'though it's usually for the prettier under-graduates.'

'Personally, I can't think of anyone who wouldn't have their mind and heart and soul, too, if you believe in souls, enlarged by Shakespeare.'

'Or completely crushed by him,' said Ivo. 'Of course, your nation thinks nothing of translating his work to a Californian high school. Strange, how many English classics have been blithely rewritten by Hollywood to appeal to the American teenager. Personally, I look forward to *Macbeth* with jocks and cheerleaders.'

'America doesn't stand or fall by the movies, Ivo,' said Daniel, in a pained voice. It always saddened him to see the way people in Europe perceived only one America, the cor-porate monolith erected by Hollywood, Coca-Cola and Microsoft. 'You should get out of New York, you know. We're a whole bunch of places and peoples, and some of us –' he hesitated, because he knew how difficult it was to get this accepted, 'quite a lot of us, actually – are pretty smart.'

'We still object to having our literature colonised by you,' said Ivo.

'*Mene, mene tekel upharsin,*' said Daniel.

'What does that mean?' asked Ellen.

'Basically, that our culture's stiffed, so we should move

over and stop whining,' said Ivo. 'Well, the same to you with knobs on, dear boy.'

'Oh for heaven's sakes, stop bickering, you two,' said Hemani. 'You're worse than the children.'

They drove in silence along the shores of Lake Trasimeno. Ivo felt guilty, but defiant. He knew he'd gone too far with Daniel now, and that he might well have damaged their friendship irreversibly, but indignation and a sense of injustice goaded him on.

They parked in Passignano, a pretty, red-roofed town tumbling down to the lake-side. The next ferry would take forty minutes to arrive, so the adults settled down to a cappuccino while the children demanded coins for the mechanical helicopter, horse and car ranged under the trees of a small park above the beach. This was so entertaining that even Betty scrabbled in her bag for euros.

'Pity you can't buy them,' said Guy. 'Hours of peace, they'd bring.'

'They'd only get bored,' said Polly. 'Whatever you buy, they play with for an afternoon, then despise. The imagination is the only toy that lasts.'

Tania, astride the black horse, could feel its sides moving beneath her calves as they galloped across the plain. Her hair whipped away in the wind, and the Native American warriors chasing her whooped in dismay as her trusty steed bore her across the unending desert, her new purple two-piece from Jayne Norman dazzling their eyes with its rhinestones as they aimed their rifles to fire.

Close beside her, Bron guided his US Army helicopter high

above the heads of the dastardly Thuggees who were swarming over Pankat Palace, attempting to regain the three precious jewels that he was going to return to their rightful owners. With his trusty side-kick fearlessly guiding the pink Cadillac, armed to the teeth with machine-guns, he would outwit the wicked Rajah, no matter how many alligators he had in the river beneath.

'Ack-ack-ack-ack, gotcha!' he whooped.

A car, a car, a real car with a steering wheel and BUTTONS, and I can make pooping noises like Mr Toad and travel the whole world in thirty seconds, it's a magic car, it's a flying car, thought Robbie, even as the music faded, and his mother dragged him off along the jetty.

'Oh, the heat,' said Polly, flapping her straw hat at her flushed cheeks. 'It's too much.'

'It'll be fine once we're out on the water,' said Guy.

The ferry sped towards them and docked, churning the blue to olive green and brown, disgorging earlier visitors to the Isola Maggiore. There was a rank smell of engine fuel as they all jumped, one by one, on board, Betty needing the assistance of a brawny young Italian in dazzling white uniform, and then they were off. For the first time since they had arrived, the cacophony of cicadas stopped. The undulating landscape swelled and receded, bleached so white that olive trees looked like the black squares on a chessboard. Far away, on the other side of the lake, seeming almost to float on the water, another town, Castiglione del Lago, sent its turrets and battlements into the sky. They stared, dazzled. The magic of Italy, so familiar and yet so strange, cast its spell on them anew.

252

'You could just see Botticelli's Venus coming out of the water over by those reeds, couldn't you?' said Ellen.

'Are you offering to strip?' said Ivo.

'Maybe,' said Ellen. Ivo gulped.

They passed an island, wild and overgrown, a single house nestling in its woods, then rounded the larger shore, and arrived. Disgorged on to a single street paved with soft, rose-red brick, where old women plied their crochet needles and thin tabby cats searched for scraps, the party wandered a little. There seemed nothing much to see, apart from the big circular nets, their colours bleached by sun and wave to soft creams and pinks, and a small church whose blue, gold-starred ceiling Tania immediately demanded to have replicated on her own bedroom. It was a gentle, sleepy place that not even tourism could destroy, for it had neither cars nor discotheques; and there was only one restaurant.

'Now, I really don't want to walk far,' said Betty, as soon as they approached the beach.

It was a small, pebbly area filled with sun-beds and umbrellas for hire, and it was plain she intended to stop there, but the children ran ahead, as usual.

'It's all level with the lake, Betty, with plenty of benches if you get tired,' said Polly.

'Of course I'm not tired,' snapped Betty. 'It's these primitive conditions.'

Polly looked at her mother-in-law's feet, and felt a reluctant admiration for her, as she certainly made no concessions to climate or terrain. She was hobbling after Ellen and Daniel like a bad fairy. Why can't she just let them be? Polly wondered, but at least she was now alone with Guy.

'Here, you need a hand with that, don't you?' said Guy, seeing her stop for a rest.

'Well, yes,' she said shyly.

'This is my good deed for the day,' he told her.

'Oh.'

She was a little disappointed to be classified as such. Of course, she had never done more than vaguely fantasise about him, like half the middle-class housewives in Britain, but after all, he had been another of her charity cases, to begin with. For it was Polly who had introduced Guy to a neighbour of hers who was a TV producer, hoping once again for romance to blossom but what actually happened instead was that Guy was transformed from gardener to presenter to, meteorically, star. He was still single, whereas nearly everyone she knew from her earlier life had paired off. It usually gives a married woman a pleasurable sensation of potential to number a bachelor or two among her acquaintance, and Polly was no exception. All she wanted was some sign from someone (other than Ivo, who really couldn't be said to count) that she was still a woman, but it seemed that she was even going to be denied that.

Ivo, by now thoroughly disconcerted, was walking as fast as he could on the circular path round the island, following the children. Their forms flitted and skipped past palm trees and cacti and umbrella pines. He had an uneasy idea that both Ellen and Hemani were following him rather too

closely for comfort, and hurried past the statue commemor-
ating St Francis, and a number of small pebbly beaches.

Behind him, Daniel, determined to speak to Ellen, also
lengthened his stride. It was ridiculous, they had spent
almost two weeks together, and nobody could ask for a
sweeter person. If he could just separate her from the others,
they could return to the mainland an engaged couple.

But how to tell her, or rather, ask? His situation was pecu-
liarly fraught with irony and self-consciousness, because all
available phrases had, so far as he was aware, been used
already. There was even an early novel by Aldous Huxley in
which a young man, in desperation, had driven three times
round this very lake before plucking up the courage to propose – an anguish of mind Daniel now felt considerable
sympathy for, seeing how very large it was. Should he propose
a similar spin to Ellen? He couldn't imagine himself doing so.
How could he propose without a thousand time-worn phrases
swarming on to his lips? The trouble with his line of business
was that you could speak in nothing but quotations. Could he
address her as Ferdinand did Miranda, hailing her as the goddess of the isle? To call a woman a goddess was not altogether
complimentary today, he suspected; it implied she had a
weight problem, similar to that of the earth mother and other
female archetypes. 'In vain I have struggled—' No, that was
Austen. So Daniel strode along, leaving Polly and Guy far
behind but not quite keeping the others in sight.

Eventually, a tumbledown castle reared up above them, its
grounds terminating in ruined marble steps and a crescent
beach. The children raced down to the shore and frolicked

there, chasing the sour green waves then skipping back. There was a brackish smell of weed and water. Ivo spotted a place where the path split and veered off to the left. It led to a round turret with a circular ledge. He walked round it and saw to his relief that it was unpeopled.

'Ah,' said Ivo aloud, stretching out both arms to lean on the railings and gaze across the lake. 'Why aren't I doing this all the time?'

'Why aren't you doing what, exactly?' asked Hemani. Startled, Ivo turned his head. She smiled at him.

'What did you have in mind?'

'Well,' she said, 'a few days ago, you did make a suggestion . . .'

'Which upset you so much you took to your bed with the vapours,' said Ivo sceptically.

Hemani shrugged, and the curves of her body deepened.

'Hi, Ivo,' said Ellen, appearing round the other side of the turret. 'Oh – I didn't think you'd be here,' she said to Hemani, who bristled at her tone.

'Why shouldn't I be?'

'Perhaps I have something to say to Ivo that I'd rather you weren't around to hear,' said Ellen sweetly.

'Perhaps I do too, and I got here first,' said Hemani. 'You're going out with Daniel, anyway.'

'Ladies, ladies,' said Ivo. 'Please, don't. I'm sure you find this highly amusing, but I don't want to be the butt of this joke any longer. Hemani, please forgive me for embarrassing you so much the other day; Ellen, I really am sorry about what happened in New York and—'

256

By now Ivo, who had glanced down and seen what was clearly impassable slabs of rock and slime beneath the turret, had jumped up on to the circular seat at its base, and was edging round. The two women looked up at him with the expressions of a pair of cats about the pounce on a small bird.

'Room for one more?' asked Daniel, leaping up on to the ledge beside him.

Chapter Eleven

❦

Polly threw the bruised, half-eaten fruit and tomatoes from the picnic into the bushes. The others had disappeared up the hill to explore the castle and the hill above, leaving her, as usual, to keep an eye on the children and tidy up. Polly's opinion of Hemani as a mother was sinking by the minute, because, personally, she would never have let a young boy run around out of her sight. She seemed to have fully recovered from her migraine now, and was behaving in an absurdly flirtatious way towards Ivo. At least Guy was doing a wonderful job of charming the Demon Queen. After her initial suspicion, Betty had been won round by Guy's shameless name-dropping of his titled clients (some of whom were royalty). If he was good enough to stay at Balmoral, he was good enough for Betty, too, and Polly watched in astonishment as her mother-in-law's frosty manner melted into what was, for her, warmth. Was that all it took? she thought. Guy (who had told her earlier an exceedingly funny story about his terror of having his underpants washed by hand by the Queen's staff, and his vain efforts to conceal them) was now solemnly assuring Betty that yes, the Queen liked roses, too.

'Now a lady with real class, like yourself,' she heard him say, 'you're really made for misty blues and pinks, and your garden should reflect that. A garden should be a background for your looks. Of course, without seeing your house on Rhode Island I couldn't say—'

'You must come,' said Betty, placing her taloned hand, with its enormous diamond ring, on his possessively. 'I insist. After all, a friend of dear Theo's . . .'

Who could blame Guy for being charming to someone who was so obviously loaded? This was the way rich people got their way, of course, by offering you things you couldn't afford and never even knew you might like, as long as you were nice to them. He was so funny and warm and entertaining that sometimes, just sometimes, Polly wondered what it would be like to stroke those furry ears. But these were not the kind of thoughts that anyone married to Theo had a right to think. In any case, there was something curiously asexual about Guy, which was why, no doubt, she felt so comfortable in his company.

'Come on, darlings, we don't want to miss the ferry back,' Polly called. The sun was now sinking into the far shore of the lake, and she didn't want them getting too tired. They giggled and took no notice. She began to repeat her request, varying the tone and volume in the hope that it would eventually get through. A small wind hissed through the reeds.

259

Tania, Bron and Robbie thought it was a great game to ignore her until suddenly, Tania began to shriek.

'Something's biting me, something's biting!'

She ran out of the water, scratching, and a moment later, Bron and Robbie joined their wails to hers.

'There's nothing there,' Polly told them, after a hasty inspection.

'Yes, there is, there is, there's insects all over me and they're biting,' sobbed Tania. She bundled a swimming towel round herself and howled. Bron and Robbie howled too, and then, to Polly's relief, Hemani appeared at a run.

'What's wrong?'

'Insects, they say. I can't see a thing.'

Neither could Hemani, but when they escorted the sobbing children into the village they were told that it was possible as there were tiny midges living in the lake, and occasionally they bit swimmers. It all sounded most improbable ('Bet it's pollution,' said Hemani) but more credible than Tania's insistence that they were inflicted by invisible people.

'Why should anyone punish you?' Polly asked.

'Because of what Robbie did,' said Tania, though what this was, she wouldn't say.

It was a thoroughly dispirited party that took the ferry back to Passignano. Betty and Guy were still discussing their extensive mutual acquaintance, while the children fought to spread a soothing cream over their itching limbs. Daniel was mystified by the way that Ellen kept giving him nasty looks if he got close to her. Ivo was desperate not to be left alone with either Ellen or Hemani. Ellen couldn't still be drunk, could she? he wondered, seeing her catch his eye and lick her lips. No, it was more likely that she had devised a new way of humiliating him. The whole thing was a put-up, and the moment he responded or took it at face-value, she'd turn on him again and say, What, you really thought for one moment I'd fancy you? Ivo, the man of whom single women remarked to each other, when desperately flicking through their address books for possible partners, 'Well, there is always Ivo Sponge.'

Ivo had long ago accepted that he was never going to be anything other than a joker in the pack. Most of the time, he didn't care. His good nature and capacity for generosity were aspects of himself that he kept hidden, as if they were something to be ashamed of, which in the world he inhabited was probably wise. He enjoyed playing the trickster and the villain, and occasionally these roles reaped him unexpected rewards, both professionally and sexually. But it was remarkably unpleasant to be pawed like that, thought Ivo, staring unseeingly as the lake shimmering beneath them. Had she been teaching him some weird, post-feminist lesson? And what about Hemani? He'd fancied her, of course, but now she was positively throwing herself at his feet, it was quite another matter.

Hemani herself was bewildered by the passion she felt for Ivo. A sensation, almost like fever, had taken possession of her. No sooner had she given herself permission to go to bed with him than it seemed she could not stop imagining what it would be like, in details so precise and anatomical that she was appalled. They filled her with desire or, rather, made her even more aware of how achingly she desired to be filled by him, so that even the faint thrum of the ferry's engines made her gasp and shudder and press herself against her seat.

I must be going mad, a part of her thought, in wonder. I don't fancy him, I don't trust him – and yet, when she remembered how he had kissed her, and how she had kissed him back, and how large and male and surprisingly, pleasingly firm he had felt, she blushed. His copper curls glowing in the setting sun, the glint of stubble on his chin and cheeks, the fullness of his lips and even the slight paunch round his middle all suggested the insatiable sensuality of a satyr. Ivo, sensing her gaze, lifted an eyebrow, which only made matters worse. She thanked heaven for the invention of sunglasses, and sat tight, counting the minutes until she could slip into his bed and relieve the unbearable hunger of her body.

Beside her, Ellen was also poised for immediate action. She remembered how she had suddenly realised that it was Ivo she really wanted. How he had, astonishingly, refused her. Or perhaps – and this was a shattering thought – perhaps he had never fancied her. All this time she had so foolishly indulged in a sort of game with him, in which he was the clumsy, ardent suitor and she the heart-free blonde, he could merely have been stringing her along after the disaster of their first date.

Ellen winced at the thought of it. She had been beside herself with fury, and why? Because the poor guy, left alone for ten minutes when she disappeared to freshen up, had been so overcome by jet-lag and champagne, he'd fallen asleep on the couch. For this, she had been mortally insulted. If any of her friends knew that Ivo Sponge – Ivo, for whom sexual failure was like catnip – had passed out even before she got down to her underwear, she would be a laughing stock too. So she had mocked him and sneered and never lost an opportunity to be unkind, and now she realised that Ivo was the one man in the world who would never bore her. Why had she looked at Daniel for a single second? Sure, he was great-looking, just like his brother, but who gave a shit about a perfect profile when the lights were out?

'Ivo?' said Ellen.

'What?'

'Ivo, would you mind very much if I sat next to you? The sun's bothering me.'

'We could swap places,' said Ivo, grumpily.

'Oh, no, I'm sure you don't need to. There!' She snuggled into him.

'Ellen, don't.'

'Why not? Don't you like me any more?'

'Not when you're behaving like this, no. Ellen, this is beyond a joke, hands off—'

'Ivo?'

'I'm reciting the seven times table. Go away.'

Ellen leant close and under Hemani's furious gaze whispered, 'Ivo, how about I do something to relieve this?'

'I'd really rather you left me in peace.'

'You don't look at all comfortable,' said Hemani, solicitously.

'I've got stuck on six sevens.'

'Forty-two,' she said promptly. 'Bron always does too.'

To Ivo's immense relief, the ferry had arrived. He sprang up.

'I say, Daniel old boy, would you mind if I sat next to you in the car? Touch of the old *mal de mer*.'

'Sorry?'

'Sea-sickness,' said Ivo, and the sweatiness of his complexion convinced his friend he was telling the truth.

It took longer to get everyone settled in the car, but Polly didn't mind. It felt so normal to be back in the driving seat again instead of having to grit her teeth at Theo's handling of the wheel, she didn't mind having Betty next to her. Guy was there, helping her mother-in-law up, and the children, and then they were off back to Cortona and the Casa Luna again.

The children had stopped sobbing and scratching, and now they fell asleep.

'Too much sun and water,' said Guy, with his crinkly grin. 'My goodness, it's hot, isn't it? I wouldn't be surprised if it rains tonight.'

'Do you think?' said Polly, staring hopefully up at the sky. It had turned the colour of annealing copper, and there was a line of dark violet far away to the west, but otherwise there were no clouds. 'The countryside certainly needs it.'

Heat choked them, and up in the hills it was little better. Even the cicadas seemed muted, fearful. Polly woke the children, who were fretful and resented being disturbed and made to eat supper and take showers.

'Why don't you all have an early night?' Hemani suggested,

in a voice trembling with suppressed eagerness. Yawning, the children agreed. Before the sun had set, they were tucked up in bed, docile, tame, asleep.

'Thank God for that,' said Polly. 'I really couldn't have taken another battle.'

She went into the kitchen, opened the fridge, and then leant her head against the open frame.

'You've had a long day, Pol, love,' said Guy. 'Let someone else take over.'

'There isn't anything much to eat except odds and ends,' said Polly.

Unexpectedly, Betty cleared her throat. 'Why don't you go out to a restaurant? I'm pretty bushed, and I don't mind staying.'

'But Theo isn't here,' said Polly, stupidly.

Daniel said, 'If Mother is willing to hold the fort, we'd all be happy to take you.'

'Excellent idea!' said Ivo. He had been wondering how to get through the next few hours unmolested, after locking himself in the bathroom. At least Ellen and Hemani would be forced to behave with more propriety in public. 'We could book at that place above the piazza in Cortona.'

'If you like,' said Polly doubtfully. She'd had a long day, and would really have liked to stay at home, being looked after and cooked for by somebody else, but this was too much to hope for. 'Are you sure this is all right?'

'The kids won't even know you're gone.'

Polly went up to check. They were still sleeping peacefully, the *spiralette* to keep mosquitoes away glowing a faint red dot in each room. It was unbearably stuffy, so she opened the windows and shutters.

'You will tell them I'll be back soon, won't you?' she said anxiously, unable to believe that Betty was finally babysitting her grandchildren. 'If one of them starts to run a temperature, there's a bottle of Calpol, you know, like Tylenol, by my bed. Oh, and check they all have water in their glasses.'

'I have raised three children of my own,' said Betty.

'Look, this is the number of the restaurant,' said Polly. 'You will check on them, won't you?'

'Sure,' said Betty. 'They're the only grandchildren I have. Why shouldn't I?'

Everyone showered and changed with particular care. The men shaved and put on the least crumpled of their shirts, and both Ellen and Hemani put on dresses. Even Polly looked less dowdy. Unable to be friendly to each other, Hemani lent her a top and Ellen insisted on applying her make-up.

'I really don't recognise myself,' she said, surprised, but Ellen said, 'You should do this every day, Polly. I'd forgotten you were so pretty.'

'Theo never seems to notice what I do and don't wear, though,' said Polly.

'Oh yeah? Well, he may find you sexy in sack-cloth and ashes, but you won't find yourself so,' said Ellen. 'You owe this to yourself. Promise me you'll do it more often?'

'Well . . .' said Polly. 'I might, I suppose.'

Then they set off, for the second time that day, in Polly's car because Daniel's was too cramped for two more adults – much to Ivo's relief.

'So romantic,' said Ellen. 'I love that the sky goes lavender here, even if lavender is so over.'

'I hardly think nature observes the latest fashions,' said Hemani.

'Well, I heard Guy saying pampas grass is the new black,' said Ellen.

Daniel sighed. When he heard Ellen say things like that, he really wondered what they had in common. Nevertheless, having steeled himself to do it, he was determined today was the day. Now, screw your courage to the sticking-point, he told himself sternly. He'd meant to propose on the island, but somehow there'd always been other people about. Ivo was sticking to Ellen like a burr, completely ignoring poor Hemani. What was it about women that they seemed to forgive and forget passes made at them, whereas it was the times you didn't make a move that really irked?

Perhaps that was why Ellen was mad at him now. As the car rounded the ascending bends to take them up to Cortona, he reached out, and patted Ellen's hand. Irritably, she shook his off. At once he felt even more foolish, making a gesture like that. He wasn't an old man, was he?

It was great to be going someplace without the children, though. Maybe marriage and kids weren't such a great idea if getting away from them, just for a couple of hours, made you feel so light and airy, like a helium balloon without a tether. Never had this town seemed as lovely as it did now, silhouetted against a sky that was turning the deepest blue, and the trees along the parterre crackling and acrid with dust and noise suddenly full of shadows, of mystery.

Daniel caught up with Hemani, who had fallen behind to prise a pebble out of her sandal. She was swearing softly, under her breath.

'Here, need a hand?'

'Oh. Thanks.'

She was flustered, and at once the memory of what she had felt like in his arms flared up in his consciousness. He said awkwardly, 'I'm glad Polly asked you.'

Hemani, steadier now, looked up in surprise.

'Are you?'

She was not wearing her glasses this evening. It was strange, seeing her eyes, so large and soft, without the usual barrier. He could see his own reflection, infinitely small, in them, and the miniature brightness of the street lamps, and even smaller specks that were swallows or bats. A whole world within a world, he thought, foolishly, and suddenly his ears were ringing. It was the town bells striking nine.

'Yes, yes. I am,' he said.

Hemani shrugged.

'Thanks,' she said, indifferently.

Daniel was surprised how hurt he felt. He was accustomed to her looking at him in a way that was more friendly. He didn't know what to make of the Hemani who was clearly impatient not to be with him. Well, of course, he thought, she probably wants to walk with Ivo. The idea made him feel strange. Ivo was his friend, and yet so was Hemani, and the concept of them together, instead of making him happy, caused a weird boiling, churning sensation.

Probably hunger, he decided. Or else anxiety, because, frankly, he didn't think someone as gentle and, well, fine as Hemani should be dating a slippery character like Ivo.

Ellen was flirting with Ivo quite shamelessly. Hemani, too, had observed this with what looked like real anger.

'Don't you mind?' she asked.

'It's OK,' said Daniel. 'Ellen's just trying to wind me up, I guess. I'm going to ask her to marry me.'

'Oh!' Hemani stopped and turned to him. She stared, then said, 'Congratulations. I'm sure you'll both be very happy.'

'If she accepts.'

'Of course she will. I know she's been . . .'

Hemani could not continue. She had never disliked Ellen, or anyone, so much as in that moment. Yet Daniel was probably right, Ellen was merely playing a game. She'd always been good at stringing men along. 'Your mother will be pleased,' she said, after a pause.

Daniel felt a sense of dread descend on him.

'Yes,' he said.

'I expect this means you'll be giving up your job in London, then,' said Hemani, not quite knowing what she was saying.

'I hadn't thought about it,' he said, lying.

'Well, I'll – I'll just take Ivo off your hands and leave the field clear, shall I?' said Hemani. She felt trapped between a sense of anguish for Daniel, being so deceived, and her own desire. She had never been more conscious of being different from Ellen than now.

Before, when she had counted Ellen as a friend, she had never resented her good looks. Hemani had her own charms and her own confidence, the confidence of having made a career for herself and won the respect of her peers against many odds. It had never crossed her mind to feel rivalrous or inferior, when their two worlds were so different. Now, though, it was another matter.

Straw doll, she thought fiercely to herself. Beanpole! Ellen might have legs to die for, but she had tiny breasts, and her hair was so thin that it was pathetic. Surely Ivo, a man of the senses if ever she saw one, could not possibly prefer this?

Yet a mixture of pride and perturbation at her own feelings made Hemani hang back. She had learnt to discipline herself in such circumstances, and it was not altogether clear that Ivo was not welcoming Ellen's behaviour. Of course, he was the sort of man who'd jump on any woman, according to reputation. Hemani could hardly wait for him to try again with her, and yet she had to preserve some dignity. It had been dreadfully hard with Bruce, of course, because there was no aphrodisiac like learning you had been betrayed. She had been privately quite beside herself on discovering about Georgie, even if Bruce had moved out a year or more before, and now she supposed the same thing must be happening with Ivo. The more Ellen flirted with him, the more furiously Hemani longed for him. She had never been more conscious of all the soft and yielding places of her body, of her own scent and moisture. Why didn't I let him seduce me the day he kissed me? she thought. Nothing would have been easier.

Although her fastidious nature disliked the idea of going to bed with him when other people were about, what was the point of being chaste?

Polly, walking behind with Guy, watched as Hemani caught up with Ivo.

'Now, there's something I can feel proud of,' she said to him.

'You've got your Mother Hen expression on,' he said, grinning.

'Well, I was rather hoping for a spot of successful match-making, you know,' said Polly. 'And it looks as if it's come off. Look, Daniel and Ellen, and Hemani and Ivo.'

'Are you sure?'

'Pretty sure,' said Polly. 'Ellen's been keen on Danny for ages, she practically begged me to invite her to stay, and Hemani really needs a chap. Not that I'd trust Ivo further than I can throw him,' she added, 'but single mothers do have a hard time.'

'Do they?'

'Oh, yes. You never get invited out as one, apparently.'

'Would you mind that very much?' Guy asked. 'If Theo left you, say?'

Polly laughed nervously. 'Oh, of course. Although I go out so little as it is, I probably wouldn't notice ... I'd mind it more for the children, actually.'

'Even if they hardly see him?'

'Why, yes,' said Polly doubtfully. 'Theo's such a good father. He – he –' Polly racked her brains to think of something her husband had actually done for Tania and Robbie.

271

He had turned up for the interviews to get them into prep school, of course, although she doubted he now even knew where the schools were. 'He takes them swimming, sometimes, you know. Oh, and helps them to find things on the Internet.'

Guy gave his strange, braying laugh.

'That doesn't sound so different from my own dad,' he said. 'Basically, he can't be buggered.'

'Oh, he did change one or two nappies,' said Polly. 'But I suppose we have a very conventional marriage. That's what we both wanted, you see.'

'Was it? Why?'

'Well, I was really quite desperate to get married,' said Polly. 'I knew I wanted children, and I wasn't really that interested in having a career, unlike my own mother. She had three of us, but she wasn't really very involved, because she was always dashing off to give papers on feminism, so I rather reacted against that because I could see that it might be as important to make sure we all went off with breakfast inside us and a vest. And Theo, he wanted to get married too. I was awfully surprised when he asked me, because I know he went out with tons of other girls before . . . much prettier and richer and so forth. And he is so successful, and clever, and handsome.'

'You thought your prince had come,' said Guy.

'Well, yes,' said Polly, blushing because this phrase always struck her as indecent. 'I am most awfully conscious of my luck,' she added. 'I never expected to be living with someone who makes so much money. I keep feeling it's like a dream, and that I'll wake up one day to find none of it is true, but so far, touch wood, I haven't. So all I try to do to deserve it is to look after him and the children, and keep everything running smoothly.'

'What a nice woman you are,' said Guy. He was looking at her with the oddest expression.

'Oh, not really,' said Polly hurriedly. 'I'm completely ordinary, and sometimes I do get fearfully ratty and resentful, inside, at least. Not of Theo, of course, but of his job, and his mother, and the children too. I do sometimes wonder whether he needs to work quite so hard, when he's already made partner. I don't really like London, or New York. I'd love to live somewhere like here, but that's an impossible dream.'

They had arrived in the main piazza, and were climbing the short, steep slope to the restaurant above it. The Loggetta was a much smarter affair than the humble trattoria and pizzeria they had visited before, and had a view of the clock tower, and its ascending stone steps, on which the students of Athens, Georgia, sketched or lolled or gossiped. In the square itself, other children darted and shrieked although the sky was now quite dark. A waiter took their orders, and then they waited.

'What a pity Theo can't be here,' said Daniel.

'Yes, isn't it? Still, there are other places – if he gets back in time. I do hope the children are still asleep,' said Polly.

'Bound to be,' said Hemani. 'I used to worry terribly about leaving Bron, I'd drive my mother crazy when I was on call. You men are so lucky, not to have these concerns.'

273

'Lucky?' said Ivo. 'I spend my life watching coloured shadows on a piece of canvas or people in bodystockings writhing about on stage pretending they're in a suburban orgy.'

'And I being one of those shadows,' said Guy, 'when what I'd really like to do is grow things.'

'Would you?' said Polly. 'Then why don't you? What's stopping you giving it all up?'

'Well, there is a small thing called earning a living,' said Ivo.

'Yes, but how much do you really need? How much do any of us? We all have so much,' said Polly. 'Cars and washing machines and clothes, and hardly any of it is really necessary.'

'See? I told you,' said Ivo solemnly. 'One of us is going to chuck it all in to grow organic wine.'

'No, no, of course not!' said Polly. 'I'm not so silly, and beside, there's the children's schooling and real life waiting to resume, but—'

'It's different for me,' said Hemani. 'I really love what I do. Even the simple things, like removing cataracts, make such a difference to people's lives.'

'So do movies, though,' said Daniel. 'Those coloured shadows, Ivo, are much more than that. Whose life hasn't been made richer, deeper, more complex or more tolerable by spending ninety minutes watching them?'

'If you saw the dross—'

'Yes, but that's why we need you, to tell us what is dross and what isn't,' said Ellen. 'Of course you're going to be wrong some of the time – and personally, by the way, I completely adored Russell Crowe in that leather skirt – but how else would we know what to see?'

'Critics are like stopped clocks,' said Ivo gloomily. 'We can always be relied on to get it right twice a day. I've praised some abysmal trash in my time, and completely failed to spot the one really good writer of my generation. At least with films it doesn't matter so much, because of the marketing budgets.'

'And most of the time you strike either twelve or one,' said Ellen, as the town clock tolled. 'But we'd still rather have you than not.'

'Well, thank you for that unexpected tribute,' said Ivo. 'I do, however, know I'm the scum of the earth – alongside lawyers, politicians and TV stars.'

'The scum of the earth could also be described as the cream of the crop,' said Hemani, teasing.

'The fat of the land.'

'Well, I certainly admit to that,' said Ivo. 'Where's my dinner?'

They waited for it, drinking more wine than they had intended, looking down on the passing Vespas, the other tourists like themselves, the local people. The feeling of well-being that Italy bestows, almost casually, on visitors crept through their limbs as they ate and drank. The air, stifling before, seemed cooler now and the full moon sailed up into the sky, filling it with silvery radiance. When they walked back towards the car, they felt refreshed and energetic again.

'Do you know,' said Daniel casually, 'this moon is so bright, I think I could walk home. I've jogged it often enough not to get lost. Anyone want to come too?'

There was a pause.

'Ellen?' he said.

'That's an excellent idea,' said Ivo, suddenly. He was thinking that a mild adventure of this kind was just what was needed in order to restore his friendship with Daniel and get away from the women. 'If you want company, that is?'

Daniel shrugged and smiled. Of course he wanted Ellen to himself, but he was too polite to say so.

'Girls and boys come out to play, the moon is shining as bright as day,' said Ellen. 'Sure.'

Hemani thought, just for a moment, of what walking a mile in her flimsy sandals on rough country lanes would do, then said, 'I'm on.'

'Well, I'm not,' said Guy. 'I want to get back to bed.'

'I almost wish I could come too,' said Polly, 'but I don't think Guy would manage to remember the roads, would you? And besides, the car is only insured for Theo and me.'

In fact, she was worried about leaving the children any longer with only Betty to look after them. In London they always had her mobile number, but her mobile didn't work here and she had a feeling of unease that, however irrational, deepened with every passing minute. It was foolish of her, she knew, to be anxious. What harm could possibly come to them, tucked up in bed in the Italian countryside? Scorpions, she thought; they could get bitten. She had forgotten to yank back their bedclothes and check, as she did every night. She imagined Robbie getting stung on the neck, and his neck swelling up in seconds so he was unable to breathe, sobbing with terror, pleading for her, and Betty telling him not to be silly . . .

All the same, when she got into the car with Guy and saw the other four setting off along the long avenue to walk in the moonlight, it was hard not to feel envious.

'Pity I didn't bring my own car,' said Guy. 'You sure about this?'

'Are you sure you don't want to join them yourself?'

'No,' he said. 'I'm expecting a call. I might have to take off again tomorrow.'

'But you've hardly spent any time here at all!' cried Polly, swerving to avoid a driver who, like so many Italians, believed it was proper to overtake on a bend.

'Shame really,' said Guy. 'Still, you seem to be coping admirably on your own.'

'Only because I have to,' said Polly. She felt a pang of disappointment.

'What about all those claims that a woman needs a man like a fish needs a bicycle?' he asked.

'Well, I've always thought that a pretty stupid joke,' said Polly. 'Because men and women do exist in the same element, unlike fish and bicycles, even if we often perceive it differently. I haven't had a single swim in the pool, you know,' she added.

'Why not?'

'I don't know. Silly of me, because I'm longing to. I suppose – I suppose I feel that if I relax and allow myself to enjoy it then nothing will get done. I'm like the Little Engine that Could,' said Polly. 'I can keep going as long as I don't deviate from the tracks. That probably doesn't make any sense to you, does it?'

Guy was silent a moment.

'No, I understand what you're describing very well,' he said. 'But, Polly, people aren't machines. They're not meant to live like that. They're alive, they're organic, they grow and develop in unexpected ways.'

'I'm not talking about how things are meant to be, I'm talking about how I survive,' said Polly. 'I tried to keep my job going, I really did, but it all became too much, and even this is too much, though it shouldn't be, just running a house and bringing up two children; it isn't as if I don't have money to help except it never seems to be enough, and it always boils down to me. So my way of coping is not to be like one of your plants, or perhaps to be more of an espaliered plum or a pleached lime. Oh, I do hope everything's all right back at the house.'

She was driving so fast now that the night-cheepings of the cicadas had become one continuous shrill in her ears. Gravel cracked and spat under her wheels. Here was the tiny hamlet at the bottom of the hill, the house with the dog running up and down on a wire, barking at every passer-by, the long straight drive between two walled estates, the slow, difficult climb that left cars coated with white dust. The MPV rocked and waddled over each hump of stone, forcing her to slow down. Up and up they went, grinding and slipping, and now the heat pressed down like a vice, seeming to throb like blood and cause all the trees to dance and jerk in the headlights.

'Sorry, sorry,' she muttered, revving the engine and wrestling with the wheel. 'It's easier when there are more passengers to stop it from bouncing about.'

'They'll be fine,' said Guy.

The Casa Luna appeared at last, its lights warm and yellow in the great furred darkness of the hills. Polly jumped out and ran to the door, opening it with her key and calling into the echoing living room, 'Hello? I'm back!'

There was no answer. Betty had fallen asleep in one of the armchairs, and when she ran upstairs to the children's rooms, their beds were empty. They were gone.

Chapter Twelve

~~~~

At first the road was straight and easy. They passed other couples, wandering out of town like themselves, kissing on the stone benches overlooking the Valdichiana or engaged in something more strenuous and steamy within the confines of a parked car. One aged Cinquecento was indeed rocking so violently that Ellen and Ivo caught each other's eye and giggled. This was a kind of no man's land, the link between the town and the countryside, and it made the prospect of walking by night seem picturesque. There were still people playing tennis in the floodlit courts at the end of the parterre, and the mosquito-like whine of Vespas, on which teenaged boys with the slanting eyes of fauns swooped and played. There were lines of cypress trees, and municipal waste-bins, there were thick iron chains and the sound of church bells.

Only when they had walked to the very edge of town, and stood on the brink of darkness did any of them hesitate, as if about to dive into a deep pool. The road curved down, faintly glimmering. On the hillside opposite, one or two lights shone like fallen stars.

'That one on the left must be our house,' said Ellen doubtfully.

'It isn't far,' said Daniel. 'I've run here and back every morning to get fresh bread.'

Nobody had thought to question where it had come from. How typical of him, thought Hemani, to do something like that and never mention it or seek praise.

'Come on,' said Ellen. 'At least it'll be something to remember about this holiday.'

'Don't you remember yours?' asked Hemani, faintly contemptuous.

'Oh, not really. The memories all blur into each other, and only something special stands out. Here, wait.'

She took out a pocket camera, and their eyes were dazzled by its flash.

'Now, take one of me with Ivo,' she told Daniel.

They paused for this, then set off down the road. Within minutes, the lights of the town were behind them, and the quiet noises and scents of the countryside were all around. Trees hissed faintly as they walked past, careful to pace themselves on the steeper inclines. Just before they came to the first farmhouse, Daniel turned off on to the verge.

'This is where things get tricky for a while, but it's worth it to avoid a psychotic dog,' he said.

They made their way through olive groves descending the hillside like a giant's steps, their legs prickled by long, stiff grasses. Sometimes, even with Daniel's knowledge, they became confused, seeking a way out of terraces that had no visible exit, and wandering along lines of wire-trained vines. As their eyes became accustomed to the light, it was possible to see shadows, sometimes bright, sometimes blurred, as wisps of cloud passed over the moon.

'Here,' said Daniel. 'You might need to go carefully now.' He turned to help the women climb down, but both preferred to cling to Ivo, who consequently lost his balance. There was a slithering, and a sound of curses. Daniel peered down.

'I've put my hand on a bloody cactus,' said Ivo.

'Maybe this isn't such a great idea,' said Daniel.

'Oh, no, having stepped in so far, etc., and besides, I'd still have a long wait if you had to walk all the way back to fetch the car. No, we're for it. Is it me, or is it becoming increasingly sultry?'

'I'm completely soaked,' said Hemani, and it was true, though how much was due to the weather and how much to her internal climate she was unsure. 'We should pair up, you know. The path is too narrow for more than two people at a time. Ivo, why don't you stay with me, so Ellen and Daniel can go ahead?'

Ellen agreed to this, though ungraciously. Since their quarrel on the ferry, the two women had hardly spoken, and even the beauty of the night had not lessened the antagonism between them.

'Do you think this was a bad idea? Coming away on holiday together?' she asked Ivo, once the Americans had pulled ahead.

'Depends. I'd never met you, so we didn't have anything to spoil.'

'But the others? I feel as if I've hardly spoken to Polly, and Ellen and I—'

'Ah, Ellen. Who can tell what goes on inside that lovely head?'

Impulsively, she said, 'Daniel's going to ask her to marry him, you know.'

'No, I didn't.' Ivo was silent for a moment. 'Well, it's what she wants. She'll accept, of course.'

'Of course.'

Their words fell with a sort of dull thud on each heart. Hemani was trembling slightly, from cold and also from the strangeness of what she was feeling. There was no point in stopping with him just now, she kept telling herself as they passed horses dozing in the starlight, a niche, another farm-house. The road was too narrow, flanked by high stone walls on one side and a deep ditch on the other, she must wait – wait.

Ivo, as he tramped along, found his mind, usually so busy and filled with schemes and stratagems, parallels and allu-sions, dismally emptied. So that was to be his perennial role, he thought: not the court jester but the fool. He was weary of it already, yet there seemed no prospect of escape. He had always had a sense of himself as a character, like most self-invented people, but it was only now that it occurred to him that it was not of his own choice and making.

'I'm sure they'll be happy,' said Hemani. 'They're pretty much made for each other, after all.'

'Do you think? Is that what marriage is for?' he said, irritably. '"And they all lived happily ever after." Well, we know the last part is a lie, and I suspect the first part is too.'

'So you wouldn't consider it yourself, ever?'

'I don't know about ever. In the right time, with the right person, in the right place, if I believed in miracles – but how long does love like that last, even supposing it comes about?'

'Have you never been in love, Ivo?'

'You are a shocking flirt to ask.'

'No, seriously.'

'Once or twice.'

'What happened?'

'I clasped her to my manly bosom and – well, let's just say it was a bit of a fiasco. The first was the worst. There was this Irish girl, Mary, and when I made my declaration I pranged my car and got knocked out by the air-bag. It would never have worked anyway. She was keen on someone else.'

Hemani laughed. 'You've been unlucky in love, then.'

'Oh, no, I've had plenty of girlfriends,' said Ivo. 'That's the weird thing. One minute, they look as if nothing could be further from their minds, the next, it's action stations and all hands on deck, so to speak.'

'I see,' said Hemani, slightly chilled by this way of speaking. If I sleep with Ivo, she thought, I'll become one of them. But how, rationally, could it be any other way?

Ahead, Ellen was fuming. She couldn't begin to say why she had suddenly gone off Daniel, but it had happened, and now she was astonished at how unappealing he was to her. They had shared the usual intimacies, and the memory made her hot with shame, an unaccustomed feeling made sharper by the unshakeable knowledge that Daniel was a nice man and one, moreover, whom she had pursued. Not that he had been unwilling, just so passive, somehow, as if allowing things to happen. Whereas Ivo had chased her, as he probably chased all girls, but at least there had been a sense of excitement. God, she thought, if I get him into bed we'll be dynamite. A guy with lips like that could do practically anything. He'd been a great kisser, she remembered, which was why she'd invited him back to her flat against all her better judgement.

'On such a night as this . . .' began Daniel.

'What?'

'I was just thinking, you know, that maybe we should, er, put this on a more formal basis.'

'What?' she said again, unable to think what he was on about. She really wanted to do an action replay of everything that had happened before Ivo had passed out, then thrown up, on their one and only date together. 'Look, are you sure we can really do this? I didn't realise the path was going to be quite so rocky.'

'The course of true love never did run smooth,' said Daniel.

'Puh-leese,' said Ellen, by now really irritated. 'Any moment now, I'm going to break a nail.'

It was true: it had been getting steadily more difficult to see where they were going. The hills, which had seemed so tame and well-cultivated from a distance, were full of unexpected folds and valleys, and now, as they slipped and tripped downwards, it was becoming evident to them both that they were lost. The groves and stone terraces had given way to thick shrubs, some prickly and others merely soft and heavy, like swathes of material that resisted when pushed aside. The ground had become softer, but curiously lumpy underfoot. The deeper they went, the darker it became, until Ellen, looking up to try and see where the lights of the Casa Luna had gone, saw dim shapes of leaves and boughs overhead.

'Oh!' she said. 'We're in a wood. No wonder we can't find our way. Honestly, Danny, this really wasn't such a great idea.'

Daniel thought it wisest not to quote Dante at this juncture. He was having some difficulty in keeping his own temper after being slapped in the eye by a branch. Thorough bush, thorough briar, he thought to himself. He was used to detaching his mind from his body, except when he was playing his cello, when the two miraculously flowed together. He stayed calm.

'It's just the wood below the house,' he said. 'We must be almost home.'

Yet the wood they found themselves in seemed vast, trackless, mysterious. The moon slipped out from behind a cloud again, and he saw massive oaks and chestnuts rising like columns. It was impossible to make out much more, though there was the sweet smell of bruised bracken from their forced passage. Everything was dappled, freckled, splashed, spattered, spangled, stippled, streaked and crazed with light and shadow, so that Daniel and Ellen, after groping forward, soon came to a halt.

'Oh, hell,' said Ellen. 'This is just perfect.'

'Careful,' said Daniel. 'I can hear water. There's a sheer drop into a pool somewhere about. If we can just find the bridge across it, I'll know where we are.'

But the sound of water, though it never left them, did not come any closer. Sometimes a sleepy bird, disturbed from its slumber, would fly away screeching and clattering, and once a white owl floated silently past, causing Ellen to gasp and clutch her companion. After what seemed like at least an hour of forcing their way over boulders and through undergrowth, they emerged into a grassy space. The moon shone directly down into it, with a light so strong it was no surprise to see that the ground was thickly sprinkled with small white flowers, open like stars. The trickling sound of water tormented.

'I'm too tired to go on looking for a way out without a rest,' said Ellen. 'This heat makes me feel quite faint. I really could do with a drink of water.'

'Sit down, then,' said Daniel. His own lips and mouth were dry as well, though whether from heat or apprehension he couldn't tell.

'But what if there are snakes?' asked Ellen.

'They don't come out at night,' said Daniel. He saw her profile, and felt the mild stirring of desire. 'If you're worried, you could come closer.'

'No,' said Ellen, briskly. 'I had enough of alfresco sex at summer camp, thanks. Anyway, I have a headache. Do you think Ivo's far behind?'

'Sure,' said Daniel. 'But, er, Ellen? Have you given any further thought to what I said?'

'About what?' said Ellen, yawning. She batted at the insects that she could see hovering in the moonlight. They hummed sleep in her ears, and she felt her eyelids closing. 'Oh, heck.'

Daniel, too, yawned, but his courteous mind was preoccupied with the problem of his proposal, so he began, 'Well, it would make Mother very happy if – it would make me happy too, that is – I mean, I don't know if you've thought about it at all, but I don't see why, all things considered, we shouldn't give a shot at seeing, er, Ellen?'

The sound of regular breathing was carried on a faint breeze. For some reason that he could not begin to understand, a sense of relief welled up in him. He stretched himself out beside her on the mossy turf, and in seconds he, too, fell asleep.

The children had been woken by the moonlight. It shone so brightly into each room that, for a moment, Tania thought it must be morning, and sprang out of bed. Only when she looked out of the window and saw the night sky, with its swirling constellations so big and bright they really did look like something from Claire's Accessories, did she realise her mistake. She turned, and saw the People. They were there, dancing, the eyes in their pale faces glowing like fireflies, their long pale green hair flowing. Their slender forms were sprinkled with pin-points of light, and they were laughing, beckoning to her.

As soon as they saw she'd seen them, they swirled into a hundred specks, and flew out of her window, where they hovered, waiting.

'I'm coming,' she whispered.

Gathering her precious potion in its bottle, she ran into the boys' room.

'Wake up, wake up,' she whispered, but they needed no telling.

'Can you hear the music?' Bron whispered back.

'Yes. We have to go outside.'

Both boys accepted this without question. In London, the idea would never have occurred to them, but here, they had lived outdoors so long that it held no terrors. They paused only to put on their sandals.

'How can we get out, though?' said Bron. 'Your gran's downstairs.'

'There's a stair outside,' squeaked Robbie. The other two hushed him, afraid he'd alert Betty, but there was no sound, other than the faint thrum of the ceiling fan. 'We can get out up here.'

It was true, and within minutes they were out, and down, pattering through the garden like shadows, following the drifting specks of brilliance, until they had melted into the shadows themselves.

'It's no good,' said Hemani, peering through the darkness. 'I've absolutely no idea where we are. I can't even see the light of the Casa.'

'Oh blast. Trust Daniel not to be able to see the wood for the trees,' said Ivo. 'I hope they're all right.'

'Should we call?'

They each felt self-conscious about doing this, but they

called, and it seemed to do no good. Although the moon still shone brightly there was a strange muffled feeling to the air.

'There's rain coming,' said Ivo.

'Oh dear,' said Hemani, moving closer, and shivering. She wasn't cold, quite the opposite. She wanted to wrap her legs around his waist like one of those smiling women on temple walls – she could think of nothing but that.

'Why do girls never wear jackets?' said Ivo, resignedly. 'Not that it doesn't have interesting side-effects,' he added, looking down at her breasts.

Hemani turned her face up to his. She waited, then opened her eyes. Ivo was looking down at her with an odd expression.

'What is going on, really?'

'I don't know what you mean.'

'I think you do. You've been giving me the brush-off every day for nearly two weeks, and then you both suddenly decide that I'm the flavour of the month, is that it?'

'No,' said Hemani. 'I just thought, I decided, that is—'

'Look,' said Ivo, 'you mustn't take this personally, but I can't, I really can't . . .'

Hemani reached out her soft, slim hand.

'Ivo, please, please, it isn't a tease. I've been so pure, so good, for years and years and when you kissed me it woke something up again and now, I—'

'You know,' said Ivo in an angry voice, 'this is just landscape and moonlight and too much wine. It's a cliché, and a rotten one at that. It isn't you, Hemani.'

The light dimmed.

'Whatever it is,' said Hemani, half-crying, half-laughing, 'why not accept it? You wanted me three days ago, what's different now? Oh Ivo, I've got so much love, I can't pour it all into my son, it isn't all meant for him, it isn't good for him, it's against all my principles to behave like this and speak like this. I don't know what has come over me but however unreal, it's true. Ivo?'

All she could hear was a crackling of undergrowth, and when the moon came out again, Hemani was alone.

Polly had raced round the house, calling and yanking open cupboard doors in room after empty room. How she could speak or move was a miracle because she felt that at any moment she would vomit up her heart. At last, she went over to her mother-in-law and grasped her thin shoulder so hard that Betty woke with a start.

'Where are they?' she shouted, her voice harsh and loud. 'Answer me!'

'What? Who?'

'My children,' said Polly. 'Your precious grandchildren, who you were supposed to be looking after. They've gone. Where are they?'

Betty put a hand to her throat.

'I don't know,' she said, dazed. 'Are you sure?'

Polly raised her own hand, as if to strike, and Guy put an arm round her shoulder, silently.

'Of course I'm sure. I've looked and looked. Their beds are empty. They've just – vanished.'

Guy went up the stairs. When he came down he said,

'You're right. The top door to the outside staircase is open. I think they got out that way.'

'Got out – or were taken?' said Polly. 'My God, do you think they've been kidnapped? I thought all that sort of thing was over in this country.'

'Got out, I think. I couldn't see their sandals. Is there a torch in the house?'

'In the kitchen,' said Polly. She looked down at Betty, who was immobile. 'Don't just sit there,' she screamed, 'do something, you silly, selfish old woman! For once in your life, pull your bloody finger out!'

She had never, ever spoken to anyone like this, least of all Betty. All the hatred, the resentment, the contempt in her had ignited and was blazing fiercely, consuming the spell of silence or inertia that had kept her docile and obedient all the years of her marriage to Theo. Why was I so afraid of her? she wondered, seeing Betty quail and shrivel, but there was no time to think about it, she was running to the broom cupboard and fumbling for the big black torch.

'I'll look in the garden,' said Guy. 'You come too. If we don't find them in ten minutes, you should call the police.'

There was no other torch, so Polly, in desperation, lit a candle in a jar, one of the ones that had illuminated so many dinners under the pergola, and ran out. The garden had become full of sinister shadows, of burglars and murderers and headless bears. She, like Guy, ran first to the swimming pool to check if there were any bodies in it, and her relief at finding none was replaced by the fresh fear that they had indeed been kidnapped, and worse, not even for money. There had been so many cases of this happening in the English countryside, why not the Italian? Why had it never occurred to her to lock the upstairs door? What would she say to Meenu, when she returned from her walk? It was like a nightmare, running in the dark clammy heat, every bush a child's fallen body, every thorn the claw of some wild beast that was even now devouring them. Her mind was full of hateful fantasies. She remembered the squirming haunches of the boar, and what Guy had said about their tusks. What if Robbie had been spitted on one? What if Tania had fallen down and broken her neck? What if they were captive in a van and being driven away together, to have the most terrible things of all done to them? Everything that had ever given her joy about her children – their beauty, their innocence, their sensitivity – now returned to torment her, so that she wished them big, ugly, aggressive, anything rather than defenceless and young.

'Tania! Robbie! Bron!' she called, and heard Guy's voice also shouting the same hopeless trio of names. In time, their voices were joined by those of others, for Betty had lost no time in telephoning the police, and soon the great dark hillside was covered with little floating points of light, which searched and did not find.

The children, meanwhile, were having a delightful time. Perfectly refreshed by their earlier slumbers, they were flitting from tree to tree, having squeezed through the iron gate at the bottom of the path. They knew it so well, they could have done it sleep-walking, which, in a sense, they were. They could all see the People, drifting and dancing in their midnight revels. It was wonderful to be free, away from the grown-ups, away from the rules and under the full moon. They capered and leapt, climbing trees and hanging from them upside-down, scuffing the thick dead leaves with their feet and playing at being wild things. Nothing alarmed them – not the small wild rabbits nibbling on grass, nor the hedgehog snuffling its way past an old fallen log, nor the fox poised, just for a second, far away with its brush standing out like a rudder from its body. They danced with the baby and the faun, they danced with the People and they danced with each other to the thin, high music of their dreams. The air was warmer than blood, and soon they had found their way down to the waterfall, where even now a thin trickle shimmered over the sheer, emerald-streaked rock into the deep pool below. There were no reeds by the waterside, only big flat rocks, encrusted with lichens and water-weed that shone faintly like precious stones.

'Let's do a wild rumpus,' said Robbie, throwing off his pyjama top. 'We can roar our terrible roar, and roll our terrible eyes.'

Tania dipped a toe in the water. She had lost one of her sandals, and not noticed. She shuddered deliciously.

'Shall we, Bron?'

Bron was about to say yes, because he'd seen a great strand of old man's beard hanging down, and he thought that if he caught hold of it, he could swing out over the pool like Tarzan, which would please him very much. But suddenly, he heard his mother's voice, calling.

'It's them,' Robbie said, snorting.

'Hide!' said Tania.

'Ivo!' called Hemani. 'Where are you? Wait for me!'

They heard her sighing, and swearing as she became caught on a thorn-bush, then blundering forward somewhere above. It was strange. She really didn't seem to be able to see where she was going, whereas they could see perfectly well. Bron put his finger to his lips, and beckoned the others to follow him. He didn't want to spy on his mother, exactly, but ever since he had found her being kissed by Ivo he had felt peculiar. He loved her so much, and he knew, in that strange, wise part of himself, that she needed another husband, but he couldn't quite see why it had to be Ivo.

The children, running along the mossy paths, made no sound but Hemani made plenty. They found this highly amusing, at least until Tania almost tripped over the sleeping bodies of her uncle and Ellen.

'Do you think they've been doing It?' asked Bron.

They all looked hopefully at the sleepers.

'Nah,' said Robbie. 'Shall we try waking them up?'

'They'd only make us go back to bed,' said Tania. 'Grown-ups always spoil our fun, don't they?'

'They're not very happy,' said Bron. 'Funny how they spend so much time fighting.'

The three children inspected each body.

'If we had chocolate, we could stuff some in their mouths to see if they're still alive,' said Robbie, remembering one Easter morning when he had experimented with this on his parents.

'Have you still got that potion?'

'Yes,' said Tania. She fished it out of her pocket, and Bron looked at the bottle with respect.

'If you put some on your uncle's lips, do you think it'll work?'

''Course,' said Robbie. 'It did last time.'

'Yes, but on the wrong people, dunderhead. Look, if we give him some now, he'll wake up, see Ellen and then it'll all be fine.'

Dubiously, Tania unstoppered the bottle and let a drop fall on Daniel's dry lips. He stirred, licked them, and parted his mouth. She was able to pour a little more in.

'That should do it. We don't want to use it all,' she whispered. 'Now we should wake him up.'

At that moment, Ivo, very much the worse for wear, stumbled into the glade, followed by Hemani. Instantly, the children hid.

'Stop, stop,' she cried. 'I need to catch my breath.'

'If you catch your breath, you'll catch me,' said Ivo. 'I'd sooner keep my trousers on.'

'Why so cold and unkind?' said Hemani. 'Ivo, look at me.'

'I'm going on alone,' said Ivo, 'and if you follow me I won't be responsible.'

He thrust her off him even as her fingers were creeping round him like ivy.

'Beast!' muttered Hemani. 'Pig! How dare you – oh! What's that? Who is it?'

She had stubbed her foot against Daniel, who opened his eyes, and sat up.

'Hemani!' he said.

Above them, the children giggled, and clutched one another. Robbie mimed a swooning effect. Bron put his finger over his lips.

Daniel looked dazed with sleep. He looked up at Hemani, standing there in the moonlight, then across at Ellen, then back again.

'It's you!' he said, surprised.

'Of course it's me,' said Hemani. 'What other idiot do you think you could get wandering about a wood in the middle of the night?'

'Hemani,' Daniel said. 'Goddess, nymph, of face and form divine. My mogul diamond from the spiced East.'

'Oh dear,' muttered Tania. 'He wasn't supposed to see her.'

'Pardon?' said Hemani.

Daniel declaimed,

> *'Reason becomes the marshal to my will,*
> *And leads me to your eyes, where I o'erlook*
> *Love's stories written in love's richest book.'*

Hemani said impatiently, 'Daniel, this simply isn't the right time for dropping quotations. We're all lost.'

'Lost! As if a man could not get lost in eyes like yours, yes, and drown, too,' said Daniel, clasping her round her knees.

'What on earth are you doing?' said Hemani, shocked. She detached his hands from her waist with an effort. He was so much bigger and stronger than she was, and she was slightly frightened.

'Daniel, have you forgotten that you were going to ask

Ellen to marry you only a couple of hours ago? You're getting us mixed up.'

He gave a howl.

'I had you mixed up before, don't you see? You're the one, you are, you.'

'Well, I'm sorry to tell you that in that case you've missed your chance,' said Hemani tartly. 'It's Ivo I fancy now.'

'What?' cried Daniel. 'That half-assed, two-timing son-of-a-bitch? That miserable hack? How can you possibly fancy him?'

The children, perched in the tree, stuffed their night-clothes into their mouths to muffle their snickers.

'*You* got it wrong this time,' said Robbie, stolidly. 'Told you.'

As Polly sat frozen with terror on the sofa, yet another car drew up.

'What the heck is going on?' asked Theo. He came into the living room, blinking and ruffled. Polly flew to his arms. 'Why are the police here?'

In a dry, cracked voice, Polly explained.

'The worst of it is that Dan and Ellen and the rest don't know yet. They're walking home from Cortona. They should have been here hours ago, so maybe they're lost, too.'

'There's no way they could have got home before you?'

'Not a chance. Guy and I came back right away in the car. I had a feeling, you see.'

'Where is Guy?'

'Out on the hillside, searching.'

Theo dropped his computer case, which he had been clenching.

'I'll go too.'

Polly said, 'Oh darling, I'm so glad you're here.'

Theo kissed her on the forehead, while pushing her away. 'Why aren't you out looking?'

Polly said, 'I have to stay, in case they come back.'

'Why can't Mother do that?'

'Your mother is the reason why this has all happened,' said Polly, her fury boiling up again. 'She was supposed to be babysitting but she fell asleep.'

Theo looked at his mother, and she gave him a tiny, apologetic shrug.

'Could've happened to anyone.'

'No matter,' he said, abruptly. 'I'll go see if one of the policemen has a spare torch.'

They had, and soon Theo too was going down through the garden. He couldn't believe they weren't somewhere close, though in his anxiety he told himself that this might just as well be wishful thinking. He hadn't really explored all the levels of the surrounding terraces, being on the whole incurious, and when he came to the bottom of the garden and found the gap in its walls leading on to the sunken lane, his breathing quickened. This was exactly the sort of place Tania and Robbie would love as a secret den. His flashlight was powerful and steady in his hand as he crunched over the leaves.

Then he reached the end of the lane, and heard a metallic noise. Guy was wrestling with the chain on a pair of large gates, his torch jammed into a hole in the wall.

'You think they're in there?' asked Theo.

'I can see something on the path. I think it's a child's sandal,' said Guy.

The two men stopped, and looked at each other.

'This is a bad situation.'

They looked at the gap between the two iron gates.

'They could squeeze through, but we can't.'

'Goddam. Is there any point trying to climb?'

Theo pointed his torch upwards, and saw there was not, though he didn't doubt that Polly would have tried. It was wreathed in barbed wire, festoons of it, sharp with rust and overgrown with creepers but still lethal. Guy had been trying to break the padlock with a rock. This was hopeless, evidently. Somewhere, my kids may be in there, lost and frightened, Theo thought, and the idea of Tania in particular with tears streaming down made him quite desperate. He thought of the times when he'd been alone and scared as a child, and it was unbearable to think of his children feeling like that. Theo did not often project himself into the felt reality of other people's lives. Nevertheless, he was surprised once again by how much he did love Tania and Robbie. He seized the gates, shaking them so that flakes of rust showered down. It was no good, but then he had an idea.

'How much do you press in the gym?'

'I don't go to the gym,' said Guy. 'But I'm pretty fit, as you know.'

'OK. Time for an executive decision. Let's see if we can lift this baby off its hinges,' said Theo.

Side by side, the two men heaved. Each felt an agonising, tearing sensation in his arms.

'Good job, keep going, we're doing great,' gasped Theo. 'One more.'

Then, as rust flaked away in a shower, the mass of ornamental iron was shifted, lifted, and suddenly fell sideways with a wrenching clash.

'Shall I run back and fetch a policeman?' asked Guy, panting.

Wordlessly, Theo shook his head, and picked up his torch.

'No. They might not be in here, after all, and, as a lawyer, I don't want to be prosecuted for trespass under some weird European diktat. Let's go by ourselves.'

'Lead on,' said Guy.

'I can't believe you're saying such nasty things about Ivo,' said Hemani. 'He's your friend.'

'Ha!' said Daniel. 'Some friend.' He glared at Ivo who, with his usual mastery of bad timing, had just crashed through into the glade. 'I found him trying to rape Ellen last night while she was practically unconscious.'

'What?' said Ivo. '*What?* What are you on about?' He looked round wildly. 'Of course I didn't. I told you before, she was drunk. If anything she was trying to rape me.'

'Oh, sure, and Elvis lives.'

Ivo opened his hands in a gesture of ruefulness.

'Not been getting enough of the old *amore* with you, I gather.'

'Now see here,' said Daniel, lumbering to his feet. 'What's

301

gone on between Ellen and myself is private, and should remain so, whatever your forked tongue says. In any case, the lady can't defend herself.'

'Where is she, then?' asked Ivo. 'For God's sake, Ellen!'

He darted forward, trying to peer into the shadows.

'She's over there,' said Daniel.

Ivo shook Ellen's shoulder.

'Ellen! Wake up! Wake up!'

Ellen's pale arms rose like two swans and suddenly pulled him down.

'Ivo, darling.'

Ivo disappeared into the shadows.

'See what I mean?' he gasped, a moment later. 'There's no holding her when she gets drunk.'

Hemani suddenly burst into tears of fury.

'Oh, I get it,' she said. 'It isn't enough for you to get Daniel in love with you, is it, Ellen? You have to have Ivo, too. Wasn't one of them enough?'

'You don't know what you're talking about,' said Ellen.

'Yes, I jolly well do. He was going to ask you to marry him tonight,' said Hemani, sobbing.

'Oh, that,' said Ellen. 'No way. I mean, you're a great guy, Danny, but I'd rather have Ivo.'

'But you can't!' said Hemani. 'Ivo's mine.'

'What do you mean, yours? Didn't you see him just now?'

'So? He snogged me too.'

'I can't believe this is happening,' said Ellen. 'Meenu, darling, this is me. Don't you remember how we shared that flat together? All those make-overs, borrowing each other's things? The double-dates, you with one guy and me with the other? And now you're behaving like this total bitch? Hello? Wake up! You can't have him.'

'I'm not the bitch round here,' said Hemani. 'Just because you've got hair like straw, you think that he could care less about you?'

Ellen's eyes blazed. 'If you think I'm going to hold back out of political correctness, then I can tell you that not only are you vertically challenged, but your dress sense is completely wacko.'

'Why are you so afraid of saying that I'm black, too?' shouted Hemani. 'That's what you want to say, say it!'

'Because you're not black, you're a sort of latte,' said Ellen. 'A regular-sized latte with plenty of cream.'

She mimed a pair of breasts. Hemani glared.

'Oh? Just because you're blonde, you think you can insult me. Well, I'll tell you what else I have as an Indian woman, and that's nails!'

She flew at Ellen, and Ellen rose as if to retaliate. Both were grabbed by the men.

'You always were a little vixen,' screamed Ellen. 'Keep her off me, Ivo!'

'Little again! Let me go, you pig, you oaf,' said Hemani, struggling against Daniel's grasp.

'Ladies, ladies,' said Ivo, trying to restrain them both, 'this has gone too far. Hemani, don't lower yourself to this kind of cat-fight—'

'Lower again?' said Hemani. 'Oh, this is too much.'

'Meenu, don't,' said Daniel. 'Ellen, this is beneath you—'

'Beneath her, am I? I can still reach her eyes—'

Daniel slackened his grasp for an instant.

'Strange, ' he said half to himself. 'This all sounds familiar somehow.'

'Ho, there, Dan, help! Don't just stand there dreaming!' said Ivo. 'You take one, and I'll take the other. We'll have to separate them.'

Hemani was beating at Ellen and Ivo indiscriminately. Daniel hesitated, then strode forwards. He picked the shrieking Hemani up, slung her over his shoulder, and blundered out of the glade. There was the increasingly distant crack of branches. Then there was silence.

At last, Ellen said, 'Ivo? Ivo, are you OK?'

'Shaken but not stirred, to coin a phrase.'

'Oh Ivo, quit it.'

'Is she having some sort of women's problem? Are you, for that matter?'

'Of course I am,' said Ellen.

'Well, that solves it. Bloody hell, I wouldn't like to have been Hemani's husband. Poor sod, probably went for him with a meat cleaver every time the moon was full.'

'Ivo,' said Ellen, 'I can't answer for Meenu, but to be honest, my only problem is you.'

'Yes, well, you've made that pretty obvious. I'll leave first thing tomorrow.'

'Must you?'

'Yes, I rather think I must. I mean, I may look like a callous, cynical, sophisticated sort of chap,' said Ivo, in tones of deep misery, 'and I've often done things I'm ashamed of, you

304

know, fiddled my expenses, made up stories just because an editor was shouting at me, porked women I didn't really like, that sort of thing. But I do have some feelings. And the fact is, Ellen, I've had a sort of thing about you ever since we met, and it's just not going to go away.'

'Why not?'

'Because,' said Ivo, 'I've never contrived to make love and be in love at the same time, but if it's ever going to happen, it's with you. I know, I know, I blew it completely when I fell asleep, and then threw up on your sofa, so now it's imposs-ible, but I just can't take it any more. So I really think I had better leave. It's affecting my work, you see. I actually found myself being kind about Tom Cruise last month. One just doesn't do things like that. It was thinking of spending two weeks with you, even if I know you're going to marry Daniel, even though he's the last chap in the world you should marry—'

'Are you completely deaf?' said Ellen. 'I'm not going to marry him.'

'You're not?'

'No. I'd much rather marry you.'

'Ellen, you do know that I am British, don't you?'

'So?'

'You know we're never any good at sex?'

'No?' said Ellen. 'Well, it's never too late to learn.'

'This is boring,' said Tania.

'Weird,' Bron said. 'Why do exercises in the middle of the night?'

'D'you think we'll ever be like them?' asked Tania.

'Nah,' said Robbie.

'Let's go and find my mum,' said Bron. 'Gosh, I hope she isn't too mad at your uncle. It looks like the potion is awfully strong.'

'What we need to do,' said Tania, 'is somehow get her to drink some of the potion then look at Uncle Dan. I bet that would undo the first lot that she had by mistake.'

'But what if she sees someone else, like one of us?'

'We'll have to be really, really careful.'

They pattered along the path that Daniel had taken, and soon caught up with him. He was still carrying Hemani over his shoulder in a fireman's lift.

'Mum?' said Bron, in a tiny whisper.

She lifted her head just long enough for Bron to brush the bottle past her lips.

'Did she swallow it?' asked Tania.

'I think so,' he said uncertainly. It had made him feel quite strange to have Hemani not see him, as if he were invisible. 'Let's follow them up and down, just to make sure. You can't rely on them not to get into trouble.'

Chapter Thirteen

By the time Daniel had found the waterfall, he was absolutely exhausted. Carrying a grown woman, even one as small as Hemani, was no joke. Just after he'd crossed over the small rattling river on a stone bridge, he decided he'd had enough of being kicked. He was dripping with sweat, parched with thirst, his back hurt and he couldn't carry her another step. The pool lay beneath him in the moonlight, deep and clear.

'Hold on,' he said, and jumped.

Hemani shrieked as they fell together, through the sticky night air and then into the water. At its touch, heat and misery fell away.

'You-you-you could have killed us both, you total idiot,' said Hemani when they surfaced, her teeth chattering with shock and cold.

'I know,' he said humbly. 'I am a stupid sort of guy, I guess. I can pass papers and write books and give lectures on the greatest writer who ever lived. That's what a genius does, he makes you believe, just for a bit, that the shining light in your mind is your own sun, not its reflection. But I know that I can't have understood the first thing about him, because I didn't understand you, Hemani.'

'You don't understand me,' said Hemani. 'You don't even know me.'

'I do know you,' he said with utter certainty. 'I know everything about you. I know you without knowing how I know you.'

Hemani glared at him.

'What do you know?'

'I know that you sleep with your hands curled, as if you're fighting off the world. I know that you love laughing, but don't do it often enough. I know that you're full of compassion for other people, without ever pitying yourself. I know that you'd die for your son. I know that you think you're in love with Ivo, but that you're not. I know that you are in exile from yourself, as I am.'

He looked so serious, even with the water streaming off him, his hair flat as an otter's.

'I don't know you, though,' she said. 'Not really.'

'I hardly know myself,' he said. 'I'm not complete. I can be that only with you. And I also believe, if it's not too vain and presumptuous, that you will only become what you could be with me. Oh,' he said in frustration, 'why can't I say what I mean?'

'I do understand what you mean,' said Hemani. All the laughter had gone out of her, and she looked at him with pity. Here was this man, good, kind, modest, intelligent, and about as much use to her as a lump of wood. 'But I couldn't trust you.'

'You were willing to trust Ivo, whom you didn't know. Couldn't you trust me?'

'I don't know, I don't know,' she said, now really distressed. 'I don't know what has happened to me. I don't know myself. I trusted someone, the man I married. I thought I could somehow make him human, but I didn't. He just froze my heart. So I don't trust feelings any more, only what I can work out intellectually.'

'How do you know, without trying? How do you know, without trusting?'

'I have tried. I have trusted. Daniel, I wanted Ivo because I can see all his flaws; they're so obvious they're endearing, and also, I just wanted to have some sex again, without complications or feelings.'

'Poor Ivo,' said Daniel, with a faint smile. 'Women only ever want him for his body.'

'Yes, it's extraordinary, isn't it?' said Hemani. 'It'd make more sense if it were you.'

They both laughed, and as the sound bounced stonily off the sheer of the fall behind them, she thought, Perhaps we can just be friends again.

But he said, 'I do mean what I said. I love you.'

Hemani said in desperation, 'No, that's not right. That's not the way it happens.'

'Why not? Why can't I say it?'

'Because I don't believe it. Why should you love me? It's

309

Ellen whom you and Ivo both want. You're just saying this out of – out of pity, aren't you?'

They both stood very still, and her stomach convulsed with misery. She gave a deep sob, and put her hands over her face.

'Just go away – leave me. You've only made things worse.'

'Listen to me, listen, I could give you a dozen speeches, and they'd all be wrong. I wish I had Shakespeare's tongue, I wish I could talk like Ivo, even, but they'd still just be words,' said Daniel, then stopped. 'Ah,' he said. 'It isn't words, is it?'

She had both kissed and been kissed before, but not like this, as if they were both melting into each other, like wax, like flame. He would not allow her to be reticent, insistent that she should stay with him, should not retreat into modesty, should yield even that. She knew so much about bodies, she had seen them cut and drawn and all their secrets revealed and yet this was a mystery to her. (It was a mystery to him, also, where this knowledge had come from, for it certainly wasn't from Ellen.) She was afraid that she would never get it right, that he would lose patience, that the flame would never catch, and then, unexpectedly, it did. The water smoked and steamed around them. I'm in a Bollywood movie, Hemani thought, when she was next able to think.

'If we stay here, we'll drown,' she said eventually.

'I'd be happy to drown.'

'Well, then, we'll both grow gills and webbed feet,' said Hemani.

'Shall we risk it?'

'Yes.'

The children peered over the waterfall.

'Swimming!' said Robbie enviously. 'Why can't we do that too? It's our pool.'

'Yes,' said Tania. 'Well, sort of.' She could see the People clustered so thick about the water that her uncle and god-mother were hardly visible through a kind of luminous, pulsing veil.

She looked away, as did the others. They all had a feeling, both of incuriosity and confusion. It was part of the grown-up world, with all its monumental simplicity and strangeness. They suddenly had no business here.

Go away, said the People, turning their backs on them.

Robbie gave a huge yawn.

'I want Mum,' he said. 'My tooth is really wobbly.'

'OK,' said Tania. It was getting wet and misty, and darker than it had been before, and even the People were fading.

They trotted up through the glades, then out through the gates, not even noticing that one was by now twisted off its hinges. Tania was so sleepy that she didn't notice her potion bottle falling out of her pocket and on to the moss. The mist became thick and opaque, like breathed-on glass. The ferns dripped moisture, and the leaves of the tunnel pattered as if a thousand small feet scampered with them. It was raining at last. They did not walk directly up the hill, but stopped to examine things, to wander off at a tangent, for they were easily diverted, but in the end the path led them back. The mist paled, swirling white, then cream, then gold and suddenly, just as they got to the gap in the garden wall, all the birds for miles around burst out singing. Every bush, every briar, every twig and every tree was alive with whistles, trills and calls, so loud that it seemed incredible that this could happen every morning at sunrise, and be ignored. It lasted only long enough to wake Polly from her stupor, but she went to the french window, and saw them emerging from the mists.

'Wow,' said Ellen. 'I feel as if we've just invented the word. Invented the world.'

The morning sun was penetrating the glade. First the roots, then the boles, then the branches were revealed as if a curtain was rising swiftly, and everything was shining and wet and new. A cock crowed, and Ivo said, 'Even if this never, ever happens to me again, I love you. I love you.'

'That makes me so happy. What is it you say? The same to you with brass knobs on?'

'Good. Do I understand that I'm allowed to rescue you from a life of scented candles and *Friends* videos?'

'Did I really say that or are you making it up?'

'Perhaps you were making it up.'

'Then, you do realise that lunges made at anyone other than myself will be terminated with extreme prejudice?'

'I don't want to lunge at anyone but you anyway,' said Ivo.

'And I don't think I'll be comfortable calling myself Sponge.'

'Of course not. You're your own woman. Only if anyone else lunges at you, I'll knock his block off.'

'Really?'

'Really. I may miss, of course, but that's the intention.'

'That sounds dandy. But I think, darling, we should leave early. I don't feel comfortable round Danny any more, or Meenu, for that matter.'

'Quite, quite,' said Ivo, blushing, for he knew that although you can have no choice over whom you fall in love with, you often have a choice as to who falls in love with you. 'A hotel would be much more . . .'

'Lungeful?'

'Exactly.'

'You know, there are some great jewellery shops in Florence,' said Ellen.

'I'm sure you'll lead me through them all.'

'I will. I'm kind of traditional about some things. There are also some really good hotels. You know, with room service?'

Ivo brightened. 'Good. I love room service.' He added, 'I can probably put it on expenses, too.'

Theo and Guy had wandered round and round the wood for what seemed like hours. They tried calling for the children, but their voices were muffled by the mist and sounded odd, and soon their mouths were cracked with thirst for it was unbearably hot. First one torch, then the other, turned yellow and flickered out. Guy trod on an old chestnut case and got a prickle from it jammed into his big toe. Theo's shirt got shredded by a particularly vicious bramble. After a while, the moon set. It became darker than Theo, a city dweller, would ever have believed possible. He was very glad Guy was there with him, and after a while, they stood still.

'Kind of ironic, this,' said Guy.

'Yeah. Even I get that.'

'You really think they're lost in here?'

'I do.'

'I do too.'

'You can't go on living like this, you know.'

'I know. It's killing me. But neither can I bring myself to hurt my family.'

'I understand, but it's you I'm thinking about.'

There was no difference between closing and opening his eyes, except that when Theo shut his he could see strange shifting streaks of violet and green on the lids. Yet when he opened them again, there was something.

'Look, there's a light!' said Guy. 'Quick, let's follow it!'

They stumbled after the winking, blinking point of brilliance. It drifted along, either near or far, as if a child were wandering a few feet away, just out of sight.

'Tania!' called Theo. 'Robbie!'

The little light seemed to pause, and wait. Desperately, the two men scrambled towards it in the thick night. Just when they seemed to have almost drawn level, it vanished, then reappeared floating just above their heads.

'Oh,' said Guy quietly. 'One of those.'

'A bug?'

'You'd call it that,' said Guy, though what he thought it

was, he kept to himself. He knew he saw things sometimes that other people didn't. 'It's led us a merry dance, any road.'

Theo clutched at his arm. 'But there's another! Much larger and brighter – that's no insect, surely?'

He plunged off again, and Guy anxiously followed.

'It's no good,' said Theo, after they had each fallen over into what felt like a large ditch or a small river. 'We're completely lost, and so are they if they're in here.'

'I'm so sorry,' said Guy. 'So truly sorry. It was my idea we should all go out to dinner. I had no idea.'

'It's OK,' said Theo. He added to himself, 'We should have brought a nanny.'

'Here, we may as well sit down on this log,' said Guy. He shivered. 'Is it me, or is it getting quite cold?'

'It could be you,' said Theo. 'Or it could be me, too. What a horrible place. I'm desperate for a drink of water.'

There was a pause.

'Does this change things?' asked Guy, yawning.

'I don't know.'

'Something always comes up, doesn't it?'

'They're so young,' said Theo. 'I do care for them, particularly Tania. If you knew what it was like – and then there's Polly. What has she done to deserve this? And then there's Mother. And work, of course.'

'And I'm an ass to dream it could ever be otherwise,' said Guy. He yawned again.

'You've seen what it's like,' said Theo.

'Love is blind.'

'So is the law.'

'So leave.'

'I don't see things the way you do,' said Theo.

The lights that had been blinking in the shrubs swarmed again, drifting and clustering, fusing into a ball of phosphorescence. By its light, they saw that they had come back to the gate. The ball drifted down, and down, and then the hairs on Theo's nape rose because it hovered just above something that he was sure had not been there the first time. He tried the torch again, and it flickered briefly, obliterating the stranger lights.

'What's that?'

'Tania's bottle. It's from her room.' Theo picked it up. 'It wasn't here before; they must have dropped it on the way back.'

He shook it.

'Look, there's even some left.'

'Bron will be getting anxious if we don't get back,' said Hemani, stirring. All through the night the apprehension of their future difficulties had risen and fallen like a fever chart, and now, like a fever, they were receding with each kiss. They were still by the waterfall, whose flow had increased during the night to a luxuriant ripple of sound. She looked up at it in the glimmer of dawn, seeing the long weeds shine, as if under glass, streaking the sheer slope of stone. The roots and branches of trees stretched out towards the spray, yearning for moisture, trembling with the faint shiver of its motion. There was no other sound, for even the cicadas appeared to have gone to sleep. The pool was limpidly dimpled all around them, as they lay like two tired swimmers in its warm shallows. Her own words came back to her, about love being like water. She had only thought of it as something to slake a thirst, not as something so plentiful, so generous that it would actually buoy you up. 'You don't mind, do you, that we'll have to tell him? I don't want to keep it secret.'

'No,' said Daniel. 'I'll have to tell Mother, too.'

'That won't be much fun.'

'I don't care,' he said.

He felt strange, yet more completely comfortable than he had ever felt, as if he had been taken apart and put back together again. This was, he knew, what love was supposed to do, though others said that you were whole before, and that it shattered your life instead. He suspected it all depended on whether it was welcome or not. Whatever Betty now thought or said was genuinely a matter of indifference. All the same, he was reluctant to leave, reluctant to put on the carapace of clothes and ordinary behaviour. It felt so natural to have nothing between them. He saw Hemani thinking, withdrawing slightly.

'She'll never accept me.'

'My mother is a strange person,' he said. 'She wants to control everything, to be at the centre like a spider in a web, yet nothing makes her happy. I used to be frightened of her. She likes to use money, you see. So the only way to be free of her is not to want it.'

'You're telling me you're going to be quite poor and ordinary,' said Hemani.

'Yes.'

317

'Well, I'm glad. Not that money isn't nice, but I don't think I'd like to live like Polly, frightened of my own shadow. I'd far rather earn it, as I always have done, and be with someone who earns it.'

'What about your family? Will they accept me?'

'I expect so,' said Hemani, her eyes mischievous. 'Beggars can't be choosers, after all.'

'You are the last woman to be a beggar,' he said. 'Golden Hemani.'

'I don't want to face them all, really. It will be awkward, staying in the same house.'

'There are always hotels.'

'Yes, but then that's harder for Bron. You do realise what you're taking on, don't you? That he has to come first, or at least first among equals?'

'I like Bron,' said Daniel. 'He's a great kid. And having waited so long to discover you, I guess I can wait a bit longer.'

'I had the strangest moment,' said Hemani, 'when you were carrying me. I thought I saw him just behind us, here in the wood.'

'What got into you, back then?'

'I don't know. I knew all along that I didn't want Ivo, that I really loved you, only I was so convinced you didn't want me I sort of made myself fancy him.'

'You're just saying that.'

'No. I didn't dare let myself begin to be in love with you, because it would have broken my heart when you left. Except that ever since, I've had this pain.'

'Where?'

'Here.'

'Is it broken now?' he said, kissing the place.

'No, it's quite mended.'

'Perhaps it's moved to the other side.'

'Perhaps, but if you do that, we'll never go back.'

Eventually they had to leave. They found the path quite quickly, and followed it.

'I know this gate,' said Daniel, 'but it's always been closed before.'

'It's fallen off its hinges,' said Hemani, clambering through the gap.

Daniel followed, then looked back. He could see the grassy path they had taken, and even the small stone bridge that crossed the top of the waterfall. The wood looked as it always had done when he had jogged past it, green and lovely, the sun casting wavering threads of light on the grass and ferns below.

'Strange, it looks so small by daylight,' he said.

The remaining policemen, yawning, had left, all in smiles at the touching reunion of Polly and her children. They were nice men – a little stiff with their own sense of importance, and their elegance too perhaps, not relishing a midnight scramble over the hills in their smart white jackets and red-striped trousers – but Italians, and therefore lovers of children. When news of the absent trio's return spread, there was a cheer that echoed across the hillside.

'*Una grande famiglia*, a big family,' one remarked sympathetically, as if this explained everything, and Polly could not be bothered to explain that Bron was not hers. They were all equally naughty, and equally innocent of the consternation and havoc they had caused. Polly had hugged them and hugged them until they became uncomfortable, for they didn't understand why she thought they could be dead simply for having got up at night. When she had seen them trailing up through the dew-drenched garden, they looked so much a part of the spellbound landscape that Polly wondered how they could live anywhere else. They did not belong to London, with it noisy cars and polluted air, or to the towering spires and hard grey pavements of New York, but to this place of long grasses and silvery leaves. How could she have believed they would come to harm here?

All three were fast asleep now in bed. Polly could not stop herself from going up every ten minutes to check that they were still there, their faces slightly flushed and dewed with the faint sweat of childhood, their hands curled like lax buds on the white pillows. She never loved them so much as when they were asleep, their lashes rayed against their cheeks, for then they were still, quiet, safe. Had she been able, at that moment, she would have put them under a spell to slumber for a hundred years. As it was, she was not allowed to sleep for, though Betty had long since gone to bed, the other adults had not reappeared.

It was obvious when Hemani returned with Daniel that now was not the time to tell her of all that had transpired. They came up through the garden by the same path that the children had taken, with the rays or the rising sun behind them. Polly had never seen either of them look so dazzlingly beautiful or, for that matter, so happy. They were not smiling, but a kind of deep joy made them shine. She guessed what had happened, and as soon as she guessed she did not want any cloud to overshadow it, so she said, 'All's well.'

'Very, very well,' said Daniel, with his slow smile. They went upstairs together. Polly heard Hemani's light footsteps travel to the boys' room to check on her son, and then there was the click of a single door.

It wasn't at all what she had planned, and a part of her would have been disappointed had she not seen them. She had hoped to have Ellen for a sister-in-law, not least because Betty seemed to like her, and that could have strengthened her own position. But she had always been fonder of Hemani, and the more she thought about it, the better it became because now Daniel would not have to leave London and Hemani would no longer be single. They would be sisters, equals, allies, family.

Shortly afterwards, Ivo and Ellen appeared, too. They were considerably dishevelled, and Ivo seemed to be limping, but they were too busy laughing even to notice her. They, also, went straight upstairs, and then Polly thought it wisest to make herself a pot of coffee and go outside into the garden, because although the house seemed to be sleeping she did not want to disturb or be disturbed.

She went down through the lavender-edged paths, carrying her mug of bitter wakefulness, and eventually sat down on a stone bench beneath a straggling white rose she knew was 'Peace'. The many sounds and scents of the garden came to her in layers. The long shadows fled like mice, the clouds that had sunk deep down into the valleys rose to become small flaws in the deep enamelled bowl of the sky, and still her husband and Guy did not appear. She lifted her face to the sun. In just two days, they would all be back on the plane for England, and this world, so completely vivid and intense, would become no more than a handful of photographs. She ought to be happy because Tania and Robbie were safe, and because all her closest friends had fallen in love with each other, but she was not.

I could actually have a swim, now, she thought. The idea became more and more appealing, until she went back to the house and found her bathing-costume. It was a plain black one-piece. She walked awkwardly to the pool, and slipped into the water. The feeling of being surrounded and held in its embrace was so intense that she wondered at how she could possibly have deprived herself of it for so long. What is wrong with me, she wondered, to be unable to accept even this? Yet it was not from an innate Puritanism, but from self-consciousness, the awkwardness with her own body. She was unhappy within her own skin, as a French person would put it, or, as Guy had said, a non-entity. Polly knew herself to be a little woman, not in the physical sense but in every other way, and this knowledge crushed her. She could not have been married to Theo, let alone had a mother-in-law like Betty, without this being borne in on her, day after day.

There were experiments, she knew, about the laws of attraction in which people had been given a number, invisible to themselves but visible to others, and told to seek out a partner with the highest possible number on their backs.

Inevitably, those with the highest scorned to pair up with lower numbers trying to attract their attention, and had to make do with others in their own scale. So it was with people, and levels of physical beauty. There were more complicated factors in real life, such as trading beauty for a partner with wealth and success that could partly compensate, but, by and large, you wound up with someone who had the same number on their back. Except that it hadn't happened to her that way. Somehow, Polly had jumped out of her own league and into one in which she didn't really belong. A beautiful woman married to a plain man is commonplace, but a plain woman with a husband as handsome as Theo was something that she knew to be strange. She sensed the envy her marriage excited, as if she had won a kind of biological lottery, undeservingly. What was such a man doing with her, when he could have had any woman? Polly had comforted herself with the perception that people didn't understand his love of the domestic, the familial. Theo needed what he himself had not had with his own family. He needed a wife to welcome him home with a warm supper on the stove, and a house that was not run by servants. He had been so happy when she had given up her own job to make this possible. Theo wanted her there, at home, at all times.

'I like that you're homely,' he had told her once. 'To me, that word has always had a good sound to it.'

Yet Ivo had called her attractive . . . Of course, Ivo was probably so coarse in his estimation of women that anyone not positively hideous would be counted by him as such, Polly thought. But Ellen had said the same, and, it made her wonder what she would look like if she did try a bit of make-up, and buy clothes that were less shapeless. She wasn't all that large now, in fact. When she had been lent that lilac top of Meenu's, which fitted instead of bagging about her hips, she had felt quite different, somehow. I'll try make-up again, she told herself. It isn't a crime to wear lipstick, after all.

She did several lengths of breast-stroke in the swimming pool before allowing herself to float. It made her dizzy, lying there and looking up at the sky, as though she were suspended in it, insubstantial as a cloud. But when she looked at the side of the pool, a shadow fell over her, for there were Theo and Guy.

'It's fine, the children were found, they're all safe,' she said, assuming the gravity of their expressions to be due to anxiety.

'We know,' said Theo, holding out Tania's glass bottle. Something about him made her unease deepen.

Guy squatted by the edge of the pool.

'Theo has something to tell you, Polly.'

'Oh? Should I get out?'

'Better not,' he said hastily.

Polly waited, feeling at once vulnerable and detached. Her husband looked down at her.

She had such a nice, honest face, he thought; not the kind of face a lawyer gets to see very often. That was where Robbie had got his eyes, and Tania her lips; he could see his children's hands and hair in her just as he could see her in them. They were forever mixed in this crucible, whatever happened.

Theo drew a deep breath, as if about to dive in, fully clothed. Guy looked at him with compassion, and with some other emotion vivid on his face.

'The thing is—' Theo said, then stopped.

Polly looked up at him, and said gently, 'The thing is . . .?'

He fell to his knees by the edge of the pool.

'I don't know that I can do this.'

'Oh, my dear,' said Polly, suddenly so full of pity for him, she wanted to take his head in her hands to comfort him, only she knew it would not work. 'Oh, dear Theo, it's better if you say it. You don't love me any more, that's it, isn't it?'

'No,' he said. 'I mean, yes.'

Polly had known it for such a long time, and yet she still felt strange. Her skin rose up in goosebumps.

'There's somebody else, isn't there?' she said. 'Do I know her?'

'Well,' said Theo, 'in a manner of speaking, yes.'

'It isn't a her,' said Guy. 'It's a him.'

Chapter Fourteen

The long wooden shutters of the Casa Luna, open to the heat of the sun, were closed one after the other, and the light of day was locked out. Polly, her back to it, tried not to weep. She had attempted to keep everything clean and in its proper place, but she had failed, and now there was dust every- where: dust from the ancient, crumbling plaster, dust from the great oak beams of the ceiling, and dust from the cars arriving to take everybody away.

'Now, Theo, if you'll just carry the cases to the hall,' said Betty.

'I can take at least one,' said Daniel.

'I'd rather your brother did it,' said Betty.

Daniel and Theo exchanged glances. It was obvious that Mother's rage at the news that Daniel was going to marry Hemani was still in full flood. It was nothing to do with Hemani herself, for who could possibly object to someone who was so beautiful, and clever and good? It was that, as far as Betty was concerned, she was going to have a coloured daughter-in-law. Daniel had never realised how deep her prejudice went, or been more ashamed of it, but he was absolutely inflexible.

'She could be purple for all I care,' he said to his mother.

'But your children, what will happen when you have children? Everybody will see they're not white,' she said. 'They'll never be accepted.'

'I think you'll find that in the twenty-first century, it'll be different,' he said. 'And if we do have children, and they're like their mother, then I'll be glad.'

'Why are you doing this?' asked Betty, and she would have wept if her tear ducts had not been frozen by injections. Even in his shame and distaste, Daniel felt pity for her, but his pity no longer made him irresolute.

'Because she makes me feel alive. I was so dull, so dead before, the biggest thing in my life were the words of a guy who's been gone for almost four hundred years. I can't be who I'm meant to be without Hemani.'

Betty sniffed.

'That's just your johnson talking, dear. If you want her as your girlfriend, then she'd be glad enough, I suppose. But marriage, no. You'll lose half your assets when you divorce, don't forget.'

'If she were to leave me, I wouldn't care about money,' said Daniel. 'And I'll never leave her.'

Betty, inevitably, moved on to threats. This was just the way she had behaved over Theo, he remembered.

'You won't find life at all pleasant on the salary of a British academic,' she said. 'You'll come crawling back after a year, and it won't be nice.'

'Other people manage,' said Daniel. 'I need very little, you know.'

'Only because you've been totally subsidised by your trust fund. You can move out of the apartment as of next week,' said Betty.

'That's fine,' said Daniel. 'I'm moving in with Hemani anyway, and then we're going house-hunting.'

'How can you afford a house?' Betty almost screamed. 'Do you know what property costs in London? You need millions of dollars even to buy a garage.'

'I have the capital I need in my head,' said Daniel. 'The rest I'll borrow from a bank, like everyone else. As long as it has a garden the size of a football field for Bron, we don't care.'

It had been impossible to keep many details of this row from being overheard, and Ellen winced. She and Ivo were, of course, relishing every moment.

'He's got more balls than I thought,' she whispered to Ivo. 'Jesus, when I think she could have been my future mother-in-law, it makes me feel like I barely escaped with my life.'

'So no regrets?'

'No, no regrets.'

'You do know that I have no prospects, really? That I might get fired from my job at any moment, and am generally regarded on both sides of the Atlantic as the lowest form of human existence?' he said.

328

'So? Nobody's perfect,' Ellen said, and he recognised the line, and grinned.

'How do I know this isn't just some sort of holiday fling for you?'

'You don't,' said Ellen; then had to spend an hour persuading him it was only a joke.

Hemani's happiness was quieter. She, Daniel, Ellen and Ivo couldn't quite remember what had happened after the dinner in Cortona, only that they had got drunk, and lost, then found again. Desire for their chosen partners blotted out everything, and each was too absorbed in private pleasures to wonder much at what had preceded it, although every one of the four felt an immense fondness for the other three. Their differences, now being so apparent, were forgotten or at least forgiven. Ellen was particularly kind to Hemani, for she, at any rate, remembered enough to feel that her friend was taking her own leavings. Hemani, on the other hand, was deeply embarrassed every time a flicker of consciousness crossed her mind that she had ever considered Ivo rather than Daniel. But then, she was wise enough to understand that what was wrong for one person could be right for another. She couldn't be jealous of Ellen's former affair, because Daniel was such a different man now – so happy, so expressive, so obviously in love. He had come into focus, the vagueness and uncertainty gone. Her greatest concern, that Bron would be anxious or jealous, was allayed by her son's evident enthusiasm at the prospect of having a stepfather.

'You really won't mind?' Hemani asked, for the fifth time after all the children had woken up from their prolonged sleep. 'Because if you do, he'll wait. We're not going to rush into anything. It's still very early stages. You don't have to see him, you know. Nothing has to change.'

'I want it to change, stupid,' said Bron. 'I'm fed up with being the man of the house.'

'You? A man?'

'Well, yes, sort of. Papaji said I had to be the head of the house, but I'd much rather have fun,' said Bron. 'Anyway, I like Daniel. He's OK. As long as you don't show him your bum all the time.'

'Rude boy,' said Hemani.

'And also, he has to play chess and tennis with me. And cricket.'

'I only know baseball,' said Daniel humbly. 'Perhaps that's something you can teach me.'

Daniel had been as good as his word, too, Bron noticed. He had taken them up to Cortona to play tennis, which was something they had wanted to do all holiday, and Bron and Robbie and Tania and Daniel had had a knockabout that other people had enjoyed laughing at almost as much as they had.

They were all leaving a day early, except for Polly and Tania and Robbie, so afterwards Bron spent as much time as he could in and around the pool. They no longer went down to the wood at the end of the lane by mutual accord. The People had stopped coming.

'You know, they probably were only bugs,' said Bron.

'No they weren't,' said Robbie. 'I lost my tooth, and one of them brought me a euro.'

He grinned, and there, on the bottom row of his teeth, was a space.

'That's just Mum, stupid,' said Tania. She was back in the hammock again, with one leg hanging over the edge. Bron was lying at the other end. 'But it doesn't matter if you want to believe in fairies, just for now. I did when I was little,' she added kindly, looking over the rims of her heart-shaped sunglasses at her brother.

'I'm not little.'

'Are too.'

'Am not.'

'Are too.'

'Anyway, you're not a grown-up, so sucks.'

'Where the bee sucks, there suck I,' said Tania, remembering Daniel's words.

'Bron! Time to go!' called Hemani. The three children looked at each other.

Bron laughed suddenly.

'You know . . .' he said.

'What?'

'You know . . .'

He bent over Tania, and just for a moment she felt his lips brush hers in a quick, shy kiss. Although they both went red and looked away, of all the kisses that had been exchanged in that place, theirs was the most blissful.

'Bye,' he said.

'Bye,' said Tania. 'You can come and see me again, in London.'

'OK,' said Bron.

'Are you her boyfriend?' asked Robbie, appalled.

'Stupid,' said Bron, and cuffed him gently, then walked up by the side of the pool and under the arch, to where his mother was waiting.

Tania lay back on the hammock while Robbie groaned.

'It's all right,' said Tania. 'You can pretend it didn't happen.'

She wondered if it would be enough to get her into Lottie's sleepover club. After all, she had been kissed by a boy, and even if they hadn't used tongues . . . even if, she could probably make something up. She could imagine just what it would be like, in fact, the more she thought about it, the more certain she became that that was what had happened, and that actually, it had really been rather nice . . .

Betty was standing in the hall, surrounded by a flotilla of monogrammed suitcases. She was wearing a silk scarf under her straw hat, and large dark glasses, and something about her set expression made Theo say, 'Mother? There's something I have to tell you.'

'Can't it wait? I can hear my car coming up the road.'

'No, it's . . .' Theo exchanged glances with Guy, who was standing next to him. 'I really have to tell you, you see. I'm leaving Polly.'

Betty looked at him. It was impossible to tell what she thought.

'Well. I see. About time, too. You've found somebody else?'

'Yes,' said Theo.

'And are you going to introduce me?'

'You've already met,' said her son, as the car drew up outside the Casa Luna. 'It's Guy.' Theo stood, quailing, awaiting a storm even more violent than that which had greeted Daniel's engagement.

Then, to Theo's utter astonishment, Betty put out her hand to his partner and said, 'My dear, I couldn't be more delighted. We must all have a little dinner together very soon.' She tripped across to the front door and said, 'Come along now, don't keep the driver waiting.'

They followed in stunned silence. At the last moment, Polly rushed up in her flustered way, dragging the children.

'Say goodbye to Grandma,' she instructed.

'Ah,' said Betty, 'the four loveliest words in the English language. Goodbye, Polly. I don't expect we'll be seeing each other for quite a while.'

'No,' said Polly, then added clearly, 'Not if I have anything to do with it, we won't.'

'Bye,' said Tania and Robbie to their feet.

'Here,' said Betty, reaching inside her purse. 'You could be doing with some of this, no doubt.'

She handed each of them a bank-note.

'Say thank you,' Polly chided, her heart sinking. She could see that this was how Betty was going to keep her grand-children under control.

Tania and Robbie looked at the piece of paper blankly.

'But, Mum, it isn't real money,' said Robbie. 'Not like I got for my tooth. See?' He grinned, displaying the gap, and showed her his precious golden coin.

'No, darling, you're quite right,' said Polly. 'Grandma was just playing a trick on you. What luck that you weren't fooled.'

Betty pressed the button on her window just as Daniel, who had finished loading his rental car, approached. He bent down, and tapped on the window, but Betty looked straight ahead and seconds later, the car began to move.

They all watched it waddle and skid down the dusty white road, and when at last it passed out of sight, they moved again, and sighed.

'So, no forgiveness there?' asked Polly.

'What's to forgive?' said Daniel, but his voice was sad. 'She is my mother. Perhaps she'll come round to us, one day.'

'Perhaps,' said Polly dryly. She didn't want to deny anyone the possibility of redemption.

'Actually,' said Theo, 'I told her about Guy, and she was really, really cool.'

'Was she?'

'Yes,' said Guy. 'You know, I think she's taken quite a shine to me. Not that it's unusual, but it wasn't at all what we were expecting, was it?'

Daniel looked from one to the other, and Polly did too, and both had the same thought: how could I ever, for one moment, not have seen this? With each second that passed, Theo seemed to be less tense and stiff, more at ease with himself, less artificial. In some extraordinary way, he and Guy now looked more like brothers than Theo and Daniel ever had, Polly realised. And they were happy. Love and tenderness, the qualities she had always perceived Theo to be capable of, shone from his eyes. How could she not forgive him for choosing honesty, when he had been so unhappy with its opposite?

Daniel drew her to one side.

'Does this mean what I think it means?' he asked quietly.

'Yes.'

'And what about you?'

'Me? Well, I don't quite know yet.' Polly said. 'It was a total shock, of course. I really had no idea. I thought, you see –' She scuffed her foot in the gravel – 'that it was my fault. And now I find out it isn't, that I was never going to be right for him, well, it isn't so bad. Whereas if it'd been another woman . . .'

She looked up.

'The children won't even notice he's gone, I expect,' she said. 'He's hardly there anyway, and I expect he'll still visit. He's always been a good father.'

Daniel put a hand on her shoulder, awkwardly.

'Did you know?' she asked.

He hesitated.

'There had been incidents. Mother thought he'd grow out of it. I know she spent a lot on shrinks, back home.'

'Poor Theo. She treated it as an illness, then.'

'Yeah. Or a passing phase. You know, prep school, being a jock, it does happen. But then he also dated girls, so . . .'

'He'll be so much happier now,' she said. 'Look at them both. They're flying back too.'

'You know, you can always call on me, if you need anything.'

'What am I to tell Robbie? And Tania?' said Polly.

'I don't have the answer to that,' said Daniel. 'They won't understand, not yet. It's the one thing children don't get, do they? They're just as smart as we are, just as full of feeling and ideas, but they don't understand sex.'

'Yet it fascinates them.'

'It fascinates all of us, at some point or other. But children are shielded from it, not, I think, by adults but by something else.'

'I'm not so sure I understand it either,' said Polly.

'I'm not sure I do. It's just a miracle when it works out.'

Hemani approached her, and hugged her. Polly hugged her back, with deep affection.

'Well, we must be going. We're driving Ivo and Ellen as far as the station. They're going on to Florence together.'

'I suppose you'll go round all the museums we never saw,' said Polly to them both.

'Not her,' said Ivo. 'She'll go shopping.'

'Well, among other things,' said Ellen, grinning broadly.

'Such a pity we never managed to go shopping together properly,' said Hemani.

'Yes. Holidays are always more work than people think,' said Polly, and they all blushed; her guests because they felt guilty at not helping more, and Polly because she knew that she had wasted a lot of time doing chores that weren't really necessary.

The house did seem so large and empty when she returned with the children from the station.

'I miss Bron,' said Tania.

'I miss him too,' said Robbie.

The heavy, dark feeling in the air increased, and suddenly there was a rumble of thunder, and a rattling sound. An open window upstairs banged, and they all jumped. Polly went round and tried switching on the lights. None would work, and so they had a hunt for the fuse-box. They couldn't find the Owner's Notes; nor could they find the torch.

'There's going to be a storm,' said Polly.

How different it looked, without good weather. Long veils of rain twisted and moved, as if gigantic figures paced up and down, scattering water on the parched landscape. The trees rolled and tossed, their branches like waves of silver cascading down into the valley. All over the house tiny leaks of water began to spurt, and now Polly and the children raced round with bowls and jugs to catch them, often getting splashed in the process. Polly let her tears flow, for in the darkness and the damp there was nobody to notice the difference, and when the storm eventually moved away, she was tired but refreshed.

It hurts, she thought, it hurts a lot, but I am going to survive this.

Slowly, as she moved around and attended to her children's needs, she began to think what she would do with her future. Now it would be she, not Hemani, who was going to be the single mother. She wondered whether her life would change for the worse, and thought with relief that at least she wouldn't have to do any more of Theo's business dinners or dreary company events. She would have to see a lawyer, but she was pretty sure she'd still have the house, and a certain amount of income, if probably not as much as before.

I'm going to have to retrain, and get a job again, she thought. The idea didn't fill her with half as much apprehension as she would have expected. What did was leaving this place and going back to London. Despite all its inconveniences – the lack of a dishwasher, the insects, the impossibly pitted floors and the absence of a video machine – she knew she was going to miss it dreadfully.

I'll never be able to afford to come here again, Polly thought, all that evening and through the night. It was blessedly cool, the perfect temperature, in fact, so that she was able to spread out on the small double bed and sleep deeply, when sleep came. She thought of moving into what had been Betty's bedroom, but really, what was the point? In the morning, both Tania and Robbie came in for a cuddle, and she had one in each arm and they were all so gentle and loving with one another, it was as if they'd never quarrelled.

After breakfast, they all went for one last swim, and then Polly began to pack. Each bedroom was full of those bits of litter that always seem to distribute themselves as soon as people move – old tissues and cotton buds, the cellophane wrappings from ironing services, tangles of discarded hair, slivers of soap and odds and ends of food. She simply couldn't do it all, not least because when she went into what had been her friends' rooms there seemed to be a kind of happiness lingering in the air, like the golden motes of dust that swirled and danced in the light seeping through the shutters.

'Can I take my potions bottle?' asked Tania.

'No, darling, it belongs to the house.'

'No it doesn't. I bought it with my own pocket money,' said Tania, outraged.

Polly did not want another quarrel, so she said, 'All right, darling, only no more raiding the spice jars for ingredients. Apart from anything else, the smell was so awful I kept having to throw them away.'

'You *what*?' said both the children together.

'I threw them away. I put water back, so you could still go on playing your game, but I was worried you'd make something dangerous.'

Tania folded her arms.

'Isn't that just typical!'

But Robbie tugged at her dress.

'It still worked, didn't it?' he said.

They went out into the garden to chase butterflies, and Polly sat down on the terrace and tried to remember as much as she could of the view. At any moment, the cleaner or caretaker would arrive, and then she'd have to hand the keys over and leave.

'Hello?' said a voice.

It was not an Italian one. Polly turned. There, standing in the doorway, was a man. He was slightly plump and balding, with longish dark hair and a short neat beard. As he looked at Polly, she thought she had never seen eyes so shining, or so dark. He was dressed in black, and had a gold hoop in his left ear.

'Hello?' he said again, and Polly was not certain whether he was English or American, or both. 'I'm sorry to disturb you. I've just arrived.'

'Oh!' said Polly, jumping up. 'Are you the new guest?'

He smiled, and shook his head.

'No, I'm the owner. Bill, Bill Shade.'

'I'm Polly Noble. I do apologise. We'll leave at once.'

'No, don't do that,' said Bill Shade. 'You look like you're part of the landscape, somehow.'

'I wish that were true,' said Polly. She sat down again, and so did he.

'So, you've been renting my place for what, two weeks?'

'Yes,' said Polly. 'Though somehow it seems much longer than that. And also much shorter, if you see what I mean.'

'I do,' said Bill Shade. 'I hate leaving. I work in Hollywood, so I can't be here as often as I'd like, but I'm always around in spirit, if not in person.'

He looked at Polly, and Polly looked at him. The miniature orchestra of cicadas began to shrill as the temperature, like the sun, rose slowly.

'I enjoyed reading some of your books,' she said.

'Did you? Good. They're there to be enjoyed. Most people just bring trash. Or else stuff they feel they ought to have read, but don't.'

'I'm not like that.'

'Me neither.'

They looked at each other again, a long, interested, measuring glance.

'So tell me,' said Bill Shade, 'did your holiday work out the way you'd planned? Or the way you wanted it to? Not that those are one and the same thing, of course.'

Polly thought. She thought of how she had arrived,

340

hoping that Daniel and Ellen would get engaged, and that Hemani and Ivo would take to each other. She thought of how she had hoped that Betty would tame her children and improve their manners. She thought of how she had looked forward to Guy's visit, and she thought about how she had hoped that her husband would love her, and make love to her again. Then she thought about what had, in fact, happened.

'Yes,' she said, 'it has.'

Acknowledgements

The first Shakespeare play I saw was *A Midsummer Night's Dream*, which my parents took me to see in the open air theatre in London's Regent's Park as a child. It remains for me, as for millions of others, the quintessence of Shakespearian genius. The play recently acquired particular resonance for me during the writing of *In a Dark Wood*, with its themes of imagination, madness and art. This novel began in the summer of 2001, when I took my own two children, then aged six and eight, to see the same play in the same place, and witnessed their immediate self-identification with the fairies and their mischief. So my first thanks are to Leonora and William for being so much more than the pram in the hall, and my second are to my husband Rob, a prince among men, for being their father. I am particularly grateful to Leonora for allowing me to quote one of her poems, because although I know very well how a child thinks and speaks I can no longer write as a child writes.

I am immeasurably grateful to the work of many scholars on the play, and in particular to Peter Holland for his introduction to the World Classics edition (OUP) of *A Midsummer Night's Dream*, and to Helen Hackett's essay on the same in the Writers and Their Work series. My thanks also to Dr Charlotte Mitchell, of University College London, for suggesting them. Jonathan Bate's magnificent study, *The Genius of Shakespeare*, persuaded me that even the Bard himself might not object to another writer using one of his best-loved plots, and John Gross's *After Shakespeare* reassured as to just how many others have taken his work as their jumping-off point. We are all dwarves standing on the shoulders of this particular giant.

Shona Abhyankar and her mother Sulekha suggested Hemani's name, as being close to Hermia, and they described aspects of Hindu background and culture that would not have occurred to me. Francesca Simon described a number of ways in which Americans misunderstand the British, as did Barbara Jones, to whom I am indebted for much concerning the life of an expatriate American lawyer. Dr Pamela Thurschwell helped further with details concerning life as an expatriate American academic. Both Elizabeth Stuart-Smith and Emma Hope helped me make Ellen a shoe designer. I am most grateful to all the above, and to the many women friends who suffer from Betty as a mother-in-law, and who told me stories about her. It should be needless to say that, this notwithstanding, all characters in *Love in Idleness* are the products of my imagination.

Those familiar with my previous novels will realise that Bron is stepbrother to Cosmo and Flora Hunter of *In a Dark Wood*, and that Winthrop T. Sheen of *A Private Place* is half-brother to both Daniel and Theo. Hemani is the sister of Laili, a doctor who appears briefly in *A Vicious Circle*, which is also where Ivo Sponge first made his entrance. Now an upstanding member of Anglo-American society, Ivo's identification with a handful of real-life British journalists will no doubt cease.

I have somehow enjoyed the support of many old friends and new ones, and wish to thank them for this. They know who they are. None has risked going on holiday with us. My parents, Dennis and Zelda Craig, gave me the benefit of their local expertise on Cortona, and much practical assistance in a number of details, as did Rupert Palmer of Classic Tuscan Homes.

I wish to thank my editor Richard Beswick at Time Warner, UK, and my editor Nan Talese and her assistant editor Lorna Owen at Doubleday, USA, for having the courage of their convictions. They and their teams have shown intelligence, sensitivity and professionalism in both the editing and composition of this novel. I would particularly like to thank Viv Redman in the UK and Carol Edwards in the US for their combined copy-editing, and my US agent, Emma Parry of Carlisle & Co.

Lastly, I would like to thank my agent, Giles Gordon, for his unflagging support. To this fount of high standards and low gossip, *Love in Idleness* is dedicated.

344